OTHER BOOKS by KASSANDRA LAMB

The Kate Huntington Mystery Series:
MULTIPLE MOTIVES
ILL-TIMED ENTANGLEMENTS
FAMILY FALLACIES
CELEBRITY STATUS
COLLATERAL CASUALTIES
ZERO HERO
FATAL FORTY-EIGHT
SUICIDAL SUSPICIONS
ANXIETY ATTACK
POLICE PROTECTION

~~

The Kate on Vacation Novellas:
An Unsaintly Season in St. Augustine
Cruel Capers on the Caribbean
Ten-Gallon Tensions in Texas
Missing on Maui

~~

The Marcia Banks and Buddy Mysteries:
To Kill A Labrador
Arsenic and Young Lacy
The Call of the Woof
A Mayfair Christmas Carol
Patches in the Rye
The Legend of Sleepy Mayfair
The Sound and the Furry
A Star-Spangled Mayfair
Lord of the Fleas

~~

Unintended Consequences Romantic Suspense Stories:
(written under the pen name, Jessica Dale)
Payback
Backlash
Backfire
(coming 2020)

LORD OF THE FLEAS
A Marcia Banks and Buddy Mystery

Kassandra Lamb

author of the Kate Huntington Mysteries

a misterio press publication

Published by ***misterio press LLC***

Cover art by Melinda VanLone, Book Cover Corner
Photo credits: silhouette of woman and dog by Majivecka, terrier mix dog by Rusu Ioana, walking sticks' display by Berkay, flea market sign by Mike Clegg
(The right to use these images purchased through Dreamstime.com; these and the cover image of this book are copyrighted. They cannot be used without express permission.)

ISBN: 978-1-947287-18-1

CHAPTER ONE

I stared at my client, incredulous. "Do what?"

Despite my tone, the cheerful smile on Derek Bradshaw's broad, boyish face lost none of its wattage. "Go to church with me tomorrow. Here, out back." He leaned forward, resting his crossed arms on the handlebars of his motorized cart. "Well, it's a prayer service, really, and we sing hymns."

Here was The Good Lord's Flea Market, where my former Army sergeant client was a vendor.

"What's out back?" I asked, stalling for time as I formulated an answer.

"The owner's trailer." He waved a thick arm toward the rear of the giant H-shaped building. "Zeke Lord—he's the owner—he runs the service. It's a good way to meet most of the vendors, when they're more relaxed, not focused on makin' sales."

Fred, a wire-haired fox terrier and something-larger-and-scruffier mix, sat beside me, waiting patiently. He turned his head as a young couple went by, with an unruly Yellow Lab pup on a short leash.

We weren't starting training with Derek until Monday, but I'd brought the dog to the flea market today to see how well he coped with the noise and chaos. So far, he was handling it better than I was. Living in a small town and commuting no farther than my backyard to train my service dogs, I wasn't used to throngs of humanity.

Still stalling for time, I pulled a hair tie from my pocket and yanked my long auburn hair back into a ponytail. The mid-November day had started out chilly, but it was warming up fast, not unusual for autumn in north central Florida.

Derek cleared his throat. "I mean, you don't gotta come to the service. I know it's not everybody's thing." His words sounded nonchalant, but his thick body slumped on the seat of his cart.

Guilt had me blurting out, "Actually, you're right. It probably would be a good way to meet the vendors." Maybe it would give me an opening to explain to everyone at once the do's and don'ts of interacting with service dogs. "Would the owner mind if I brought the dogs?"

"No problem. This is a real dog-friendly place."

As if to prove his point, a Chihuahua, in the arms of his rather large, muumuu-wearing owner, started barking ferociously at Fred.

The terrier's brown and white ear flicked slightly, but otherwise he paid the yappy little dog no mind.

The muumuu wearer made me a bit homesick for Mayfair, and my neighbor Edna Mayfair, whose standard attire was a muumuu and flip-flops.

I didn't get why I felt homesick already. I'd only been here, or rather in the nearby town of Williston, for a day and a half. I'd come early, with my mentor dog and four-legged best friend Buddy, to visit with my two-legged best friend Becky and her family, before starting the training with Derek and Fred next week.

You're missing Will. That's a good sign. My mother's voice inside my head.

Good sign of what, Mom?

After a beat of silence, the snarky part of me, whom I'd long ago dubbed Ms. Snark, chimed in. *Maybe she's worried about your marriage.* Her tone was mildly sarcastic, as usual.

Your marriage, not *our* marriage. More and more lately, Ms. Snark seemed to deny that she and I were the same person. What was that about?

Hmm, she said internally, *could be because you threatened to buy a human-sized muzzle.*

Derek interrupted the voices in my head. "The service starts at six-thirty."

"In the *morning*?"

"Yeah, we all have to be back at our stalls by seven-thirty." He straightened on his cart, which reminded me of the kind you see in grocery stores. "The early birds start showin' up around then."

He zipped the cart backward, stopping abruptly just inches from a display of walking sticks.

I winced.

He chuckled. "Don't worry. I know this stall like the back of my hand."

I already liked the guy. Now, I warmed even more toward him, for using one of my mother's favorite sayings. And one that I used too…I'd picked up a lot of her speech patterns.

Will teasingly called them my motherisms.

My chest ached a little. I was definitely missing him.

As a distraction, I walked over and pulled one of the brightly colored walking sticks from the display.

Fred automatically followed, and even though he wasn't on duty at the moment, he turned and sat in the *Cover* position. He was literally watching my back—a maneuver designed to help hypervigilant veterans feel more relaxed in public. If anyone approached from behind, the dog would signal their approach with a tail thump and an ear twitch.

I smiled down at Fred, then examined the stick. It was golden oak, painted with long, slender flowers, in shades of blue and purple. "This is gorgeous work."

"Thanks."

I looked up, surprised. "You made these?" The sign over them said *Hand-Whittled and Painted*, but I hadn't realized he was the whittler/painter.

His boyish cheeks pinked. "Yup." He self-consciously ran a hand over his light brown buzz cut.

He was thirty, only a few years younger than myself, but I tended to see him as much younger—he seemed such an innocent.

I only knew a little of his background, that he'd been raised by a single mom, which is probably where he'd learned *his* motherisms. On his eighteenth birthday, he'd signed up for the Army. His mom had died a couple of years later. But somehow his sunny personality had remained undimmed by that tragedy, and by the experiences of war in the Middle East and almost being blown up by an IED.

He definitely had PTSD—nightmares, anxiety and anger issues, among other symptoms—which is what qualified him for one of our service dogs. But he didn't seem to have the depression that all too often went with traumatic-stress syndrome.

Another walking stick caught my eye, or maybe this one would be considered a cane. It was quite different, a deep mahogany stick, with a silver head in the shape of a dragon.

I picked it up to examine it more closely. The dragonhead was formed from an intricate design of thin silver wires.

Down inside the wires, a dark substance was stuck to one of them. A short internal debate—who knew what yucky substance that was? But curiosity overrode caution. I inserted my pinky finger between the wires and scraped at the dark spot with my fingernail. It came away with something black under it.

I held it up close to my eyes and made out a small dry flake of something. It wasn't black after all, but rather a dark reddish brown.

Did Derek get stain inside the dragon when he was finishing the wood?

I glanced at the price tag, and my mouth fell open. "Is this really worth five-thousand dollars?"

"Probably more. It's about a hundred years old, accordin' to the friend who gave it to me."

So obviously Derek had not stained the wood. It was far older than he was.

"Five thousand is how much someone would have to offer me before I'd be willin' to part with it. I have it out there mainly to attract attention."

"Well, it certainly attracted mine." I rubbed my fingers on my jeans, wishing I'd worn something cooler. "But I didn't see it earlier when I walked by."

"I don't leave it out if I'm not at my stall, even for a few minutes."

I nodded. "I guess shoplifting's a real problem at a flea market."

Derek's perpetual smile faded. "Yeah, but…" he dropped his voice, "things have been disappearin' around here overnight lately."

"Overnight?" I echoed, in a matching low voice.

"It's gotta be an inside job." Maybe it was a trick of the glaring overhead lighting, but it sure looked like his gray-blue eyes had gone shiny. His lips thinned into a grim line. "Nothin's been stolen from me. Yet."

Fred whined softly. He was picking up on anger or anxiety coming from Derek. Or maybe both. Curious as to what he would do, I dropped his leash. He trotted over to Derek's cart and put his chin on the man's knee.

"Hey boy." Derek's smile resurfaced, as he patted Fred's head and scratched behind his ears.

Little did he know his new service dog had just demonstrated one of the many helpful tasks he could do for his owner.

~

During the fifteen-minute drive to Becky's house, I tried to keep my mind focused on planning Monday's training session.

But this was *my* mind, after all. It kept stubbornly circling back to that antique dragon cane, and then on to the mystery of why Derek would be so upset over the thefts.

I touched my tongue to my front teeth, as if they were the figurative "sore teeth" that I couldn't leave alone. Then I laughed at myself.

Fred cocked his head at me from the backseat.

I turned into Becky's driveway and decided to put Derek and the flea market out of my mind for the rest of the day. I had godchildren to play with!

Becky was sitting on the front porch of the clapboard rancher she and Andy were renting. They hadn't decided yet if they were going to stay in Williston proper, where Andy had recently joined the police force, or move to somewhere in between Williston and Ocala. The latter would make it easier for Becky to resurrect her massage therapist practice, since most of her former clients were in Ocala.

Fred trailing behind, I stepped up onto the porch—and quickly hid my disappointment. The twins weren't there.

Becky held up the monitor for the nursery. Of course, it was nap time.

"Lemme change," I said. "These jeans are too hot."

Becky nodded, her dark curls bouncing around her heart-shaped face.

I suppressed the usual spurt of envy. My best friend was gorgeous. And she was just as beautiful on the inside.

She grinned up at me.

"Did I say that out loud?"

"Say what?" she asked.

I chuckled, and Fred and I headed inside. In the guest room, Buddy, my Black Lab-Rottie mix, rose from the rug next to my bed.

"Hi, boy." I beelined for the bathroom and splashed cool water on my hot face. Grabbing a towel, I glanced in the mirror. A freckle-faced, thirty-five-year-old imp smiled back at me, water dripping off her nose.

I quickly changed into shorts and a tank top. Five minutes later, both dogs in tow, I was back on the porch, iced tea glass in hand. Unsweetened. When it comes to sweet tea, I am a staunch Northerner.

I flopped into a wicker rocker, and Fred and Buddy settled on either side of it.

Becky was wearing one of her many sundresses, this one denim with red trim around the bodice and straps. Her shapely legs were propped up on the edge of a large pot, which contained a brown, desperate-looking plant.

I pointed to the sad thing. "I see you still have a black thumb."

"Afraid so, and it's too bad. Here…" she gestured to the large swath of lawn in front of us, "I could have a garden. Wouldn't it be wonderful to be able to eat fresh organic vegetables every day?" She sighed wistfully.

I suppressed a grimace. Becky was a vegetarian. I thought of vegetables as a necessary evil.

"So, how was the flea market?" she asked.

"Busy." I told her a little about it, including the antique dragonhead cane. "I've got to get to bed early tonight. I'm going over there at six-thirty tomorrow morning."

"Why? I thought you weren't training until Monday."

"Um, I'm going to church."

Becky shifted in her chair to stare at me.

"It's a prayer service, actually."

She gave a slight shake of her head. "I thought you'd given up church for Lent six years ago and never looked back."

"Well, it isn't that I'm anti-church, I'm, uh…" I trailed off. Having grown up as a pastor's kid, church had been an ordeal for me. Even the post-service coffee hour, a mainstay at Episcopal churches, had usually ended up garnering me disapproving stares from parishioners when I talked too loud or ran across the parish hall. I'd inevitably hear someone snap, "Walk, don't run."

To my parents' credit, it was rarely them, unless I was truly doing something dangerous. As strict as my mom was, she got how hard it was for me—being the daughter of a Methodist minister herself.

I'd gone to church sporadically during my first marriage, but once I was free from two-timing Ted and I'd moved away from Maryland, I stopped going at all.

As for God, I didn't *not* believe in him. He and I had settled into a relationship of mutual benign neglect.

Although my mom claims he must have assigned an angel exclusively to watch over me. What else would explain how I'd survived all the scrapes I kept getting into?

Scrapes was her euphemism for almost getting myself killed a few times. Either Florida was the homicide capital of the world, or I'd developed really bad luck since moving here.

But then again, I'd met Will down here, which was the best luck of all.

"Earth to Marcia." Becky broke into my reverie.

I smiled. "I was thinking of Will."

She smiled back. "Always a good sign."

I stifled a sigh. Why was everybody so worried about my marriage?

"Your first anniversary's coming up," Becky said. "You decided what to get him yet?"

"No." But my mind immediately flashed to that intricate dragonhead. I found it fascinating, but I wasn't sure he would. Indeed, he'd probably be insulted if I gave him a cane.

It was a moot issue. No way did I have five-thousand dollars to spare.

"I gotta come up with something soon," I said, "but I want it to be really special."

"How about a gift certificate for a massage, at a new office opening in Ocala?"

I turned in my chair, excitement bubbling in my chest. "Really? That's awesome."

She grinned. "I hope to open next month, for a couple days a week to start. My mother-in-law's retiring and moving down here. She's gonna watch the kids."

"That's great." My enthusiasm wasn't totally selfless. I'd been Becky's guinea pig for new massage techniques. I missed those free massages.

Rustling, gurgling sounds emanated from the baby monitor. "Break time's over," Becky said, with a small groan.

I smiled, resisting the urge to rub my hands together. Time to spoil some rug rats.

~

The next morning, I expected to have trouble staying awake during the prayer service. As a kid, I'd always found the readings and prayers the most boring parts of church. Even the sermon was better, because my dad had a good sense of humor. I didn't always know why the adults were laughing, but it was fun to be able to make noise for a few seconds, off and on during his sermons.

Today, I was pleasantly surprised. The sixty-something man, with a stringy gray ponytail hanging below a baseball cap, kept things hopping. I assumed he must be Zeke. He was a skinny guy, wearing an overlarge green Army jacket and clutching a tattered leather-bound Bible in his weathered hands.

He'd read a short passage of scripture or say a short prayer, then launch us into another hymn. They were popular ones, and I remembered most of the words. Which was a good thing, since there were no hymnals.

Only forty or so souls singing their hearts out, from narrow folding chairs crammed into the house trailer's living room. Even with all the other furniture removed, the room was way too small for the crowd, but that didn't seem to slow anybody down.

By the third hymn, everyone was standing, arms in the air, swaying back and forth. I stood with them, feeling a little foolish. But by the last hymn—a rousing rendition of an old Sunday School favorite, *This Little Light of Mine*—I found my hands were creeping up and my hips were bopping back and forth.

The song ended abruptly and heat crept up my cheeks. I lowered my arms.

Zeke raised his hands in the air. “Hallelujah and amen!” he shouted.

“Hallelujah and amen,” everyone yelled back.

And suddenly the organized rows of worshipers dissolved into a gaggle of folks, shoving folding chairs aside, shaking hands, slapping shoulders, exchanging hugs, and all talking loudly.

“Come on,” Derek shouted above the noise. He moved off, balanced between two walking sticks, his jeans-clad legs seeming too thin to hold up his bulk. The crowd parted for him and greeted him warmly, smiling, patting his arm, exchanging a few words.

The dogs and I trailed behind and waited for introductions in each small cluster of folks.

Most people, especially the women, leaned down to fuss over the dogs. No way was I going to try to explain, under these circumstances, that they shouldn’t be treated as pets. It wasn’t something you wanted to yell at the top of your lungs.

I’d go through the drill tomorrow with Derek about making it clear when others could or could not pet Fred, and we’d devise a plan for setting those limits with the vendors and customers.

I wasn’t going to remember all these people’s names and faces, but it was good to know my client was part of this community. It was too easy for combat veterans, especially ones with PTSD, to end up isolating from people. I’ve heard more than one variation of “others haven’t seen what I’ve seen; I don’t fit in with normal society anymore” from my clients.

Derek didn’t seem to have that problem. And now I better understood his upset over the thefts. The “insider” who was stealing things was breaking faith with this tight-knit group of vendors.

He was one of its youngest members. Most of the vendors were middle-aged or older. About half the men, and some of the women, wore military insignia on jackets or baseball caps.

Which explained why Derek did not have that all-too-common isolation issue. More than a few of these people had probably seen combat.

Two people stood out in my mind enough that I remembered their names. One, Denny, was a robust gentleman with a loud voice.

Like Zeke, he wore a Vietnam Veteran's baseball cap, which meant he had to be at least in his sixties. His wife was rail thin, with too-evenly-dyed dark hair. I didn't catch her name.

Then Derek lingered a bit with a woman around his age, whom he introduced as Nell Benson. Hers was one of the few introductions that included a last name.

She wore a gray sweatshirt and loose jeans—which only somewhat disguised a great figure—with long blonde hair, big blue eyes and a porcelain complexion. She reminded me of the china-doll collection my grandmother had passed down to me, and I had passed on to my niece.

She seemed shy and ducked her head a lot as Derek chatted with her. I couldn't tell if he was just being kind or if he was attracted to her.

Eventually, the group started to break up, people wandering off to open their stalls. We moved out onto a poured-cement porch, the dogs following.

"See ya later, Nell," Derek said. She gave a small wave and jumped off the porch, then walked around the outside of the flea market building.

I glanced up. A small wooden steeple had been added to the house trailer's roof. It sat at a slight cant, perhaps as a result of some tropical storm. That and its flaking white paint made it look a little sad.

Zeke appeared and followed us as Derek maneuvered his way down the ramp with his walking sticks. At the bottom, he steadied himself beside his motorized cart, loaded the sticks into the plastic basket attached to its front, and climbed aboard.

We headed toward his stall, Zeke keeping pace with us.

"Hope you enjoyed the service," he said in a gravelly voice devoid of a Southern accent. Another Northern transplant like myself maybe? It was hard to tell. Some natives retained the Florida Cracker accent while others, especially those who'd spent any amount of time up North, did not.

"Yes, very much so," I said, and found that I meant it.

We came to a stall that was surrounded by make-shift curtains of heavy chain-link fencing material. They met in the middle and were held together with two combination padlocks. Zeke unlocked them and shoved the fencing curtains aside.

Inside was a rough-hewn wooden table covered with a gruesome array of knives. One section was for kitchen knives—everything from paring to steak to butcher, some in blocks, some in cases. On the other half were every kind of cutting instrument imaginable—pen knives, hunting knives, daggers. Some were probably antiques, with ornate patterns on their handles and sheaths.

On the back wall, various swords were displayed. Zeke reached up and touched the blade of one of the unsheathed swords. "Ouch." He snatched his hand back and put a finger in his mouth.

"That baby's my good luck charm," he said around his wounded appendage, "I touch her every day, but half the time she bites me back." He grinned at me. "Kinda reminds me of a cat I once had."

I gave a weak smile back. I wasn't sure how I felt about this guy. He had a certain charisma, but…

Derek obviously liked him. His face beamed as he shook Zeke's hand goodbye.

The dogs trailing along, he and I moved on to his stall. It had a fancier mesh-metal curtain around it. Derek dug a small remote from his pocket and hit a button. The curtain, hanging from a track, slid smoothly aside and retracted along the sides of the stall.

"If Zeke's the owner," I blurted out, "why doesn't he have a nicer gate like this?"

My inner mom tsk-tsked at my rude curiosity. Heat rose in my cheeks.

But Derek didn't seem to mind my nosiness. "I think a previous vendor added this one at their own expense." He pulled his walking sticks out of the cart's basket. "Could you put these back in the rack for me? I rotate the ones I use, to show them off."

I smiled at him and took the sticks. He might seem like an innocent, but I was starting to think he was a pretty savvy marketer.

I walked over to the display. "Where's the fancy one?"

"Getting it out now." Derek headed for the back of the stall. He maneuvered himself off of the cart and, hanging onto a railing along the very back wall, disappeared behind a curtain.

I looked around at the other vendors, bustling about their stalls. Nell's was across the aisle and two down, stuffed with all kinds of kitchen gadgets.

Feeling the lure of all those gizmos promising to make food prep sublimely easy, I took a step in that direction.

A bellow thundered behind me. I jumped an inch. *Crapola!*

Whirling around, I raced in the direction of the yelling…toward the back of Derek's stall.

CHAPTER TWO

Hanging onto the railing across the back of his stall, Derek stood over a steamer-type trunk, his face beet red, cursing a blue streak.

I hate swearing—another trait I'd picked up from my mother—but now was not the time to convey that to my client. "What's the matter?" I had to raise my voice to be heard.

"It's gone," he yelled, gesturing toward the trunk. "The dragonhead cane is gone." He turned, letting go of the railing, and lost his balance. Grabbing for a set of metal shelves beside the trunk, he nearly brought them over on himself. Tools and chunks of wood rattled, a few of the latter tumbling to the ground.

I held out my hands in a placating gesture. "Take it easy. Are you sure you put it in there?"

"Of course, I did," he yelled, not quite as loudly. But his face was still red. I worried he'd give himself a stroke.

He took a deep breath. "I always keep it locked in there," he said, his volume closer to normal. "The padlock's been cut off."

"Can I take a look?"

Derek backed out of the narrow space between the curtain and the back wall. He glanced my way, then ducked his head. "Sorry I yelled at you."

"No problem." Telling the dogs to lie down and stay, I slipped past him to the open trunk. A padlock lay on the floor, its shank cleanly cut, most likely with bolt cutters.

Inside the trunk was some folded cloth on one side, and on the other, a metal cashbox and a couple of small power tools—apparently expensive enough to merit being locked up.

"They didn't take the other stuff." He'd moved up behind me. His voice sounded rough.

I looked over my shoulder. "You should call the police."

He shook his head. "Zeke might not like that. He's not fond of cops."

That surprised me some. As a military veteran, I'd expect Zeke to be pro-law-and-order.

"We need to at least tell *him*," I said.

Derek hung his head. "He's gonna be pissed that I lost his cane."

"*His* cane?"

"He was the one who gave it to me."

"Well, you didn't lose it. You had it locked up, but it was stolen." I patted his arm that clung to the railing. "You finish setting up your stall. I'll go get him."

~

Zeke wasn't particularly upset about the stolen cane. He seemed rather blasé about the thefts in general, but I didn't know him well. Maybe that was only his surface reaction.

He took a couple of photos of the trunk and the cut lock with his phone. Then he picked up the lock in his bare hand.

I winced. Now his prints were on it, and the thief's prints were probably smudged.

"I'll hang on to this as evidence," Zeke said, "in case we ever do catch whoever's doing this."

That isn't gonna happen anytime soon, Ms. Snark commented internally, *with this guy in charge.*

I nodded slightly to myself, then realized, with some consternation, that I'd been agreeing with Ms. Snark a lot lately.

"I wish you'd sold the dang thing," Zeke said. "I gave it to you 'cause it fit in better with your stuff than mine. You should've priced it right and made some money off of it."

Derek pressed his lips together and swallowed hard, but didn't say anything.

Meanwhile I was trying to make sense of Zeke's words. Why would he give away such a valuable item just because it wasn't a sword or knife?

Aha! Maybe he'd wanted to help Derek out financially, but in a way that allowed him to save face.

Zeke gently patted the younger man's shoulder. "Don't worry about it. It is what it is." He walked away.

I was a little worried about Derek. He seemed so shaken by the theft.

I ushered the dogs behind the curtain to where he had set up a large dog bed and water dish, at the opposite end from the steamer trunk. I signaled for them to lie down.

Fred's dark brown eyes watched me from his lighter brown face. He rested his chin on a white paw. Most of the rest of his wiry coat was white, with flecks of gray and a wide swath of black across his back, like a saddle. He wasn't a particularly attractive dog, but he had a cute face, and he was smart as a whip.

I smiled down at him. "Stay," I said, holding my hand up, palm out.

Buddy promptly closed his eyes and went to sleep, but Fred's gaze followed me as I left the back area.

Out front, Derek, on his motorized cart, was conversing with a customer. The elderly man seemed interested in a cane that was hanging from the rafters above the stall.

Derek maneuvered his cart under it, then stood, holding onto the edge of a table for balance. Hefting a long-handled mechanical grabber in his other hand, he snagged the cane off its hook and brought it down.

The old man's face had shut down. "Why're you in that cart, pretendin' to be crippled?"

I shot him a dirty look, which he ignored.

"You tryin' to get people to buy your stuff 'cause they feel sorry for you?"

I heard a low growling sound and looked around for Buddy. He wasn't there. I realized the sound was coming from my own throat.

Meanwhile, Derek, whose cheeks had reddened, was saying in a calm voice, "I've got back and balance issues."

"From a war injury," I added, glaring at the old man.

His cheeks turned red. He gave the cane a perfunctory glance, mumbled something about he'd think about it and wandered off.

I took a deep breath to calm down.

Derek shook his head. "I get that sometimes. People have trouble with the idea that you can be partially paralyzed. If they see me first in my wheelchair or on the cart, and then I stand up…they get all weird about it."

"What causes that exactly, the partial paralysis I mean?" I told myself the information would be useful to me, as the trainer of his service dog, but mostly I was curious—a chronic condition that my mother frequently reminds me can be lethal to cats. Thank heavens, I'm not a cat.

"I've got what they call an incomplete spinal cord injury," Derek said in a matter-of-fact tone.

"What's that?"

"An IED went off a ways behind me. The shock wave damaged my spinal cord but didn't sever it. My doc described it as someone takin' a hammer to a hot dog, but not quite hard enough to smash it completely. It's smushed in the middle."

That mental image did help me to understand, but it also made me shudder. And I suspected I'd be off hot dogs for a while.

"My left leg doesn't really listen all that well to my brain's signals to move," Derek said, "although I can swing it from the hip. The right leg, the muscles work okay, but it doesn't have much feeling. So I gotta be careful I don't overdo, 'cause it can't tell me when it's tired." He looked down at that leg. "And I've cut or burned it a few times, and didn't realize it right away."

The information *was* actually useful—I made a mental note to teach Fred to stay on Derek's right side instead of the left, where service dogs of right-handed owners usually walk, so he wouldn't impede Derek's ability to swing his paralyzed leg.

But the info also made me sad.

As a distraction, I grabbed up one of the wooden toys from the table. It was a train engine, brightly colored, with big, googly eyes on the front end. "This is cool."

The gesture worked. Derek's face brightened. "I've got the rest of the train up there." He pointed to a shelf.

My mouth fell open. Each car in the train was made to look like a different animal, but it was still somehow a train car. The lion and tiger were both box cars, with their stubby legs ending at wide wooden wheels. And the giraffe sat on a flatbed car, long legs tucked under him. A tanker car was an elephant, and the caboose was a bear with a reddish-brown coat.

"Awesome. Did you make that?"

He nodded with a self-effacing smile.

How much is the whole train?"

"For you, free."

I shook my head. "I'm not allowed to take gifts from clients, but thank you. I'd like to buy it, though, for my godchildren for Christmas."

"Forty dollars."

I knew darn well that was lower than the normal price, but the look on Derek's face kept me from arguing. He was totally tickled that I wanted the train.

He used the long-handled grabber to gently lift each car down, and then nestled them in tissue paper in a box.

One major Christmas present taken care of. If only I could find an anniversary present for Will so easily.

Hmm, the first anniversary present was traditionally supposed to be paper. Maybe a gift certificate was a good idea. But I wanted it to be for something grander than a free massage from Becky.

I glanced at my watch. Speaking of Becky, she'd be wondering where I was.

A huge grin splitting his face, Derek rolled his cart over and handed me the box.

"Thanks so much." I paid him. "I gotta run. I'll be at your house bright and early tomorrow."

"Sounds good."

With dogs in tow, I carried the box to my car, a distinct bounce in my step. The kids would love playing with the train, and its nature-based motif would appeal to my best friend.

Becky's husband had the day off. It was cool watching all of them around the lunch table. Andy's light tan skin and tightly curled dark hair spoke of his African-American heritage, but a slight copper tone—brought out even more by the Florida sun—said there was a Native American or two in his family tree somewhere.

Winston and Jasmine—Winnie and Jazzie to me, but Becky didn't allow anybody else to call them that—had cream-colored skin and looser curls, more like Becky's.

They were now rambunctious almost-toddlers, and they sat in matching high chairs, with Becky in between them. Her fair skin was flushed a bit, I suspected with the pleasure of having all of us at home at the same time. Andy's hours were unpredictable.

Over dessert, I asked, "Andy, have you heard anything about thefts at the flea market?"

He shook his head. "No, but I wouldn't necessarily. We stay in pretty close contact with the Levy County sheriff's department, but the flea market's just over the line, in Crystal County."

"It is?" That was news to me.

He nodded and forked a bite of Key Lime pie into his mouth. After he'd chewed and swallowed, he said, "You want me to ask around about it?"

"Um, no. I was just curious if you knew anything."

"What's been stolen?"

"I think it's been different things, and mostly taken after hours." Now I was wishing I hadn't brought it up.

But Andy's police instincts had been activated. "The sheriff down there has no doubt run the backgrounds of the vendors. I wonder what he's found out?"

Panicking butterflies fluttered in my chest. If the thefts hadn't been reported, I didn't want to get Derek in trouble with Zeke by drawing the law's attention to the flea market.

I waved a hand in the air. "I don't think it's been anything all that expensive." My other hand was tucked behind my back, fingers crossed to negate the lie. "Not sure they've even reported it. Boy, this pie is delicious, Beck."

She gave me a pointed look, one eyebrow in the air. "You haven't tried it yet."

I grabbed up my fork. "Um, no, but it looks delicious."

Winston chose that moment to drop his sippy cup of juice on the floor. Andy leaned down to grab it up.

Becky tilted her head to one side, staring at me.

I shook my head slightly.

Sippy cup's spout wiped off and the cup restored to Winnie's grasp, Andy picked up his napkin and patted his lips. "Honey, would you hate me if I took a nap?"

Becky gave him an indulgent smile. "No, of course not. Marcia's here…" she gave me a meaningful glance, "…to help me clean up, so go on."

Once babies' faces and hands were washed and dishes were rinsed and in the dishwasher, we took Winnie and Jazzie out on the porch. Jazzie lay in her mother's arms and plucked at the top edge of her sundress top, as if she were remembering the good old days when her meals came from mama.

I bounced Winnie on my knee. They wore matching white onesies that had *I'm so cute, God made two of me* printed on them. They'd begun the day with little pairs of blue jeans pulled over the snapped bottoms of the onesies, but the day had warmed up enough that Becky had taken the mini denims off.

"Don't bounce him too hard, with a full tummy." Becky said. "So, what gives with these thefts at the flea market?"

I sighed, wishing I'd never brought it up. "I fudged a little earlier. I don't know about the other things, but my client had something valuable stolen last night. He was pretty upset."

"I'm sure the Crystal County sheriff is looking into it."

"That's just it though… The reason I brought it up, to see if Andy had heard anything about it. I got the impression the thefts haven't been reported. At least, the one discovered this morning wasn't. And the flea market owner's reaction, um, it seemed kind of off."

Becky turned her head toward me. Her eyes bore into mine. "Marcia, don't go getting yourself involved in something crazy again."

Eyes wide, I feigned innocence. "*Moi?*" I pointed to my own chest.

Winnie chose that moment to bounce harder and almost propelled himself off my knee. I grabbed him again with both hands.

He chortled, and I grinned.

"I guess you're right. It's none of my business. It's just that…"

I trailed off. Saying more would be a breach of confidentiality. I wasn't supposed to talk about my clients' psychological issues.

But Derek was such a sweet guy. I hated to see him upset.

"Mar-see-a," Becky dragged out my name, emphasizing each syllable, the way Will did when he was annoyed with me for "poking around" in a law enforcement investigation, "what are you thinking of doing?"

Something shifted inside, and I knew exactly what I should do. "I'm going to find out more about what's been stolen, and then I'm going to anonymously report it to the sheriff of Crystal County."

Jasmine squirmed on her mother's lap. Becky put her down on the smooth wooden porch floor. The little girl started trucking on all fours toward me and her brother. She was perfectly capable of walking, but at sixteen months, crawling was the better established skill and therefore faster.

Becky stood up, hands on hips and frowned down at me. "And exactly how are you going to find all that out?" Her tone said she was assuming I would poke my nose in people's business and get said people pissed off at me.

I shook my head. "Simple. I'm going to ask my client."

She took a step toward me and breathed out a sigh. I wasn't sure if it was a relieved sigh or an exasperated sigh. Maybe some of both.

Then she reached for Winston. I gave him up and scooped Jazzie up onto my knee.

The babies thus swapped out, she went back to her chair.

"And once I've tipped off the sheriff down there, I will be done with it." I said it with conviction. A conviction I even felt at the time.

~

The best laid plans of mice and men and independent women.

I'd assumed it would be easy to pump Derek for details about the other thefts, but he'd suddenly gone from Mr. I'm-An-Open-Book to Mr. Circumspect. He sidestepped my first couple of questions, then changed the subject.

I decided to get on with the training and come back to the questions later, when he'd relaxed some.

On Derek's double-wide driveway, I ran Fred through his paces, showing Derek the tasks he could do. I concluded the demonstration by dropping down on my side onto the cement.

A neighbor, driving by on a golf cart, almost ran into a street sign, he was staring so hard at Derek in his wheelchair and me lying on the ground, with Fred barking his head off.

"It's okay, boy," I said, and the dog quieted. "That's to attract attention if you've fallen," I told Derek, "to get help."

Derek opened his mouth. I held up a hand. "*Or*, you can tell him to *Brace*." The last word was the signal for Fred to stand next to me, his long legs spread to brace himself. I mimicked using his back to push myself to a sitting position, and then to a stand, without putting any actual weight on the dog, since I'm able-bodied.

"If you fall," I said, "you can assess whether or not you're hurt. If you think you are, let him keep barking. If not, tell him to brace instead."

Derek screwed his face up into a grimace. "I try really hard not to fall. And my doctor always insists that I get checked out after I do. There's a piece of shrapnel lodged in the muscle near my spine. It's in a tricky place so they left it alone. Too much risk of doin' more damage if they'd tried to take it out. My doc gets all worried that it might shift and do more damage, if I fall."

"Yikes." I was at a loss as to what else to say. How awful to live with the knowledge that at any moment you could become even more paralyzed.

The guy in the golf cart came by in the other direction, still staring our way.

"That's why I suggested workin' on the cement out here," Derek said, "because it's even underfoot. But now I'm not so sure." His gaze followed the golf cart as it went on down the block.

"Let's go around back," he said, "where it's more private."

I was wishing we could work inside, but his house was pretty small. We'd be tripping over ourselves and the furniture, and other clutter—the guy was a bit of a slob.

While Buddy snoozed on the back porch, we worked in the backyard for the next half hour. I helped Derek get down on the ground, so he could practice the *Brace* maneuver. "Try not to put too much weight on him, if you can help it," I said.

He nodded. "Mainly, if I can use him for balance and get my good leg under me…." With a grunt, he made it to his knees and then to a stand.

"That's awesome." He beamed at me. "No more havin' to call 911 if I take a little tumble."

I gave him a concerned look. "Maybe we shouldn't practice that too much though."

"Don't worry. It's been two years and that shrapnel hasn't shifted yet. And I do plenty of twistin' and stretchin' to move things around in my stall. I think it would take a bad fall to jar anything loose. My doctor's bein' extra careful is all."

We moved on to the *On Duty* and *Release* signals. The first was merely holding one's hand out for the dog to touch the palm. The latter involved crossing one's arms at the wrists, uncrossing them, and then crossing them again—a gesture that people would not normally make by accident.

"I also taught him a verbal signal, for times when you're using your canes and your hands aren't free. It's the word *Release*."

Fred immediately flopped down on his butt and scratched his ear with a back paw.

I laughed. "And for that reason, you need to train yourself to avoid using that word in everyday conversation. Use *off duty* when you're talking about it but don't want to actually release him."

I asked Derek to walk with his canes a short distance, with Fred and me beside him. Fred was trained to walk on my left side, but sandwiched between us this way, he was on Derek's right.

I'd added a verbal *on duty* signal as well, for times when Derek couldn't hold his palm out for Fred to touch.

"Okay, I'm going to stop in a few steps. You give him the verbal reminder that he's on duty and keep walking. We'll see what he does."

I stopped, and Derek said, in a firm voice, "Fred, *on duty*."

The dog gave me a slightly confused glance, but then he touched the side of Derek's hand, where it clutched the cane handle, with his nose.

I resisted the urge to cheer, which would distract the dog. Fred might be kind of funny looking, but he was one incredibly smart boy.

Derek took several steps, and Fred stayed right with him, on his right side.

Well, that was easier than you thought it would be, Ms. Snark commented.

I nodded and opened my mouth to call for a break.

Slamming car doors out front interrupted me.

Derek and Fred turned and moved back toward the house, but it was slow going from the far end of the yard. Whoever was out front would have to be patient.

I was about to offer to go see who it was, when two men rounded the corner into the backyard. Both wore uniforms, one dark blue and the other the dark green that most sheriff departments in Florida wear.

The guy in green stopped. His hand went to his holster.

The one in dark blue called out, "Mr. Bradshaw?"

I recognized the voice. "Andy?"

At that same moment, the guy in green yelled, "Drop those poles in your hands! Get down on the ground."

I blinked, unable to process what I was seeing. The sheriff's deputy had pulled his weapon, and it was aimed at Derek.

My stomach clenched, my heart rate soaring.

Derek had frozen in place. Beside him, Fred had gone into the *Cover* position, facing behind him. On the porch, Buddy jumped up growling.

"Stay, Buddy!" I ran forward and inserted myself in front of Derek. I'd like to say I was bravely defending a veteran, but honestly my first thought was that this deputy might shoot one of the dogs by accident.

"Is that you, Marcia?" Andy called out.

I decided that was a rhetorical question. My focus was on the crazy deputy with his gun drawn. *Sorry, Andy.* I let Ms. Snark rip.

"You idiot," she yelled at the deputy. "This man can't do either of those things without doing himself harm."

Andy held out a hand in the deputy's direction. "Easy, Joe."

The deputy ignored him. "Get out of the way, Miss. This man's a person of interest in a murder case."

Murder? Crapola!

CHAPTER THREE

"Is this your client?" Andy called out to me.

"Yes!"

"Joe, lower your gun." Andy had a touch of steel in his voice now.

"Not until he drops those poles," the guy in green said. "He can use them as weapons."

"They're canes, you nitwit," I screamed. "If he drops them, he will fall down."

The deputy, Joe, seemed unimpressed. "That's where I want him, on the ground." His pistol remained pointed at us.

"Deputy Harrison, I know these people." Andy sounded a little desperate. His hand had gone to his own holster. Was he going to draw on another law enforcement officer? "You're in my jurisdiction," he said in a firmer tone. "Now lower your gun!"

The deputy's hand slowly sank, and I blew out the breath I'd been holding.

What a total jerk, Ms. Snark said internally.

No argument from me.

Andy walked toward us, as Derek moved up beside me.

"Murder investigation?" I said when Andy was close enough I didn't need to shout. My voice shook a little.

Grim-faced, Andy looked at Derek. "Mr. Bradshaw, do you know Ezekiel Lord?"

"Yeah." Derek swallowed hard, his Adam's apple bobbing in his thick neck. "Has somethin' happened to him?"

"I'm so sorry." Andy sounded like he meant it. "I'm afraid Mr. Lord has been murdered."

Derek wobbled. "Murdered?"

Andy was next to him in a heartbeat, gently grabbing his broad shoulders and steadying him.

"No, no." Derek kept shaking his head. "It can't be. Zeke *can't* be dead."

Fred looked at me as if to say, *What do I do now, boss?*

I gave him the release signal and patted my thigh. Best to get him out of the way.

The next few moments were a blur as somehow we all made our way to the back door, Andy half holding Derek up. We crammed into his small kitchen.

I pointed to a corner, then held my hand out flat and lowered it toward the floor. Both dogs trotted over and laid down.

Andy settled Derek at the table and poured him a glass of water from the faucet.

As Derek took a few sips, Andy said, "The Crystal County sheriff needs you to come to the flea market and unlock your stall. They're searching the whole place."

I turned my back partway to the jerk deputy. "Why are *you* here?" I asked Andy in a low voice.

An odd grimace flashed across his face, so fast I thought maybe I'd imagined it. "Since Mr. Bradshaw lives in our jurisdiction, protocol requires the sheriff's deputy here to coordinate with our department. Our Deputy Chief sent me along."

I squinted at him, beyond curious. Why didn't they just give the deputy permission to pick Derek up?

Andy gave a slight shake of his head.

Okay, this is getting interesting, Ms. Snark commented internally.

"I need you to come with me," Deputy Harrison said to Derek in a crisp tone.

Considering the deputy's recent behavior, I had some trepidation about Derek willingly entering his jurisdiction. "I'm going with," I announced.

Harrison puffed out his chest. "I'm not allowed to transport civilians who are not related to the case being investigated."

Moments like this, I wished I cussed. I stared at Andy.

He gave another small shake of his head. This time it seemed more a gesture of confusion. He'd probably planned to extract himself from the situation once Derek agreed to cooperate.

He held my gaze for a long moment, then nodded slightly.

I put a bowl of water down next to the dogs and told them to stay.

Derek led the way out through the front of the house. In the living room, he pointed to his wheelchair. "Can you bring that? It collapses."

"No room for it," the deputy snapped.

"He needs it," I snapped back.

"He can use those pole things."

"He can't walk–"

Derek interrupted me. "I can only walk for a limited time, or I get too tired."

I gave him an apologetic look. I needed to rein in my mama-bear routine, as Becky called it.

Andy had folded up the wheelchair. "It'll fit in the backseat."

Deputy Harrison pointed at Derek. "He goes back there. Against the rules for anybody to ride in the front seat."

"Your trunk then," Andy said, sounding slightly irritated.

"Full of equipment."

Meanwhile, I was gritting my teeth and counting to ten. I was on nine and it wasn't helping much.

Andy glanced at me as he held up a hand. "It'll go in *my* backseat," he said in a hard voice. "We'll follow you. Come on, Marcia."

In his cruiser, I said, "That guy is a piece of work."

"He's a piece of something." His expression grim, Andy stared out the windshield. "Don't repeat this or you'll get me in trouble, but the Deputy Chief took me aside and told me this guy's a jack… I mean, a jerk. That's why he sent me along." He shook his head. "But I sure didn't expect him to pull his gun on Mr. Bradshaw."

"Um, I didn't want to correct you in front of the jerk deputy, but it might help to call him Sergeant Bradshaw, to remind folks that he's a veteran."

"Duly noted." Andy sighed. "Harrison wasn't totally out of line, at first. We're trained to react to any potential threat and neutralize it. But when you pointed out they were canes, he should've stood down."

He shook his head again. "I'd heard rumors before, but I didn't quite believe them. Now I do. Seems a few years back, Harrison tazed one of his father's pigs, just to see what would happen."

I stared at him, horrified.

He briefly glanced my way. "The pig was okay. No permanent damage."

"Didn't he have to be tazed himself when he went through training?" Will had told me that was protocol for new officers in most law enforcement agencies. He'd had to endure it when he'd joined the Marion County's Sheriff's Department.

Andy nodded, his gaze flicking my way again. "I think he got out of it. Harrison's father is a county commissioner."

"Ah, which explains why the jerk hasn't been fired."

I hadn't even met the Crystal County sheriff yet, and I already felt sorry for him.

~

On Sunday, the flea market had been a beehive of activity with customers and vendors. Today, Monday, it was closed to the public, but it was a beehive nonetheless, of sheriff's deputies and crime scene techs, plus a few vendors hanging around.

As we neared Derek's stall, I got a queasy feeling in my stomach. The florescent overhead lights glinted off an intricate silver dragonhead, in the center of the display of hand-carved walking sticks.

Derek's mouth turned up, but the smile didn't make it to his eyes. They were cloudy with worry. He seemed unsure if he should be happy or scared about the cane magically reappearing. He hit the button on his remote, and the wire-mesh curtain retracted.

He pushed his wheelchair forward, as the rest of us took a couple of steps.

Andy's arm flew out in front of me. At the same time, Deputy Harrison said, "Stop, Mr. Bradshaw."

The queasy feeling got a lot worse. The dark spot down in the wires of the dragonhead had grown in size, and it was redder than it had been, as if someone had poured red paint inside the cane's handle.

Only I knew it wasn't paint.

Deputy Harrison gestured to a crime scene tech, who took several photos of the display.

"Lemme guess," I whispered to Andy, "Zeke died from the proverbial blunt force trauma."

Andy shook his head. Why was he unwilling to give out that information when the evidence was right there in front of us?

With bright blue rubber gloves on her hands, the tech gingerly lifted the dragonhead cane from the display's center.

I gasped. Derek's mouth fell open.

"He was stabbed in the chest," Andy whispered back.

I blinked, but the object did not morph back into a cane.

Below the intricate dragonhead handle was a thin saber.

CHAPTER FOUR

Andy gave me the name of a criminal defense attorney. "I don't know how good he is, but his face is plastered all over some billboards on I-75."

I found his number online and called him, as Andy drove us to the Crystal County Sheriff's Department.

Once the lawyer arrived, he, Derek and a detective went into an interview room and closed the door.

"I really should be getting back," Andy said.

"I know. Sorry I dragged you into this."

"Not your fault. I might've come along anyway, the way things went down. They're probably gonna want to talk to you too, since you were there yesterday when the cane's theft was discovered."

I'd filled him in on those details while we were on the road.

I should've brought my own car. I shook my head. I'd never dreamed that Derek might be a suspect.

I looked past the short counter that separated us from a bullpen of gray metal desks. Two uniformed deputies hunched over paperwork. A plain-clothes detective sat at another desk, a phone receiver glued to his ear. I said, "Surely someone can give us a ride home later."

"Maybe, maybe not," Andy said.

I wasn't totally sure what that meant, and I wasn't crazy about the dogs being closed up in an unfamiliar house for a long period of time.

I waffled for a moment, but the thought that the sheriff's department might *not* give Derek a ride home—if he wasn't arrested—decided me. I wasn't going to leave him stranded here by himself.

"I don't suppose they have Uber out here in the boonies."

Andy let out a small snort. "If you can't get a ride, call me and I'll come back for you."

I nodded.

He put a hand on my shoulder and squeezed gently. "Try not to worry. His lawyer won't let them railroad him if he's innocent."

That did not bode well—another law enforcement officer was even considering the possibility that this sheriff's department might try to railroad a suspect. But I thanked Andy for his efforts at reassurance. He took his leave.

The sheriff himself interviewed me. I wasn't sure what that meant. I was hardly a key witness.

Maybe it was just a courtesy, since I was married to a Marion County detective.

The sheriff was a tall man, at least six-four, and big all over. I suspected he'd played football once upon a time, and he was slowly losing the battle of keeping muscle from going to fat. But despite his size, he didn't come across as intimidating. His hair was gray, with a little sandy mixed in—I pegged him as about my mother's age, mid-sixties. His weathered face wore a tan and, at the moment, a friendly enough expression.

He sat down across from me at a wooden table in a glass-walled conference room and dropped some papers in front of him. Then he asked me to tell him exactly what happened on Sunday morning, when the "sword" had gone missing.

"Sheriff, we didn't know it was a sword. We thought it was a cane."

He pursed his lips. "Okay, when the cane went missing."

I described coming back from the prayer service and Derek

finding the trunk open and devoid of the dragonhead cane.

He told me to run through it again. I did.

"You believed Mr. Bradshaw's dismay was legitimate?" he asked.

"Yes, sir. *Sergeant* Bradshaw was quite upset. That cane has strong sentimental value to him, because Zeke Lord gave it to him." I was trying to make the point that Derek and Zeke were close.

"Hmm, but you see, we found some paperwork amongst Mr. Lord's things. Looks like the prov-e-nance…" he dragged the word out emphasizing each syllable, "…for that sword, I mean cane. It was worth a pretty penny, so why would he give it away?"

"He said yesterday that he'd expected Derek to sell it. I think it was Zeke's way of trying to help out a friend financially, but without making it seem like charity."

He'd also said that the cane fit in better with Derek's merchandise than with his, but that wasn't true. Did Zeke not know that it was a disguised sword?

"Did the provenance describe it as a cane or a sword?" I asked.

The sheriff glanced down at the papers in front of him. "A saber hidden inside a mahogany cane sheath," he read, "with an ornate silver dragonhead handle."

The slight twinkle disappeared from his eyes, making them look less friendly. "Why do you ask?"

I repeated Zeke's comment about why he had given it to Derek. "I also got the impression that Zeke felt Derek had it way overpriced at five-thousand dollars." As had I, at the time.

The sheriff lifted a sandy-gray eyebrow and tapped the papers on the table. "According to this, it's worth three times that."

My chin dropped. "Fifteen thousand?"

The sheriff nodded.

"Then why in heaven's name did Zeke give it away?"

"That is a very good question." The sheriff's voice had gone hard. "And I intend to find the answer."

A knock on the conference room door. A young deputy stuck his head in. He barely looked old enough to vote.

"Sheriff," he said in an excited voice, "they found some stolen stuff, in some woman vendor's trailer."

The sheriff shot the rookie a scathing look. The kid's face turned beet red, then he disappeared and the door shut, probably a little harder than was good for his career. Although I suspected he'd already blown his first promotion by talking out of turn in front of a civilian.

The sheriff rose from his chair. "I'll arrange for someone to take you home."

"And Derek as well."

His hesitation was so slight, I wasn't sure if I'd imagined it.

"And the sergeant too. Mrs. Haines, your reputation precedes you. Please, do *not* interfere in my investigation." It was couched as a request, but his tone said he would not go easy on me if I disobeyed.

Ah, that's why the sheriff talked to you himself, Ms. Snark commented internally. I could've sworn I heard her snicker.

"Um, Sheriff, I go by Banks-Haines."

Although I was rethinking that strategy. It was a little bit of a mouthful.

~

The rookie drove us back to Derek's in one of the department's SUVs. I asked him a few questions, trying to sound like a curious tourist merely trying to understand the dynamics of a Florida county sheriff's department.

But he answered me in monosyllables, followed by "ma'am." Either the sheriff had torn into him, or he'd figured out for himself that he was already in enough trouble.

It was late afternoon by the time I got myself and the dogs back to Becky's. The house seemed quiet from the outside. I took the dogs around back for a bathroom break, and while they were at it, I stuck my head in through the kitchen door, which was rarely locked.

Still as an empty church inside. I surmised that babies and mama were napping, and decided that was a lovely idea.

After retrieving the dogs, I took them with me to the guest bedroom, gestured for them to lie down and flopped fully clothed on top of the bedspread on the antique double bed.

Lovely fragrances woke me awhile later. I splashed water on my face in the bathroom, then the dogs and I followed our noses to the kitchen.

"Hey there, sleepyhead." Becky stood by the kitchen table, a stack of plates in her hands. The twins were already in their high-chairs, slobbering over teething biscuits. I winced a little as Winnie threw part of his across the room.

Becky didn't bat an eye. "How'd the training go today?"

I took the plates from her and started setting the table. She grabbed a paper towel, scooped up the yucky biscuit and tossed it in the trash can, all in one fluid motion that said she did this kind of thing several times a day.

I tried not to let her see the shudder that ran through me.

As much as I love my godchildren, being in close proximity to their bodily fluids over the last few days had not improved my attitude toward having children of my own.

"Things were going pretty good, until my client almost got arrested."

Becky, now at the stove, whirled around toward me. "Seriously? What happened?"

I gave her a synopsis of the afternoon's adventures.

By the time I'd finished, Andy was coming through the front door. "Hey, Marcia," he greeted me, then gave Becky a peck on the lips.

"Hey, little ones." He kissed his children on the tops of their heads. Jazzie looked up and gave him a toothless, slimy grin, but Winnie was busy pounding the remaining half of his biscuit into tiny crumbs with his fist.

Who says some gender differences aren't innate, Ms. Snark quipped internally.

And then they get reinforced. I kept that observation to myself. Most of the time my masters degree in psychology comes in handy, but sometimes I notice things I wished I didn't.

Sure enough, Andy grinned back at his daughter, but didn't interact again with his son.

He headed for the living room where I knew his first action would be to lock his service weapon in the gun safe in the corner.

Once we were all seated, a savory pasta dish in the middle of the round table, I asked Andy, "Did you hear anything more about the you-know-what at the flea market?" I really didn't want one of my godchildren's first words to be *murder*.

He frowned and shook his head as he scooped food onto his plate, then handed me the serving spoon. "No reason I would. Not my jurisdiction."

I tried a different approach. "Hmm," I said as I served myself, "I wonder how I can find out about the forensics at the scene." I put the spoon in the casserole dish, the handle pointed in Becky's direction.

She was currently cutting thick noodles into bite-sized pieces on a plastic plate shaped like a cow's head—and flicking her gaze back and forth between me and Andy.

He took a bite of pasta and veggies, chewed slowly and swallowed. "Delicious, honey." He turned to me. "I can't think of any *legitimate* way you could get that information."

Uh, oh. I'd stumbled over a line. I stared down at my plate, studiously examining the bits of green, purple and yellow stuff scattered in the creamy sauce adorning the alfredo noodles.

And felt an all too familiar jolt of envy. Not only was Becky gorgeous, she was a better cook than I was. Of course, that wasn't saying much.

I glanced up, assuming Andy would be focused on his food or his family. But he was still looking at me. "Marcia, why do you want to poke around in this?"

His choice of words made me wonder if he and Will had discussed my proclivity for getting involved in investigations. Because that's what Will annoyingly called it—*poking around.*

"I'm worried about my client."

Andy nodded once, a slight dropping and then lifting of his head. "I get that. The fact that he wasn't charged today is a good sign." He paused, spreading butter on a piece of whole-grain bread. "Deputy Harrison may be a jerk who jumps to conclusions, but the sheriff down there has a reputation for being methodical."

"He did ask me if I thought Derek was genuinely surprised that the cane, I mean sword, was gone."

"And what did you say?"

"Yes, definitely. He was visibly upset."

Andy gave me a there-you-go look and forked food into his mouth.

"Do you know if they found the cane sheath?" I asked.

He swallowed, then blew out air. "I got the impression, before I left to return to my *own jurisdiction*, that they had not."

Becky had been eating quietly, while keeping an eye on the

twins and also glancing at her husband and me occasionally. Now she stared at me.

Okay, I get it, Beck. I'll back off.

"So, did anything else interesting happen in Williston today?" I asked Andy.

One end of his mouth quirked up and his face lost the stony-cop expression. "Nope. Wrote a few parking tickets and caught a couple of kids vaping behind the school."

"Is that such a big deal these days?" I said. "I thought most high schools even have smoking areas behind the school."

"This was the elementary school."

"Crapola."

He smiled.

Becky's shoulders relaxed considerably.

And my chest was tight with guilt. I'd almost put her in the middle.

Derek hasn't been arrested, and Andy says that's a good sign, I told myself. And the sheriff in Crystal County did seem to know what he was doing.

I really didn't need to investigate.

That's it. No more poking around in this.

CHAPTER FIVE

With my no-poking-around resolution in mind, I vowed to myself that I would not ask Will about the case—even though Marion, Levy and Crystal Counties were all adjacent, and he might very well have heard something about it.

Ironically, he brought it up when he called Monday evening. “Seems you had a little excitement over there today.” His tone was casual, but I didn’t trust it.

“Did Andy call you?”

“Of course he did. We used to work together.” He was reminding me they were friends in their own right, not just because of the connection between Becky and me.

And technically, Andy had worked *for* him, as a deputy when Will was sheriff of Collins County, and then he’d succeeded him as sheriff. When Will decided not to run for reelection, that had left only two viable candidates, Andy, a light-skinned black male whom the residents knew fairly well, and a more recent newcomer, Jamilla Price, a darker-skinned female. No way was poor Jamilla getting elected in small, rural and somewhat bigoted Collins County.

But Andy had only lasted a few years as well, before he felt he had to get his family out of that insular environment. You'd think after losing two sheriffs in a row, the county would realize they needed an attitude adjustment.

"Did you know the guy who was killed?" Will pulled me back to the current reality. "This Ezekiel Lord?"

"I met him once, on Sunday." Was that just yesterday morning? It had been a long thirty-six hours. "My client's pretty upset. I think they were close, in a kind of father-son way."

"But you're not getting involved, right?"

"Not intentionally," I said, trying not to sound defensive. "The sheriff himself interviewed me." I opted not to mention that he'd also warned me about interfering.

"What'd he ask you about?"

"The theft of the murder weapon the day before."

"Andy said it was some kind of a sword."

I described the antique cane/sword to him. The image of the bloodstained dragonhead handle popped into my head. A shudder ran through me.

To cancel out that image, I intentionally brought up my husband's rugged face in my mind's eye, his baby blues sparkling with amusement.

"Harumph," Will said in my ear. "Never ceases to amaze me the creative ways people can kill each other."

My inner Will's eyes lost their sparkle, and he shook his head slowly, mournfully.

The real Will cleared his throat. "I don't like you hanging around there while a murderer's on the loose. Can't you come home until after whoever did this is caught?"

Now I was shaking my head. I'd figured this was coming. "Do you know if they have any leads?"

"No, and I'm *not* going to ask."

"Then I don't know how to answer your question. This whole thing could drag on for weeks, or months. I've got to train Derek at some point."

And there was another timing factor that I didn't bother to go into. As of next week, the flea market would be open on Wednesdays as well, until Christmas. And Derek had said his stall got quite busy. All that would seriously cut into available training time.

"Look," I said, "tomorrow and Wednesday, I'll be training at

Derek's house. After that, I'll only be at the flea market when it's open and there are lots of people around. I'll be fine."

Silence for a beat, then Will said, "Actually, stabbing is a pretty personal way to kill someone. It was most likely someone the vic knew, not some random murder."

"Exactly, so I'm not at risk."

The sound of air being blown out in a sigh. "Not as long as you keep your nose out of it."

"I fully intend to. Don't worry."

A low chuckle. "Easy for you to say. You're not married to *you*."

I laughed. "Good point, but I do promise to behave this time. The sheriff is a good ole boy, but he seems competent."

Another small sigh. "I'd better get to bed. Miss you."

"Miss you too. Goodnight, love." I disconnected and smiled at the phone. That conversation had gone much better than similar ones in the past. Apparently, Will was getting used to the idea that I could take care of myself.

Well, most of the time.

My smile faded as I realized that now I perversely wanted to call the sheriff in Crystal County and ask about leads. Indeed, I really, *really* wanted to call him.

I could use the fact that Will is nervous for my safety as an excuse for asking.

But it was way too late to call tonight.

I shook my head at myself and gritted my teeth. "I'm not going to get involved," I said out loud.

Buddy and Fred both lifted their heads from where they'd been snoozing on the bedside rug. Buddy gave me his patented what's-up look, head cocked to one side.

"Nothing, boy. Absolutely nothing is up."

~

For the next two days, I distracted myself from temptation by focusing on the training with Derek. It went well.

On Thursday, we took Buddy and Fred to the flea market, so the latter could get used to the place. That's all we were really aiming for today. Tomorrow between customers, we would practice any tasks that Fred might need to perform while here.

At the sight of her kitchen gadgets stall down the aisle a bit, I of course thought of Nell. I had a strong suspicion she was the woman vendor who'd had "stolen stuff" in her trailer.

"Have you talked to Nell lately?" I asked. "Did the sheriff's people question her?"

Derek's usual cheerful smile sagged into a frown. He turned his cart away from me. "Yeah, it seems she was the one who was stealin' things around here."

He sounded sad but not all that surprised, as he straightened items on a table. Was that the reason for his earlier upset about the thefts? Had he suspected Nell all along?

But I wasn't about to ask those questions out loud. Instead, I said, "I wonder how she got past your locked curtain to get to your trunk and the dragon cane." The mesh-metal curtain hadn't been damaged.

He glanced my way, shaking his head. "She swears she didn't steal the cane. And she's real worried that the sheriff's department's going to arrest her, even though…"

I was kind of surprised they hadn't already done so.

I tuned back in to the end of Derek's sentence. "…she says it was somebody else's idea."

"What was whose idea?" I asked.

He was now setting out some new wooden toys he'd brought from home. "I guess it was somebody else's idea to do the stealin', but she won't say who." Again, he sounded sad, and maybe a little worried.

"Hey, are you two an item?" Ms. Snark blurted out before I could stop her.

Derek looked at me funny. "An item?"

"Sorry, I sound like my mother sometimes. I meant, are you and Nell dating?"

Derek ducked his head and his cheeks flushed. "No, but I… I guess I'd like to ask her out. Haven't gotten up the nerve yet."

Dang! That would be a complication he really didn't need in his life right now, especially if she was about to get arrested.

"So, what did the detectives say to her about the thefts? Do you think they *are* going to arrest her? And what exactly did they take out of her trailer?"

Curious, much? Ms. Snark commented internally.

Hey, you were the one blurting out nosy questions a few seconds ago.

"They said they *could* arrest her for receiving stolen goods, at the very least. But they were still investigating to see if there would be additional charges." Derek shook his head again. "She got kinda cagey when I asked about what they confiscated. That's when she said it was somebody else's idea."

The fact that the sheriff's department hadn't arrested her struck me as odd. They had the goods on her, quite literally. Rather than arresting her, had they put a tail on her to see if she led them to her accomplice?

"Hey," I said, "while you're finishing opening up here, how about I take Fred for a walk around the flea market? Get him used to the sounds and smells and such."

"Sure," Derek said in a distracted voice. He was trying out different walking sticks in the center hole of the stand, looking for the one that was most likely to draw customers' eyes that way.

The dragonhead cane/sword had been taken as evidence, and it was unlikely he would get it back anytime soon. I wondered if he would still treasure it as a gift from Zeke. Or would it now be a reminder of his friend and mentor's death?

Buddy, Fred and I set out to explore the flea market. Both dogs wore their red service dog vests, and most people abided by the big letters along their backs that spelled out *Do Not Pet*.

Only one teenage girl approached, her hand out. "Oh, they're so–"

I held my hand up in a stop gesture. "They're working right now."

"Oh," she said, "sorry."

"No problem. Thank you for understanding."

The flea market would not officially open for another fifteen minutes. I figured as the crowd grew, I'd encounter more well-meaning people who wanted to pet the dogs.

Normally, my clients have certain people who are in their lives on a regular basis, and they could convey to those people that their service dog was not a pet and should not be fussed over while on duty. And when out in public, they could ward off unwanted efforts to pet the dog without worrying too much about offending people, since they were strangers.

But in Derek's case, those strangers were potential customers. Hmm, how to get people to back off without taking offense? Most weren't as quick to get it as the teenage girl had been.

As I chewed on that question, we wandered the aisles of the two adjacent buildings that made up the flea market. There was also a section that joined them in the middle, making a big H.

Coming out of one end of Derek's building, we rounded the corner to go into the back end of the other one. I paused, noticing that the stalls had back doors, with a short step down to the ground. Many vendors had sheds or tents just outside the doors. Others had their cars or pickup trucks pulled up close. Vendors and their helpers walked back and forth, carrying merchandise into the stalls.

I spotted a small camp trailer, the old-fashioned kind, rounded on top. It had once been silver but had faded to a dull gray and showed rusty spots in a few places.

The trailer's door opened, and Nell stepped out. She held a medium-sized cardboard box in front of her as she carefully stepped down the two steps to the ground. Leaving the trailer door ajar, she went through the back door of her stall.

We walked over. "Stay," I told the dogs, and then stepped up on the lowest step to peek inside.

A small table—pressed wood with a veneer surface—was directly across from the doorway, with benches on either side that were barely big enough for one person. To my right, crammed against the front wall of the camper was a twin-sized mattress, covered by a slightly rumpled blanket.

Does she live here?

I took another step up and craned my neck around the edge of the door. A tiny sink and small square of counter, with doll-house-sized cabinets over and under, and beyond that a rough-hewn plywood wall that was most definitely not part of the original layout. In the wall was a wooden door, with a hefty hasp at eye level. An equally hefty padlock hung from it, unlocked.

The thump of a tail against the metal steps. I glanced down. Buddy had taken up the *Cover* position, as had Fred beside him. Both were twitching their ears.

Someone was behind me.

"What are you doing?" Nell's voice, slightly annoyed.

"Sorry, I was only curious." I ad-libbed, "You know, to see how the camper was laid out inside. Very efficient." I gave her a big smile.

She frowned. "Ain't nothin' left to see in there. The cops took all my collections."

"Your collections?" I stepped down to the ground.

"Yes." She leaned slightly toward me. "I mean I was storing some stuff for somebody else, and maybe some of that stuff was stolen. How would I know?" She shrugged, but her feigned innocence didn't quite ring true. "But they had no right to take my collections too."

"So, what kind of things did you collect?"

Her gaze dropped to her feet. "Just things I liked."

"Things you liked?" I echoed.

"Yeah, nothin' that was worth all that much, but they were pretty."

"Uh, *they* what?"

She looked at me like I had switched to some foreign language.

"What kinds of pretty things?" I repeated.

She shrugged. "Rings, and little boxes, and stuff like that."

I nodded. "Well, I'd better let you get on with opening your stall."

She gave me a shy smile. "Okay. See ya later."

I stepped aside, patting my thighs to signal that the dogs should follow me. We went around the corner and entered the building.

I spotted the heavy chain link fencing surrounding Zeke's stall. The dogs and I headed that way.

I stared through the links, only mildly surprised to see an empty table and walls. All the knives and swords were gone.

More tail thumps from the dogs. I turned.

"Good morning," said the vendor in the next stall. It was the older fellow, Denny, whom I'd met on Sunday after the prayer service. His stall was full of baseball caps, of every imaginable color, with every imaginable decal or logo on them. All the sports teams, a dozen countries' flags, and several well-known corporations, like John Deere, plus many more.

"How's it going?" Denny asked in a booming voice.

"Okay. How you doing?"

He shrugged, his hands palm up and slightly out to the sides. "Can't complain. Looks like it's gonna be a nice day."

"Yes. Hopefully a little cooler than the last few."

Having exhausted all the small talk that two strangers can come up with, he squinted at me. Gesturing toward Zeke's stall, he said, "You know anything about what's going on?"

For a moment, I thought he meant regarding the space. Did he want to expand his own set-up?

"Any word on how he died?" the man asked. His face was pinched, his eyes cloudy.

Seriously? This guy didn't know Zeke had been murdered?

Or is he fishing, to see if you have any info? Ms. Snark said in my head.

Wow, we might have to rename you Ms. Paranoid.

Nonetheless, I decided ignorance was the best approach. I shook my head.

Denny pulled out a handkerchief and wiped sweat from his brow, even though it was in the low sixties, this early on a November day. "Well, let me know if you hear anything."

"Okay, sure."

Hmmm, I guess the guy could just be concerned because his stall was next to Zeke's. No doubt they'd gotten to be friends, or at least friendly, over time.

But there was something slightly off about his reactions. I tucked that observation away for later contemplation, and the dogs and I headed back to Derek's stall.

He had finished setting up.

"Hey," I said, "before things get busy, can I get some pics for the agency's newsletter. They send it out quarterly to our donors, to show what their money is paying for."

"Sure." Derek took Fred's leash from me, rubbed his head affectionately, then told him to sit next to his cart in front of the stall. He gave me one of his signature smiles. It didn't quite reach his eyes though, which wasn't a big surprise. He was putting on a good show, but he was grieving for his friend.

I snapped a few photos as the stream of customers began to pick up.

One fellow, by himself, seemed vaguely familiar. He also seemed to be hanging around Nell's stall. He wore jeans and a blue-striped dress shirt, collar open and the sleeves rolled up.

Another rather beefy guy, also on his own, was even more out of place. Instead of jeans or shorts like most people at the flea market sported—vendors and customers alike—he wore black dress slacks, neatly creased, and a green polo-style knit shirt that looked as if it had been pressed.

He was hovering at the stall next to Derek's. I wondered if these two were plain-clothes deputies, sent by the sheriff to keep an eye on Nell. Or maybe Derek as well.

My throat tightened at that thought.

"Hey, Derek, do you know anything about Nell's 'collections?'" I made air quotes.

"Not really. She's mentioned them once or twice."

"Have you ever seen them?"

"Nope."

"Have you ever been in her trailer?"

His cheeks flushed. "Once or twice."

"Have you been in that locked room?"

He shook his head. "She acts like it's a bank vault."

"Could you see if you can find out more about her collections?"

"Now?"

I hadn't meant now, but why not? "Yes, if you don't mind. I can watch things here."

Derek nodded and pointed his cart toward her stall.

I took the dogs back behind the curtain and signaled for them to lie down. Buddy plopped down on the cement.

Fred started to follow suit, but I said, "No." I pointed to the dog bed. Might as well get him used to it. "Lie down."

Fred looked at me, tilted his head, then complied. Have I mentioned he's one smart dog?

Smiling, I went out front to help a customer.

~

A half hour later, I was straightening some wooden toys on a table—a grandmotherly type had just pawed through them but hadn't bought anything—when shouts of "Hey!" and "Watch out!" came from the building's aisle.

I headed toward the noise, and almost got run over by Derek and his cart.

"Yikes." I jumped back.

He stopped less than an inch from a twelve-by-twelve wooden post, one of many that held up the building's massive metal roof.

I ran to his side and stopped, gawking at him.

His red face was screwed up into a mask of anguish and fury. I was pretty sure I heard teeth grinding.

"What happened?" I gasped out. "Are you okay?"

His lips pinched together in a straight line. Without a word, he backed the cart up, swinging it in an arc, ignoring the people hustling to get out of its way.

When the cart stopped beeping, realization dawned that he was about to shoot forward again. Heart pounding, I stood in the middle of the aisle, arms out, trying to stop him.

He moved straight toward me. "Get out of my way, Marcia," he yelled.

I jumped to the side. The cart raced past me at top speed, which wasn't all that fast. But in the now crowded aisle, it was a very bad idea.

Frozen to the spot, I stared after Derek and his cart as they disappeared out the end of the building.

Shaking myself slightly, I ran back to the dogs. "Stay!" I grabbed the gate's remote control off the shelf where Derek kept it during the day and ran out of the stall. Hitting the button, I didn't wait to watch the curtain close. I bolted after Derek.

I caught up with him at his white SUV. His arms were on the handlebars of the cart, his face buried against them, the muscles in his back so tense I was half expecting his shirt to tear down the middle, like The Hulk's.

"Derek?" I said gently as I approached.

After a beat, he lifted his head and swiped a massive forearm across his face. Through gritted teeth, he growled, "Take the cart back, please."

It was couched as a request, but the sharpness of his tone had me wanting to salute and say, "Yes, Sir." Instead I intentionally gentled my voice, "Sure, but are you okay?"

He shook his head and maneuvered himself off of the cart and into his SUV faster than I'd ever seen him move.

This time I had the good sense to stand back.

The engine roared. Tires spewed gravel as he took off.

Worried butterflies fluttered in my stomach. What if Fred had been in the truck with him?

I stared after him for a couple of beats, then went to the cart. It took me a little while to figure out the hand controls. In fits and starts, I managed to get the cart back inside without running over anybody.

But as I neared Derek's stall, my mouth dropped open and a heavy sense of dread spread through my body. One side of the mesh-metal curtain had snagged on some wooden stools, leaving a substantial gap.

And someone had taken advantage of my absence to ransack the place.

I brought the cart to a jerky halt and climbed off. Closer up, I could see that mainly the walking sticks display had been disrupted. Canes and walking sticks were scattered all over the floor, and a few had been thrown onto the tables of toys, knocking them around.

I raced into the back area—and screeched to a stop. It was a mess, stuff pulled off the shelves and some of the contents of the trunk yanked out and dumped on the floor.

I whirled around to the dogs' area, and my heart stalled. I couldn't breathe.

Fred stood on his bed, quivering. But Buddy was gone.

CHAPTER SIX

Stomach in knots, I stood amidst the chaos in Derek's stall. I was getting more and more antsy. I wanted to be looking for my dog, and I was worried about Derek.

His file had said he had anger issues, not unusual in PTSD, and especially in veterans. Their anger at all they had seen and endured had to be kept under tight control while they were fighting in a war zone. And then, when they came home, they were expected to go back to "normal" life, like nothing had happened.

All that pent-up rage tended to come out at unexpected times, and sometimes at inappropriate targets.

But even with the notations in his file, I'd been surprised by Derek's anger. He was normally such a cheerful guy. Then again, maybe *because* of his natural easygoing personality his anger was that much more suppressed.

I also worried that whoever'd trashed the stall might go to Derek's house to continue their search. I was pretty sure they hadn't found what they were looking for, because I was pretty sure I knew what it was—the dragonhead sword/cane.

But why had the searcher taken Buddy?

I'd had a heck of a time convincing the dispatcher to take me seriously. At first, she chastised me for calling 911 over a lost dog. "He isn't lost. He was stolen," I said. "And he's a valuable animal, a trained service dog, worth thousands of dollars."

She'd remained unimpressed, until I mentioned his theft might be related to the homicide at the flea market Monday morning. "Deputies are on their way," she'd said. "Stay put."

I was having more and more difficulty following those instructions. Heart beating faster than was healthy, I tried to pace but kept tripping over the scattered canes. I desperately wanted to clean up the stall, both to have something to do and so Derek wouldn't see it this way. But that would be tampering with evidence.

For the third time, I called Derek. For the third time, it went straight to voicemail. He must have his phone turned off.

A woof from behind me. I whirled around. A man had Buddy by the ring in his service vest.

Lightheaded with relief, I yelled, "Buddy!"

The man let go of him, and the big black dog bounded over to me.

I dropped to my knees, crying, "Thank God, thank God," as I squeezed his neck.

He squirmed some, then licked my cheek.

I laughed. "Sorry, boy. Didn't mean to strangle you."

The man was standing by, an indulgent smile on his face.

"Where'd you find him?" I asked.

"He was chasing some dude, barking his head off. I grabbed the edge of his vest as he went by. He didn't resist me hanging onto him."

"He wouldn't. He was just in protect mode, trying to chase the guy away."

The man looked around, his mouth hanging open a little. "That guy did this to Derek's stall?"

I nodded, standing up. "It must have been him, if Buddy was chasing him. What'd he look like?"

"White guy, not real tall but heavyset. Dark hair, cut real neat." He shook his head slightly. "Even running, it didn't fly around. Dressed real neat too. In his fifties, I'd guess."

"Overdressed for a flea market?"

"Yup," the guy said.

One of the two men I'd suspected earlier of being sheriff's

department detectives. But why would a detective be searching Derek's stall? And why would he run away when Buddy came out of the back? Was he afraid of dogs?

Wait a minute! The back had also been searched. How did that happen when Buddy had chased the man away?

I shook my head, more confused than ever. "Hey, can you watch the stall until the deputies get here?"

"Yeah, my wife is covering ours."

I handed him the remote for the gate. "Thanks. I gotta go check on Derek. He went home. Um, he wasn't feeling well. And thanks for catching my dog for me."

"Sure thing."

I called for Fred, who bolted out of the back like a demon was on his tail.

I felt a little sick to my stomach, and yet proud at the same time. The dog had to have been terrified, but he'd obeyed my last command to stay.

Once we were on the road, I used my Bluetooth to call the sheriff's department. I kept insisting that I had to talk to the sheriff himself.

When he finally came on the line, I said, "Do you have two men in plain clothes at the flea market?"

A pause. "I'm not answering that question."

"Was one or both of them instructed to search Derek's stall again?"

"I'm not answering that either. What's this about, Miz *Banks-Haines*?" He exaggerated the hyphenated last names.

Ignoring that, I filled him in on what had happened.

"I'd heard there was some disturbance at the flea market," he said, when I'd finished. "My deputies are on the way." His voice was crisp. "Stay there until they arrive, please."

"No can do. I'm on my way to check on Derek Bradshaw at his house."

Another pause, a bit longer. "Then stay there. Someone will be over in a while to take your statement." He disconnected.

"Thanks a lot," I grumbled under my breath.

My precipitous race to Derek's house turned out to be unnecessary. There were no strange cars hanging around. No vehicles, except his truck, anywhere in sight. The nearby houses even had empty driveways.

I knocked on the front door, and when there was no answer, I tried the knob. It wasn't locked, which didn't particularly surprise me. People often left their doors unlocked when they were home in rural Florida, sometimes even when they weren't home.

I nudged the door open and stepped inside, the dogs right behind me. "Derek?"

Rustling noises came from the kitchen. We moved in that direction, my nerves on high alert.

But again, nothing there but Derek, sitting at the table in his wheelchair, staring into space.

"Hey," I said softly.

His face turned toward me, and his eyes slowly lost their faraway look. "Hey."

"You okay?"

He shook his head at the same time as "Yeah," came out of his mouth.

Ho boy, talk about mixed signals.

He glanced away. "Sorry I yelled at you."

And almost ran us over, Ms. Snark added.

Oh, so it's us *now,* I said internally.

Well, I would've been flattened too.

I ignored her, trying to decide what to address first.

Begin at the beginning. My inner mom's voice this time.

"Um, what happened when you talked to Nell?"

He shook his head again, his eyes morphing from dull to shiny. "Remember I told you my father ran off when I was just a little kid?"

I nodded and slipped into the chair across from him. Under the table, I held my hand out parallel to the ground, then lowered it, signaling for the dogs to lie down. They complied and promptly went to sleep. It had been a strenuous morning for them.

Derek and I'd had a short conversation about his background, when I'd brought Fred here six months ago, to see how they got along. I'd asked him why he went into the Army. He said it was the only way he knew to make decent money to support his single mom, who was too sick to work herself. He'd mentioned his father abandoning the family when he was little, and then he'd changed the subject.

Now, he said, "I don't remember much about my dad, but my mom told me all these wonderful stories about him when I was a kid. She said he was a few years older than her. He'd fought in Vietnam, right out of high school, and had decided to become career Army. Later, he was killed in Desert Storm."

He paused, sucked in air. "When I was thirteen, my aunt told me that he'd actually come home from that war, but he was a changed man. He drank too much and couldn't hold a job. And he finally ran off with the female bartender at the local dive."

Derek paused again, staring right at me now. He swallowed hard. "You can't tell anyone this, Marcia, what I'm about to tell you."

"Okay." I was bound anyway, by agency rules, to keep anything regarding our clients' mental health to myself. I figured childhood wounds fell into the same category as combat-induced issues.

"You promise?"

I held my right hand up in the air, as if I were swearing to tell the whole truth in court. "I promise."

Derek took another deep breath. It came out rather ragged. "I hated my father after that, with a hate so pure—it was like this shiny black stone I found in a stream one time. Hard and cold and dark."

I nodded. With a cheating ex-husband in my own history, I got how love could turn to hate.

I felt Fred's body brush my knee. He was defying my order to lie down, which usually implied a "Stay" as well. But if he did what I suspected he was about to do, it would be one of those times when a service dog was supposed to defy that order.

"My mom used to tell me to let it go," Derek continued, "that the hate would eat me up inside. Instead, her worryin' about me ate her up. She got cancer and when she couldn't work no more, she went on disability. Most months we had to choose between paying the rent or getting her pain meds…" He trailed off, his eyes shiny again.

The tablecloth moved a little in front of Derek, and I saw the very tip of Fred's nose.

I hid a smile. The dog was doing exactly what he was supposed to do.

Derek looked down. "Hey, boy." He patted the dog's head.

Fred pushed up farther, his chin now resting against his master's broad chest. Derek absently stroked his ears.

"We were about to be evicted when I turned eighteen. My aunt said she'd take mom in and take care of her, if I wanted to go into the Army. I dropped out of school and joined up. I would've graduated in two months, but that didn't matter. I could send enough money home to pay for my mom's meds. That's what counted."

He shook his head slightly, still petting Fred. It seemed to be having the desired anxiety-reduction effect. Now Derek looked mostly sad.

"After my mom died, I took a pillow and I pretended it was my father's chest. I stabbed a steak knife into it again and again. Then I told myself I'd killed him and I didn't have to think about him anymore."

I suppressed a shudder. This guy's anger began long before his combat experience.

He met my eyes again. "And I hardly ever did think about him after that. Until today. After I came home in this," he smacked the arm of his wheelchair, "I was in a real dark place for a while. Thought about offing myself more than once. And then I met Zeke Lord. He took an interest in me, got me set up as a vendor at the flea market. And one day he told me he loved me like a son."

Derek had a strange grin on his face now—too wide, too forced—and tears were running down his cheeks.

Fred licked his chin and whined softly. Derek resumed petting him.

The lump in my throat was so big, it extended down into my chest and wrapped around my heart.

"I cried like a baby, just like I am now," Derek said. "Then I told Zeke about my father, and how much I'd hated him, and how he, Zeke, had somehow filled up that hole inside of me—where the stories my mother used to tell me had lived, once upon a time."

He snorted. "Zeke got real quiet while I was talkin', and then he said he was honored that he could help me heal from all that. But today, Nell told me…" He choked up and looked away.

"Told you what?" I said quietly.

"That she's my half-sister."

I sat back in my chair, stunned. But also confused. It was a lot to process. Was he truly in love with Nell and so upset now because he couldn't have her?

Then the other shoe dropped. The pain in my chest intensified.

The strange, forced grin was back. "And guess who our dear father is…was?"

I didn't have to guess. I knew. "Zeke," I breathed out.

"Yup, good ole Zeke."

The rest of the story came out in bits and pieces. Nell was the product of Zeke's short encounter with the alcoholic bartender. He took off before she was born and hadn't known she'd been diagnosed with fetal alcohol effects—a milder form of fetal alcohol syndrome. She didn't have the facial features of those with the full-blown syndrome, but she did have learning deficits. All this she'd apparently told Derek today.

I added a mental note that fetal alcohol effects usually meant poor impulse control as well. That could explain her kleptomania.

Nell's mother had drunk herself to death when Nell was sixteen. She'd spent a couple of years in foster care, and then she was on her own.

My heart squeezed in my chest again. This time for her. Apparently, her disability hadn't been deemed severe enough to merit putting her in a group home for the mentally-challenged. So she'd been cut loose.

"She'd told me before," Derek said, "that she was homeless when Zeke took her under his wing, six years ago. He co-signed to help her buy her camper and paid for the inventory to start her kitchen gadgets stall."

It didn't take Sigmund Freud to figure out part of Nell's appeal for Derek. He'd spent a good portion of his teens taking care of his mother, had even sacrificed his high school diploma for her. Of course, he'd be attracted to a woman who needed him to look out for her.

He had paused, his lips in a tight, straight line. "Today, she told me that four years ago, he'd confessed he was her father and that he'd intentionally been searchin' for her when they met. She said it was the happiest day of her life."

He suddenly banged his fist on the table in between us, making me jump.

Fred whined. A growl rumbled from beneath the table.

Under its edge, I gave Buddy the nonverbal *it's-okay* signal, a circle made with thumb and index finger, two other fingers sticking up like a K.

He laid his head back down, on my foot this time. His way of saying, *I'm here if you need me.*

"Today," Derek ground out between clenched teeth, "is the worst day of my life." He dropped his head down onto his crossed arms.

I let the emotional dust settle for a few moments, then I cleared my throat. "Fred, lie down." I felt him plop down next to my other foot.

Now might not be the ideal time to bring this up, but if this wasn't going to work out with Derek, I needed to know sooner instead of later. As gently as possible, I said, "I know you've had a really rough day, but we need to talk about your anger."

His head jerked up.

"Your dog can help you with it," I said, "but only if you can control it well enough to keep him safe."

"What do you mean?"

"I need to be sure that you won't hurt him or put him in harm's way, because you're angry."

He stared at me for a couple of beats, his face still tense. Then he swallowed hard. "I'm working on the anger. I go to a support group that really helps. I skipped the meeting this week because of our training."

"That's good to know, that you're going to that group. But I can't let you keep Fred if you might abuse him."

His mouth dropped open. "I wouldn't ever."

I nodded slightly and let the silence stretch out between us. He needed to know I was serious about this. At the first hint that a veteran might be abusive to their service dog, I had to stop the training process and report to my supervisor, Mattie Jones, that there was a problem.

"Fred can help with the anger?" Derek said, his expression and tone now neutral.

I nodded again. "Petting an animal, especially one that you're strongly attached to, can calm feelings, help you get them better under control. As you've just observed."

He gave a half-hearted smile. "I didn't realize he was trying to comfort me. I was trying to calm him."

I smiled back. "He's trained to respond to anger as well as anxiety, by encouraging you to pet him, like he just did, by whining, and putting his head or his paw on your knee. When he senses you're angry–"

"Wow. How did you train him to sense that?" Derek's face had completely reverted to his usual expression, with a touch of amazement mixed in.

"Dogs can sense human emotions based on how we smell when we're feeling a certain way." I let out a low chuckle. "I thought about my lying, cheating ex-husband, while I was training him."

Derek gave me a small grin. "Sorry you went through that with your ex, but cool that you can use it now in your training."

I grinned as well. The Derek I knew, and had come to like, was back.

"Unfortunately," I said, sobering some, "we're going to have to make you think about what makes you angry in order to transfer that training from me to you." With a side agenda of observing whether he indeed had enough self-control to not hurt his dog when angry, or do something irresponsible like drive off without him.

Derek grimaced. "Considerin' the day I had today, it shouldn't be hard for me drum up some pissed-off feelings."

I shook my head. "We'll deal with that next wee–"

Buddy jolted to his feet, jostling the table. Thrusting his head out from under it, he looked past me, growling.

I jerked around in my chair, then jumped up, my heart rate skyrocketing.

Buddy inserted himself between me and the man in the kitchen doorway.

"Did ya know your front door's sittin' ajar?" the man said.

CHAPTER SEVEN

A corner of my brain registered that Fred had inserted himself between Derek and the intruder. But mostly I was focused on the latter—the leaner of the two guys who had looked out of place at the flea market.

The rolled-up sleeves of his blue-striped dress shirt revealed a tattoo on his right forearm. It rippled as he quickly reached for his pocket.

My insides twisted in panic. Was he pulling a gun? "Protect!"

Buddy barked, showing his teeth, the hackles up on his back. He took a step forward.

The man quickly backed up, hands in the air. "I'm a cop," he yelled.

"Sit, Buddy." The dog instantly stopped barking and dropped his butt to the floor.

The man looked at him and then at me. "Wow."

He held a thin leather wallet in one of his raised hands. I recognized it. He flipped it open and sure enough it held a gold detective's badge, similar to the one Will carried.

"Did ya know it's not a good idea to sneak up on people?" Ms.

Snark said in her best snide tone. I didn't feel all that guilty about letting her slip past my guard.

"Sorry," the cop said. "When I saw the door hanging open, I thought maybe something bad was going down."

I glanced toward Derek. He was breathing hard and fast, at risk of hyperventilating. Fred now had his chin on one knee and a paw on the other, whining softly.

"Pet him," I said, "to bring your heart rate back down." I figured that was the most face-saving way to point out that he was having an anxiety attack.

He placed a hand on Fred's head. But his eyes were out of focus. He was either partially dissociated, maybe having a flashback, or he was about to faint.

Keeping one eye on him, I said to the cop, "I must've left the door open by accident when I came in." Because *I'd* also been afraid that something bad was going down inside.

"Are you Ms. Banks-Haines? I was told you'd be here. You called in the burglary at the flea market?"

"Burglary?" Derek said.

I turned back to him. His eyes were in focus now, and his chest wasn't heaving anymore. But he looked exhausted as he slowly stroked Fred's ears.

Suddenly I wanted to cry. "Brace yourself," I said and swallowed hard. "Your bad day's about to get worse."

I filled Derek in. Despite the disturbing news about his stall being ransacked, he visibly became more grounded as he petted his dog.

After the detective had asked a few questions, I suggested Derek stay home and rest. "I'll go back over and straighten up your stall."

"You don't need to do that," he said.

"It happened on my watch. I feel responsible."

Derek shook his head, but he didn't say anything else.

"Turn your phone on," I said gently.

"And keep your doors locked," Detective Young added.

Derek nodded.

The detective and I left him at his table, slumped in his chair and staring at his hands.

I was tempted to leave Fred with him, but it was too soon in the training process, and we hadn't fully dealt with the anger issue yet.

Out in the driveway, Detective Young turned to me, the remote for Derek's stall in his hand. "Thanks for your cooperation, Ms. Banks-Haines."

I took the remote. "Call me Marcia. It's less of a mouthful."

He flashed a quick smile that significantly improved his lean face. "Then I'm Rick."

Bet he's only trying to put you at ease so you'll let something incriminating slip, Ms. Paranoid Snark said in my mind.

Or he could just be a friendly person, inner Mom responded in an acerbic tone.

I ignored the battling voices in my head as we walked to my car, parked in front of the house. The dogs trailed behind on loose leads.

"I'm glad your dog chased the guy off, before he could do any more damage," Rick said.

"I wish he'd caught him," I said.

"He might've been armed. He could have hurt the dog."

A shudder ran through me. "True. One part of all this doesn't make sense, though. The back area, where the dogs were, it was also searched." I looked down at my dog. "I'm not sure why Buddy would've let the guy do as much damage as he did, and *then* start barking and chasing him."

The detective watched me, unblinking, as if he expected me to say more.

Despite Ms. Snark's paranoia, I obliged. After all, I didn't *know* anything incriminating to let slip. "At first, I thought it was you guys who did it, that you came back to search Derek's stall again. And Buddy chased one of you off, then the other searched the back room."

"The other?"

"The other plain-clothes detective."

Detective Rick cocked his head slightly. "I was the only one assigned there today."

"Then who was the other guy?"

"Good question." His expression was grim.

Then he flashed another smile, probably meant to be reassuring, but it didn't quite reach his eyes. "Most likely just a customer."

~

Back at the flea market, I closed the mesh curtain around Derek's stall, with me and the dogs inside, and began putting the place to rights. It wasn't as bad as it had looked. Nothing seemed damaged, only scattered around or knocked over.

My mind churned the whole time I worked, going over Derek's story of his childhood and his discovery that Zeke was his long-lost and much-hated father.

I was between a rock and a hard place.

That was not a motherism. It was one of my dad's sayings, when describing a moral dilemma.

My eyes stung. My late father was a gentle man who saw the world as a simpler and kinder place than it actually was. I tried to imagine growing up without him in my life—and failed. Which gave me a taste of what it must've been like for Derek.

What to do? I was now privy to information that was very much related to a homicide investigation. Two adults were abandoned by Zeke as children, which could give either of them a motive for murder. Although Derek's upset said that he hadn't known about the connection until today.

Nell, however, had known for several years. She told Derek that she was thrilled to have her father in her life, but she could've lied. Or she and Zeke might have gotten into an argument, and she lost her temper and struck out with the first thing at hand.

Wait, the body had been found out behind the flea market, so the dragonhead sword would hardly be the first thing at hand—unless one of them had taken it back there for some reason.

Maybe Nell wasn't particularly thrilled that her father had given Derek the valuable sword/cane. Maybe she took it and then confronted Zeke, a case of good old sibling rivalry.

Zeke had told Derek that he'd found God and AA about twelve years ago. That's when he'd gotten sober.

And apparently that was also when he'd started searching for his lost children. He'd found Nell six years ago, and Derek two years ago, after his discharge from the Army and return to the area.

Hmm, maybe there were more deserted children out there.

But I couldn't tell any of this to the Crystal County Sheriff's Department. I was bound by the confidentiality rules of the agency I trained for, and by my promise to Derek, made in all innocence.

However, I was not a counselor, so that confidentiality was not protected by law. If the sheriff ever found out that I'd withheld relevant information, he could charge me with obstruction and withholding evidence.

For a moment I paused in my clean-up efforts and imagined Will's reaction as they carted me off to jail. A chill ran through me.

Moving into the back area, I took a deep breath and dove into the process of cleaning up there.

The clothing, which I'd noticed in Derek's trunk before, turned out to be a set of camouflage fatigues. They had been unceremoniously dumped by the opening in the curtain. I lifted the shirt up in front of me to fold it—and froze.

These were not Derek's. They were too narrow, the fatigues of a teenager…or a thinner man, like Ezekiel Lord.

I folded them carefully, holding my breath. They smelled of mustiness and old sweat, and had a couple of odd faded-out areas on them. I understood the fatigues might be a keepsake from Zeke. But why did Derek feel the need to keep them under lock and key?

~

I returned to my home away from home. Stepping through the front door, which they didn't bother to lock during the day, I called out softly, "Becky, it's me."

No answer. I stood in the middle of the spacious living room and listened to the unnatural quiet. The house wasn't all that big, a three-bedroom rancher. It didn't even have a formal dining room, just a large eat-in kitchen.

Was Becky napping, along with the twins, in the bedroom area on the back of the house?

I moved quietly into the kitchen. On the table was a note saying she and the kids were out running errands and inviting me to help myself to anything in the fridge for lunch. But my stomach was so knotted, it wasn't interested in food.

While driving from the flea market to here, I'd come up with a tentative game plan. If I could find a different, and preferably better suspect for Zeke's murder, rather than Derek or Nell, it would become a moot issue that I had withheld information from the sheriff's department.

I went to my room and fired up my laptop. On the police shows on TV they always say, "Start with the victim." I ordered a background check on Ezekiel Lord from a company I had used before.

I considered emailing Will and asking him to see what he could find out about the investigation. When we'd talked Monday night, I'd had no idea that there would be all these threads linking my client to the murder victim.

He'd caught a new case since then, and we hadn't had a chance to talk. The best he'd managed were a few cryptic text messages to let me know he was okay.

Maybe he could find out if the sheriff had any viable suspects, other than my client. I could use the excuse that Derek was worried about his friends at the flea market coming under suspicion and that was distracting him during our training sessions—which was at least partially true.

I decided not to go there yet. However carefully I worded the email, Will would see through it.

With nothing better to do, I opted to take a nap. It had indeed been a strenuous morning. I slipped off my shoes and flopped onto the bed, on top of the bedspread.

The dogs were all for the nap idea. They laid down on the rug, and within minutes, we were all snoozing.

My growling stomach woke me awhile later.

Or at least, I thought it was my stomach that woke me. The dogs were standing by the closed bedroom door.

"You guys need to go out?" I swung my legs off the bed and searched with my toes for my shoes.

A low rumble, coming from Buddy's throat.

My sleep-fogged mind finally got it that the noises coming from the living room, which I'd assumed were signs that Becky had come home, might be attributed to another cause.

Buddy let out a loud woof.

The noises stopped abruptly.

Insides shaking, I found my shoes and ran to the door. But instead of opening it, I put my ear to the wood.

Nothing but the pounding of my own pulse in my ears.

I debated what to do. Was the person out there the same one

who'd searched Derek's stall? I should call 911. But what if it was Becky or Andy out there?

Or what if one of them came home while the searcher was still in the house? My heart stuttered in my chest.

"Becky," I called out, trying to sound nonchalant. "Is that you?"

A quick series of thuds.

Gesturing to Fred to stay, I opened the door. Buddy took off, barking loudly.

"Wait!" I yelled.

He stopped, but he was quivering all over, eager to chase away the intruder.

I caught up and then followed him as he raced to the mud room on the back of the house.

The back door was standing open.

CHAPTER EIGHT

"Wait, Buddy." My dog stopped in the doorway and looked back at me.

Beyond him, a dark form barreled across the backyard. Probably a guy from the way he was running. And probably heavyset, but he wore a black hoodie that flapped open at the sides, disguising his build some. Despite his bulk, he vaulted over the back fence like it was nothing.

There was no point in giving chase. I doubted we could catch him, and the guy might have a weapon.

I closed and locked the door. Then I did the same with the front door.

To my surprise, the living room was not a mess. The searcher had been much more subtle here. If I hadn't caught him in the act, I would have assumed the minor disruptions—the skirt on the sofa flipped up in one spot and several books on the shelf put back upside down—had been caused by Becky or Andy.

Or the twins, in the case of the toys scattered on the floor in front of the mesh thingie in the corner. Winnie and Jazzie wouldn't stay in the portable playpen anymore, so it was used solely for toy storage.

I was pretty sure the toys had been inside of it, when I'd passed through the room earlier.

The kitchen was even less obviously disturbed, with only a few of the vegetarian cookbooks a little out of line on the shelf above the stove.

If I hadn't interrupted the intruder, it was likely no one would have even noticed he had been here. Or it could be a *she*. I hadn't gotten a good look at the person, and their clothing had disguised their build. Height was hard to judge too, when someone was running full tilt away from you.

I was just assuming it was the same man Buddy had chased away from Derek's stall at the flea market.

And I'd also been assuming that the object of his search had been the dragonhead sword/cane. But there was no way it would have fit on the small shelf where Becky kept her cookbooks.

Watch that assuming, my inner mom said. *It makes a you-know-what out of you and me.*

My mom was so adverse to cursing, she wouldn't even say the a-double-s word when quoting that old line about assumptions.

Ms. Snark chuckled. *And you won't even say it inside your own head.*

I ignored her and turned my brain power to deciding what to do. Should I call the Williston police or the Crystal County sheriff? And what would I tell them?

It was likely the whole thing would be dismissed as me interrupting a burglar who'd thought the house was empty.

Except my car was parked at the curb.

My car! Buddy and I jogged out front.

The car hadn't been locked, and again the disruption was subtle. But someone had definitely stirred the contents of my glove box. I always kept my GPS and the car's registration card on top of the otherwise disorganized pile of papers in there.

I popped the trunk open. Things had been moved around in there as well, but nothing seemed to be missing.

And the presence of the GPS said this wasn't an attempted theft gone wrong.

And now I was pretty sure the search was at least partially directed at me. This person thought I might have something that they wanted.

What had he or she planned to do if they didn't find what they were looking for in the rest of the house? Would they have come after me in the bedroom, tried to take me by surprise?

They must've known the dogs were in there with me.

I dug out my cell phone and called Will, thinking that I could use him as a sounding board about what to do, who to call.

I got voicemail, which meant he was most likely still involved in his new homicide case.

No way was I going to try to explain all this in a message. I just said that I missed him and to call me when he could.

I opted to call Andy.

He listened without interrupting until I got the whole convoluted story out, including the conclusions I had come to.

"Marcia, I hate to be a bad host," he finally said, "and don't take this the wrong way, but you need to go home."

I had been thinking the same thing, and also trying to decide what to do about that. I was supposed to stay until tomorrow evening, getting Fred used to the flea market during the day, and doing some training with Derek in the late afternoons after it closed.

Then go home for Saturday and Sunday to be with Will—although he might be tied up with his case through the weekend.

"I agree that I need to leave," I said to Andy. "But I'm not sure that whoever this is will realize I'm not at your house anymore."

A long pause, then a soft chuckle. "I guess a big sign on the door—*Marcia Is Gone*—would be a little weird, huh?"

I smiled at the phone, despite the gravity of the situation.

I really liked Andy. He was pretty unflappable. The only time I'd ever seen him anything less than calm, cool and collected was when one of his children had been in jeopardy.

"Do you think this is drastic enough to move Becky and the kids elsewhere?" I asked.

The sound of air being blown out. "I don't know. I'm headed home now. I'll text Becky and we'll figure that out once I see what's what."

"Should I call the Crystal County sheriff?"

"Lemme decide that after I see what was disturbed. Don't touch or move anything."

I stared down at the plastic truck in my hand. Without thinking, I'd picked it up and had been about to pitch it back in the playpen.

"Um, sure. Okay. See you soon."

I disconnected and leaned down to carefully put the truck back where I'd found it.

~

Becky had protested, but I had insisted on moving myself and the dogs to a bed and breakfast in Williston that accepted pets.

Andy had said he'd handle contacting the Crystal County Sheriff's Department. "They'll take it more seriously if it comes from me."

I totally agreed with that and was happy to let him do it.

Once the dogs and I were settled in, I called Derek. I opened with the obligatory question. "How are you doing?"

"Okay, I guess. I'm not goin' back to the flea market today." He sounded tired and maybe depressed.

I felt for him, but in that moment, I was more concerned about protecting all of us from the man or woman who was desperately searching for something. "Hey, do you have anything of Zeke's, something small he may have given you for safekeeping?"

A pause. "Why do you ask?"

I thought that an odd response, but I obliged with a recital of what had happened at Becky and Andy's house.

"Why do you think," Derek asked, "that whatever this guy is lookin' for is small?"

"Because he also searched the glove box in my car."

Another pause.

I said, "So, can you think of anything Zeke may have given you, that someone might want badly enough to break and enter to get it?"

No answer.

I added, "It might be something he talked about giving you, but then didn't?" Maybe that's why the guy or gal would still be looking for it after searching Derek's stall. The object wasn't there because Derek didn't actually have it.

"I've' been wrackin' my brain," Derek said. "Can't think of anything he gave me, or talked about giving to me."

"Okay. Well, be careful. Whoever this is may come to your house next."

Unless they'd already searched there earlier. "Have you noticed anything out of place in your house or truck?" I asked.

His chuckle sounded a little forced. "I'm such a slob, I'm not sure I'd notice if someone had tossed this place." Yet another pause. "Maybe you should go home, Marcia, until they catch whoever killed Zeke. We can finish my trainin' after that."

"I'm seriously considering doing that. I'll let you know what I decide."

"Okay. In the meantime, *you* be careful."

"I will be." We disconnected, and I stared at my phone for a moment.

I had a nagging feeling. Not everything about that exchange had rung true.

Oh, I believed Derek's concern for me was real, and he definitely was a slob. I'd seen the inside of his house. But…

For the first time since I'd met him, I was pretty sure Derek Bradshaw had lied to me. I suspected he did know what the elusive intruder was searching for.

CHAPTER NINE

My stomach rumbled unhappily, protesting the fact that lunch had never happened. I glanced at my watch. It was almost three o'clock—the time that the flea market closed.

Since I needed to go find myself a late lunch anyway, I figured I might as well swing south and check on something. With the dogs in the backseat, I went through a fast food drive-thru, then ate my burger one-handed as I navigated the country roads to Crystal County and the flea market.

Most vendors were still packing up, although a few of the make-shift chain-link gates were closed and locked already.

But the mesh-metal curtain around Derek's stall was open.

Why are we not surprised? Ms. Snark said inside my head. At least, she was using *we* now.

Rustling noises came from the back area. The hair stood up on Buddy's ruff. He growled low in his throat.

Fred was oblivious. Which was a good thing. I tried to train the protective and territorial instincts out of my dogs. They needed to remain focused on their owner and their duties and not react to strangers out in public.

Buddy, however, had lost some of that earlier training since he'd returned to my possession, and Will and I had decided that was just as well, since I had such a tendency to get into "scrapes," as my mother called them.

I silently signaled for both dogs to lie down at the front of the stall and to stay. I tiptoed toward the rear.

A whirring sound from the back area. I jumped back barely in time to keep from being run over.

From his cart, Derek gave me a startled look. Then his wide eyes relaxed. "Should've realized I couldn't fool you."

"Why did you try?"

His expression turned sheepish. "I don't know. I guess I wanted to buy myself some time to think."

"And to see if it was still here?"

He nodded and maneuvered his cart closer to me. Glancing past my shoulder, he held out something on the palm of his hand.

It was a small glass vial, with a metal screw cap. Inside were some flakes and powder that looked like rust scraped off of metal.

I took it from his hand. Intentionally blocking the view of anyone in the aisle with my back, I examined it more closely. My heart rate kicked up a few notches.

"Zeke called it his little pot of gold," Derek whispered, "said to hide it good. I carved out a chunk of wood and hid it inside, then put that in a box with other wood scraps. It was down on the bottom shelf next to where Fred's bed is. Forgot all about it, until today."

This guy had a really bad memory. Had he suffered some brain damage from that IED explosion? Or was there more to it than that?

Also keeping my voice low, I said, "The guy searching earlier probably didn't get that far before Buddy chased him off."

I swallowed hard. "Derek, we've got to give this to the sheriff. I think it's…" For some reason, I was reluctant to say out loud what I thought the flaky powder was. "Um, I think it might be a clue to why Zeke was murdered."

~

I grabbed the dogs' safety straps and service vests from my car, and we took Derek's SUV, since he had his wheelchair in the back.

At the Crystal County Sheriff's Office, I really wanted to speak to the sheriff himself. Unfortunately, we first had to get past the obstacle that was Deputy Harrison, standing in the middle of the department's lobby. He insisted we tell him why we were there.

"We have some potential evidence in the Zeke Lord case," I said.

The deputy held out his palm.

Derek shifted in his wheelchair, reaching for his pocket. I put a hand on his shoulder to stop him, still trying to decide how far to push this confrontation.

Harrison hadn't seemed to notice Derek's hand moving toward his pocket. He was too busy staring at *my* hand on my client's shoulder. A smirk slowly spread across his face.

I resisted the urge to jerk my hand away and gave Harrison an exasperated look. I'd been starting to waffle some, until the smirk. "We're not turning it over to anyone but the sheriff," I said firmly.

His gaze shifted from my hand to my eyes. "You ever heard of obstruction of an investigation?"

"Yup, I'm a detective's *wife*." I came down hard on the word *wife* and took the opportunity to move both hands to my hips. "I'm quite aware of the concept, and this doesn't qualify."

It had only half-registered in my peripheral vision that the receptionist had picked up her phone. Now, I heard her mumble a few words into it.

The deputy and I had a staring contest for a couple of beats.

The door to the inner sanctum opened, and the sheriff stepped out. "There a problem here, Harrison?"

The deputy put on his cop face before turning around. "No, sir."

The sheriff made a come-here gesture with his fingers. "Ms. Banks-Haines, Sergeant Bradshaw, follow me."

"Call me Marcia, Sheriff," I said to his back as we made our way down a wide hallway. "It's easier."

In the same glass-sided conference room as before, the sheriff gestured toward one side of the table, I sat and signaled for the dogs to lie down on either side of me.

The sheriff, meanwhile, had pulled the chair on the end out of the way, making a space for Derek's wheelchair.

Derek stopped short of the table's edge, lifted himself up on one elbow on the chair's arm and dug in his pocket. Then he wheeled the chair one-handed to the table and set the small vial on its surface.

"We believe that is what the guy was searching for today," I said, "in Derek's stall and elsewhere."

Derek filled the sheriff in on how he had come by the vial and where it had been hidden.

"Buddy must've chased the guy off before he got to that side of the back area," I added.

The sheriff frowned, which made his broad face kind of jowly, like a bulldog's. "Why didn't your dog go after him as soon as he started searching the stall?"

"Service dogs have their protective tendencies trained out of them, because they can't be reactive to strangers out in public." I didn't go into the fact that I'd intentionally let that training slip in Buddy's case, or that Will and I had taught him some additional protective tasks, similar to those used by police canine units.

"I think Buddy wouldn't have liked it that a stranger was pawing through Derek's stuff, but he probably wouldn't do more than growl, until the guy came toward the dogs. Maybe he made a threatening gesture to get them out of the way. Buddy would've gone on the defensive if he thought they were about to be attacked."

The sheriff nodded, pulled out a handkerchief, and used it to pick up the vial. My cheeks heated a little. We shouldn't have handled it with our bare hands.

He lifted his glasses onto his forehead and brought the vial close to his face. "Do you know what's in here?"

I looked at Derek. "No," he said, "but we can guess."

I recalled the dark red flake under my fingernail, that first day I'd handled the cane/sword. "Was there more than one person's blood on the dragonhead?"

The sheriff glanced my way, a sandy-gray eyebrow cocked in the air. "Why do you ask?"

I told him about finding something down in the intricate wiring, and how I'd scraped some off with my fingernail. "I thought it was mahogany stain at the time."

"Why?" the sheriff said, sounding surprised.

Surprised by his surprise, I said, "Because the cane was dark wood." Then guessing the reason, I blurted out, "You still haven't found the sheath, have you?"

The sheriff hesitated, then shook his head. I warmed a bit more toward him. He could have told me that he was the one who would ask the questions, thank you very much.

"Do you think the murderer took it with them?" I asked.

"Most likely," he said.

I leaned forward. "Sheriff, could you please let the media know that this has been found, so the murderer stops looking for it? Derek and I are in danger until then, as are Officer Matthews of Williston PD and his family. I was staying with them until their house was searched."

"We don't know that the person searching for something is also the murderer," the sheriff said. I opened my mouth, but he continued, "And what's this about Matthews's house being searched?"

"This afternoon. I woke up from a nap to sounds of someone in the house. He ran off. The search was not real obvious, unless you knew where things were normally kept."

The sheriff's face had been turning red as I talked, causing butterflies to line up for the *macarena* in my stomach. But I couldn't imagine why he was getting mad at me.

"Harrison, get in here!" he bellowed.

Derek and I both jumped a little in our seats. Buddy lifted his head and gave me his what's-up look.

"It's okay, boy."

Deputy Harrison entered the room, without his usual swagger.

"What's this I hear about a break-in at the Matthews's house earlier? Why wasn't I informed?"

"Andy," I interrupted, "I mean, Officer Matthews said he was going to call you all."

"Um, he did," Harrison said. "You were out of the office, sir, so I took the call."

"And you didn't deem it important to tell me?" The sheriff's tone was still angry.

"Uh, it didn't… I mean it happened in Williston. I didn't think it was relevant to any of our cases."

The sheriff stood up. "I'll deal with you later, Harrison. Get out of my sight."

Harrison's face was now the red one. He hustled out the door, without closing it behind him.

The sheriff turned to us. "Thank you for bringing this in. And yes, I will hold a press conference saying we've received new evidence, but I can't really say what the evidence is—since I don't quite *know* what it is yet." He handed each of us a card. "My cell phone number's on the back. If you think of anything else, or if anything else happens, call me directly."

"Thank you," I said pumping some extra gratitude into the words. He was being quite gracious.

"And Ms. Ba–"

I held up a hand. "Marcia."

The ends of his mouth twitched upward. "Mar-see-a…" he dragged out my name, like Will sometimes did, "…you should consider going home until this case is resolved."

Third person today, Ms. Snark commented internally.

"I am considering that, sir. Thank you for your concern."

Outside the building, Derek abruptly stopped his chair and turned it toward me. "I knew I'd seen that guy before."

"Who?"

"That deputy. I saw him a few times talkin' to Zeke at the flea market. But he wasn't wearin' a uniform."

"Harrison? He and Zeke were friends?"

Derek shook his head. "I asked Zeke if his friend was an old Army buddy. He had that kind of bearing, you know?"

I did know. Both military veterans and law enforcement officers seemed to carry themselves differently.

"He said the guy wasn't old enough to have been in his unit, and then he added, 'and he ain't a friend.' He said it real emphatically."

"Maybe just a customer then, and I'm not surprised Zeke didn't like him. Harrison isn't exactly a likeable guy."

Derek nodded slightly. "Maybe a customer, 'though I never saw him buy nothin'."

I'd muted my phone while we were in conference with the sheriff. It had vibrated once, so I pulled it out of my pocket now and checked for messages.

There was a text from Will. *Andy called re: latest developments. You need to come home now!*

The fourth person to tell me that.

CHAPTER TEN

The tone of the last sentence in my husband's text kind of pissed me off. But I talked myself down. He got like that sometimes, when he was worried about me.

While Derek drove us back to the flea market, I called Will. It went straight to voicemail. Great, Andy could get through to him, but I can't.

I left a message. "I *am* planning to come home earlier than expected." My voice sounded a little terse to my own ears. I decided that was okay. "Tomorrow morning maybe." I was still considering bugging out this evening, but I wasn't ready to commit to that.

"Call me when you have a few minutes. I'll fill you in." I disconnected.

I was also still debating how much to tell Will. I had promised to keep what Derek had told me about Zeke being his father to myself, and then there was the training agency's confidentiality rule. But neither the promise nor the rule protected me legally.

And if I told Will what I now knew, I would be putting him in the same bind. But I desperately needed a sounding board.

Mom was not an option. She'd get all worried if she knew I was once again embroiled in a murder investigation.

And Becky was too close to the situation. She would want me to spill everything, since the sooner the sheriff closed the case, the sooner her family would be out of danger.

"Sorry I dragged you into this, Marcia." Derek was staring straight ahead, his right hand clenching the steering wheel.

"You didn't drag me into it."

No, you jumped in with both feet, my inner mom pointed out.

"Yeah," Derek said, "but you got into it because you were worried about me. I don't think I'm high on the sheriff's suspect list anymore, though." His left hand pushed a lever sticking out from the steering column. It must be the brake, because the SUV slowed. "I think you should go home tonight."

Grabbing a knob on the steering wheel with his right hand, he deftly made the turn one-handed into the flea market parking lot.

I daydreamed for a moment about sleeping in my own bed, riding my horse tomorrow in the cool morning air. A small sigh escaped my lips.

And then it dawned on me who I could talk to.

Derek pulled up next to my car.

"I think I will go home tonight. I'll come back Monday morning, depending on where things stand with the case. But you need to start locking your doors, and be on guard."

"Oh, I will be. And don't worry, I know how to take care of myself." His grim expression said he wouldn't mind taking on Zeke's killer.

Had he gotten over being mad at Zeke that fast? Unlikely, since he'd hated his absent father for most of his life. But his relationship with Zeke was complicated.

I gave a slight shake of my head. Not my business.

I pulled the handle to open my door. "I'll call you Sunday with an ETA for Monday."

"*You* take care, Marcia."

I nodded and got out to unload the dogs from the backseat.

~

By nine-thirty the next morning, I'd shared a brief breakfast with my husband, who'd gotten home at two in the morning to catch a few hours of sleep, than had risen at six-thirty to take off again, chasing a new lead in his case. I'd assured him that I had no intentions of getting "directly involved" in the investigation over in Crystal County.

I would go back over on Monday to continue Derek's training, assuming there had been no more breaking-and-entering incidents by then. But I would keep a low profile.

I'd also gotten in a nice long ride on my mare, Niña, through the fields and woods behind our house, with Buddy trotting alongside.

Derek's situation and Zeke's death were beginning to feel like a grade B movie I'd stayed up too late to watch. I had almost convinced myself that I didn't need a sounding board after all.

But feeling more distant from the events in Crystal County didn't change the reality that I knew something I should be reporting to law enforcement.

I stepped out on the front porch of my "training center." I always thought of it in quotation marks. It was actually my former house. Will and I had hired a contractor and linked our two older cottages together into one big house.

Bedrooms and our study area were in what used to be his house and the twenty-by-forty-foot new construction in between housed our living/dining room and an open kitchen.

I had fetched a fresh cup of coffee from the latter before venturing outside. The morning was a pleasant seventy-four degrees, but it was supposed to get a bit warmer as the day progressed. I blew on my steaming cup to cool the coffee before taking a sip.

I was rehearsing openings in my mind when my neighbor, Sherie Wells, stepped out onto her front porch.

I let out a relieved sigh. Perhaps this wasn't going to be as awkward as I'd feared.

"Good morning, Marcia," she called over as she inspected her hanging plants. Satisfied that they didn't need anything at the moment, she walked over to the railing, no more than twenty feet from me.

"Good morning." I stepped down off my porch and sauntered over.

"Welcome home," she said, a bright smile on her brown face. As usual, her silver-streaked black hair was pulled back in a chignon. She wore a long-sleeved white cotton shirt over jeans.

Whereas I had donned a tee shirt and capris after I'd showered off the horse sweat. And therein lies one of the differences between those born in the South and Northern transplants like myself. True Southerners like Sherie considered anything under eighty degrees as chilly. Not that they didn't welcome the relief from the heat, mind you.

Sherie and I spent a few minutes in idle chit-chat, as required by Southern manners before diving into more serious topics. When we'd exhausted the subjects of the weather and the latest news of the doings in Mayfair, which wasn't much, I took a deep breath. "Can I ask you a hypothetical question?"

"Sure."

"It's really more of a hypothetical situation, and it's kind of complicated."

She flashed me another smile. "Well, come on in then, so we can be comfortable while you tell me about this *hypothetical* situation."

When I'd first moved to Mayfair, I'd assumed that Sherie—whom I'd called Mrs. Wells for the longest time, too intimidated to use her first name—was a gossip, since she always seemed to know everyone's business, including mine. But after a while, I'd realized that she only repeated things that were innocuous or were already common knowledge.

She wasn't one who enjoyed *telling* people about what was going on, she only liked to *know* everything that was going on. She had taught school in Jacksonville for thirty years. I suspected that was where she'd developed the habit of carefully observing her students, looking for signs that something was off, and then probing to make sure it wasn't a serious problem that she should be doing something about.

"Um, a friend of mine has a dilemma," I said, once we were settled on Sherie's navy velveteen sofa in her living room. "She was told, in confidence, some information about a murder victim, something that could cause law enforcement to suspect the person who told her, even though she doesn't think he had anything to do with the crime. She was going to investigate the situation herself, but then some things happened that spooked her. And the sheriff on the case is pursuing other leads now. So she's trying to decide if she should continue to investigate—she could do some probing from afar…" I was thinking of the background check I'd already ordered, "…to see if she can clear her friend. But she's not sure if she should tell the sheriff the info she has about her friend's connection to the victim?"

"And what is that connection?" Sherie asked.

I took a deep breath. "My friend's friend just found out that the murder victim is his father, who deserted the family when he was little. And she promised, before he'd told her, that she wouldn't repeat what he was about to say."

Sherie frowned. "That would be a big deal, to break a confidence like that, but… Well, I can see your friend's dilemma. The information could be important to solving the case."

"Um, the sheriff doesn't really suspect her friend at this point."

"But maybe he would if he knew what she knows."

"Yeah, I guess. But there would be other ramifications if she breached confidentiality and told. It could affect her job."

Sherie was shaking her head. "Things told in confidence can't always be kept that way, as I well know. I've had students tell me about things happening at home that constituted child abuse. And I was mandated by law to report it. I would have anyway, to protect the child."

"Well, I would too, I mean, my friend would, if she thought someone would be in danger if she didn't tell."

"And the more time that goes by," Sherie said, "without her telling, the worse it might be if she has to tell later."

I sighed. "I know. So you're advising that my friend should tell the sheriff what she knows?"

"Nope." She shook her head again. "I'm not advising a thing. This is a real sticky wicket. Only your friend can decide what to do, what her conscience can live with."

"Sticky wicket" was another of my mother's favorite terms. She and Sherie were around the same age.

"You said your friend maybe could 'probe things,'" Sherie made air quotes, "from afar."

"Some, maybe."

"Might be worth doing, if that won't get her into trouble or put her at risk."

I nodded. "At least I can validate for her that she isn't overreacting, that it really is a *sticky wicket*." I smiled a little.

Sherie gave me a gentle smile back. "Just be careful, child."

I said goodbye to Sherie and went back to my house. My laptop sat on the kitchen counter.

I fired it up and checked my email. Nothing back yet from the background check company. I emailed them, asking if it was too late to put a rush on the order.

A few minutes later, my phone rang. I didn't recognize the number and would normally let it go to voicemail. Too often these days, it was a telemarketer or a scammer.

But on a hunch, I picked it up. "Hello."

"Hi. Is this Ms. Banks?"

"Yes."

"This is Elise, from E and R Electronic Investigations. I, um, *we* haven't gotten the report back to you yet because we ran into a snag. We can only get information for the last twenty-four years on Ezekiel Lord. Before that, he doesn't seem to exist." She cleared her throat. "It's a really hard name to research because all that keeps coming up are references to the Ezekiel in the Bible. I did find an Ezekiel Ford who would've been about the right age, but he died in the Vietnam War."

I was silent for a few beats, digesting what she had told me.

"Do you want me to send what I have?" Elise said.

"Yes please," then I thought to ask, "Did anything else unusual come up?"

"Well, I always try to verify through the appropriate state's motor vehicle administration if the person has a driver's license. This guy supposedly had one. A photocopy of it is attached to the lease he signed for the flea market property. But Florida's Department of Highway Safety and Motor Vehicles has no record of him."

"The driver's license is a forgery?"

"Maybe. Probably. I'll send copies of those documents along with the report."

"Thanks, Elise. By the way, who's the R in E and R Electronic Investigations?"

"Um, Rocket." A beat of silence. "He's my dog."

I laughed out loud. "You're kidding?"

"No, but please don't tell anyone. I make it sound like there's more than just me so people will take me seriously. Often folks won't believe that one female geek can track down so much info so quickly, but as geeks go, I'm pretty good." There was a touch of pride, well-deserved, in her voice.

Still chucking, I said, "Your secret's safe with me, and I'll bet Rocket makes a better business partner than some people I've known....Say, I have another search for you. Could you do a quickie on Derek Bradshaw? He's thirty, honorably discharged for medical reasons from the Army. I think he grew up in Florida, but I'm not sure about that."

"Sure. I'll rush it, no extra charge."

"Thanks. Mostly I'd like to find out about his family." We said goodbye and disconnected.

I waited impatiently for the report on Zeke to come through. Sure enough, it didn't have much in it. He'd led a fairly low-profile life for the last twenty-four years, renting the land on which he'd built the flea market from a local farmer. The report said he had constructed the original building himself. Then once it was a going enterprise, he'd had a contractor add the other building and the connecting section that made it an H.

The Good Lord's Flea Market was a sole proprietorship. There was a checking account, through a small Florida credit union, in Zeke's name. A few years back, a lawsuit had been filed against the flea market by the estate of one Charles Dudley, over a two-thousand-dollar check, written at an estate sale, that had later bounced. The suit had been dropped after a few weeks, when Zeke made good on the check.

That was pretty much it.

I knew it would drive me crazy waiting for Elise to send me more, so I opted to take a walk.

I'd already decided to give Fred the day off from training, but maybe he could use some exercise. I walked over to his crate. "Hey, boy. Wanna take a walk?"

I could've sworn that dog grinned at me. I put a regular harness on him and gave him a quick scratch behind his ears.

Buddy lifted his head from where he lay in his favorite spot under the front picture window.

"Stay, boy. You've already had your exercise for the day."

I was surprised to run into Edna Mayfair so late in the morning, along with her two Springer Spaniels, Bennie and Bo. She usually walked them much earlier.

"No guests at the motel today?" I'd surmised this from her typical off-duty attire of a brightly colored muumuu and, in deference to the somewhat cooler weather, moccasins instead of flip-flops, and a black cardigan.

She shook her head, which made tufts of her gray hair stick out even more than usual. "Things tend to slow down about now, until after the first of the year. Except the weekend of the extravaganza."

Hoping to distract her from that topic of conversation, I said, "New muumuu?"

She smiled and twisted one way and then the other, as if modeling it on a fashion show runway. "You like?"

"I do," I said, keeping the thought to myself that I'd like it better if I were wearing sunglasses. It was neon lime green with hot pink hibiscus blooms on it.

Bennie and Bo were alternating between sniffing Fred's butt and jumping around playfully. Leashes were already getting tangled, so I let Fred off of his. "Stay close," I said.

The three dogs romped in the motel's parking lot, while Edna and I did the obligatory chit-chat about the weather and such. Meanwhile, a part of my brain was still chewing on Sherie's advice.

Edna suddenly interrupted herself midway through a description of her nephew Dexter's new job. "You seem preoccupied this morning, Marcia."

Dang. Edna might be in her eighties, but she didn't miss much.

"Um, I do have something on my mind."

When I didn't continue, Edna stared at me, wide-eyed and eager.

I shook my head slightly. "It's confidential." I hated to disappoint her, but unlike Sherie, she did tend to tell the gossip she heard.

"Is it about anybody here in town?" Her tone was concerned. She considered the town of Mayfair her personal responsibility, since her now-deceased brother had founded it in the 1960s, and then the demise of his tourist-trap alligator farm had left it almost a ghost town.

"It's about a client," I said.

She nodded, one quick up and down of her head, but her stare was still unrelenting.

"I found out something about his family, something he asked me to keep in confidence, but it might affect a legal case."

Edna narrowed her eyes at me, but I resisted saying more. Even that much was probably more than I should have said.

After a beat, she said, "Two thoughts. One, is keeping this confidence worth getting into legal trouble?"

That was indeed the royal question.

"And two," Edna continued. "I know from personal experience that keeping family secrets can do a lot of harm. Are you really doing this client a favor by keeping the secret?"

My heart squeezed in my chest. She was referring to the events of two years ago, when Will and I had discovered that her niece, Susanna, whom Edna had long since thought dead by her own hand, was alive and more or less well, illegally institutionalized for almost four decades.

I braced for Edna to push for more information, but bless her heart, she changed the subject. "So, are you ready for this year's Christmas bash?"

I suppressed a sigh. The answer to that question was no. I was never ready for Mayfair's holiday extravaganzas, designed to bring in tourists and bolster the town's economy. We'd actually pulled off three so far—a year ago on Halloween, last Christmas and most recently, this past Fourth of July. At two out of the three, something significant went very wrong.

We'd skipped Halloween this year—too many bad memories from the previous year—but Edna was determined to make this year's Christmas affair bigger and better than ever. I shuddered slightly.

I listened while she chattered for a few minutes about the plans for the bash. Then I said I had to get home, which was a fib. I had no particular tasks I needed to do, since I hadn't even planned on being here today.

But I was feeling antsy. I'd thought I had the whole mess sorted out after talking to Sherie. I'd keep Derek's confidence, but I'd find out what I could from afar via background checks. Now, Edna's comments had me doubting that decision.

A few minutes later, I was definitely second-guessing it. Once home, I'd checked my email. Already there was a message from Elise. It read: *I'm still double-checking some things, but this is what I have so far.*

I clicked on the attachment labeled *Preliminary Report–Derek Bradshaw.*

It included his birth date and birthplace, Crystal City, Florida. Plus his mother's maiden and married names, his Army records, and the fact that his father had left the family when he was three.

I was staring at the father's name, when my laptop pinged, announcing a new email.

It was also from Elise, with another attachment. I clicked on *Supplemental Report–Derek Bradshaw*.

Its contents had my jaw dropping, along with my stomach.

CHAPTER ELEVEN

I'd been surprised to see Derek's father's name listed as Jacob Bradshaw. I'd assumed that his mother had taken back her maiden name and changed Derek's last name as well, when her husband had deserted the family. Thus the discrepancy in the last names between Bradshaw and Lord.

But that wasn't the case, and Elise's supplemental report had shocked me even more. She'd looked into Derek's father's background.

Jacob Bradshaw had a sealed juvenile record in Connecticut. Elise couldn't get into that, but she had plenty to tell about his later activities.

In 1968, at sixteen, he was tried as an adult and convicted of forgery, larceny and fraud. He'd gone to prison for six years, until 1974—the time period when Derek's father had supposedly been fighting in Vietnam. He'd moved to Florida in 1977 and married Derek's mother a decade later. A year after that, he was incarcerated again for possession of stolen property, and was gone for the first two years of Derek's life.

I sat back and tapped my lips with my index finger. That was also around the time of Desert Storm, so it would've been impossible for him to have served during that conflict—the war that had supposedly "changed" him. Probably what had changed him was that second stint in prison.

In 1992, the Bradshaws filed for divorce. Jacob was already living with his bartender girlfriend. Then he disappeared six months later and was never heard from again.

I emailed Elise. *No indication that Jacob served in the military?*

The answer came back in seconds. *Nope. You want me to check further?*

Not yet. Thanks.

My stomach growled. I glanced at the time on my computer screen. 11:33. It had been a long time since the early breakfast I'd shared with Will before he'd taken off again to chase bad guys.

Crapola. Will! It would be hard to explain to him why I was going to do what I was about to do.

I tried his number and wasn't surprised when it went straight to voicemail. "Call me when you can," I said into the phone.

I made a quick decision. If I left right now, I could be back by dinnertime.

But first… I typed out where I was going and why and sent the document to our wireless printer in the study. I retrieved the single sheet of paper and sealed it in an envelope, then hand-wrote a message on the outside of it.

Leaving Fred with a chew stick in his crate, Buddy and I headed out.

First stop was my friend Jess Randall's diner. The lunch crowd wasn't in high gear yet, but it would be soon. I told Buddy to stay by the door and went in to wait by the cash register until Jess could shake loose and come over. Her petite frame was enveloped in a chef's jacket that no doubt had been white this morning, but was now smudged with various colorful food items. Her dark hair was pulled back in its usual short ponytail, with a hairnet over it.

I asked for a grilled cheese and tomato sandwich on wheat to go. "And wrap it so I can eat it in the car, please."

Jess handed the order off to her waitress, Lisa, and turned back to me. "Where are you going in such a hurry that you can't sit down to eat?" Her tone was light, and she wore a slight smile.

I was relieved to see her looking and sounding so normal. She'd lost her fiancé a few months ago and, understandably, had been fairly down ever since.

Too bad I had to worry her with my mess. I handed her the envelope.

She read the writing on it out loud. “If I haven’t called you by six, call Will and read this to him.” She looked up. “What’s with all the cloak and dagger?”

I sighed. “It’s complicated. I need to drive over to Williston and take care of something related to a client, and let’s just say that things could potentially get tense.”

Jess frowned. “Then maybe you should wait for Will to go with you. Or me, after I close for the day.”

I hesitated. But she didn’t close the diner until four-thirty. I’d miss the sheriff at his office and might or might not be able to track him down at home. I shook my head. “This really can’t wait.”

She pressed her lips together in a thin line. “Okay, but you call me the second,” her voice was firm, “the *very* second you’ve done whatever it is and are headed home again.”

“I will. I promise.”

Lisa brought me my sandwich, wrapped in foil and I bid them goodbye.

I was twenty minutes down the country road that led to Williston and had finished the grilled cheese, when my phone rang. The dashboard screen informed me it was Will.

I took a deep breath and answered the call.

“Hey there, what’s up?” Will said, his voice casual.

“How’s your case going?” I was stalling.

“It’s not. Another day or two like today, with no decent leads, and it will end up in the cold case pile. What are you up to?”

It was an innocent enough question, but I suddenly felt defensive.

Maybe because you’re doing something you know he won’t like, Ms. Snark pointed out.

I stalled. “So the lead this morning didn’t pan out?”

“Nope, we spent several hours chasing our tails.” A brief pause. “What’s up, Marcia?” His voice was now a bit wary.

Okay, dragging this out wasn’t making things better. “Um, I’m headed over to talk to the Crystal County sheriff. I found out some things about his murder victim that he needs to know. Some of it came from my client and was told to me in confidence."

Another brief pause. "Why not call him?"

"Well, it's kind of complicated. And I need to talk to my client first, in person, so I can see his reaction."

"I take it that means you think he might react negatively."

"Maybe, but I'm hoping I can help him understand why I have to violate his confidence and tell the sheriff what he told me."

A couple of beats of silence. I imagined Will shaking his head, trying to make sense out of what I'd said. "Could he become violent?" he finally asked.

I thought about Derek's anger, but I doubted he'd intentionally hurt anyone. "No, he's not the violent type."

"He was a soldier, Marcia. He's been in combat," Will said, his tone one of forced patience. "That may not make him the violent type in general, but he can certainly go there if need be."

"True, but I can't imagine him going there with me." Well, a part of me could, after seeing his anger in action yesterday. I decided to talk to him in a public place, not his house.

And I had Buddy with me.

"So, what is this thing he told you," Will was saying, "that you need to tell the sheriff?"

"Um, I can't tell you."

He sighed into the phone. "You make me crazy, woman."

"Will, I haven't told you, I can't tell you, not only because it was told to me in confidence and it's related to a client, but because you would then be in the same bind I'm in—either break that confidence or withhold information from law enforcement."

"That's a no brainer."

"For you, it is." *Which is another reason why I haven't told you.* I kept that thought to myself. "But like I said, it's complicated."

"Look, I get it that you can't discuss clients' personal business. But in this case, that personal business is putting you at risk."

My turn to heave a sigh. "Says the police detective."

"Okay, okay. Truce… I just can't stand the thought that you're not safe."

And I try real hard not to think about the fact that you're not safe every time you go to work. Another thought I kept to myself.

"I'm only going to talk to my client and the sheriff. Then I'll turn around and come home. And I have Buddy with me."

Another pause. "Call me when you're headed home."

"Definitely. See you later. Love you."

"Love you too." His tone was now resigned.

I disconnected. That hadn't gone as badly as I'd imagined it might. But a niggling worry made my stomach uneasy. Will had somehow sounded off.

I shrugged. Probably because his case wasn't going well.

Just after the underpass for I-75, I called Derek to tell him I was coming to talk to him.

He was at the flea market. "It's a little crazy today. We're getting into the busy season, with people starting to shop for Christmas gifts."

"This won't take long." At least, I hoped it wouldn't. I hoped he would understand that I had to tell the sheriff what we now knew about his parentage.

~

When I arrived, he was helping a customer, and two other people were examining the merchandise in his stall.

I waved, and Buddy and I moved on past. During the last few minutes of the drive, it had dawned on me that there was someone else I should talk to as well.

There were a few people examining Nell's merchandise, but no one was demanding her attention at the moment.

"Hey Nell," I said.

"Oh, hi." Her china-doll face was as beautiful as always, but her eyes were dull.

"How you holding up?"

She shrugged. "I think it's finally hit me that Zeke's really gone."

I nodded sympathetically. "You two were close?" A round-about way of asking about their relationship, since I wasn't supposed to know he was her father.

I'd meant that they were close as friends, but I hadn't counted on her concrete view of the world. "Derek told you then?"

I nodded again. What else could I do?

"He was sooo mad when I told him."

"I think he'll get used to the idea," I said. "Did you remember

Zeke at all from when you were little?"

"No. He was gone by the time I was born."

That jived with the timetable Elise had spelled out in her report.

"He told me he was called up in '93, when my mom was pregnant. His reserve unit was reactivated because of the terrorists. And then we moved, and he lost track of Mom and me."

I guessed that made for a plausible story, since the first attack on New York's World Trade Center—a car bombing—had occurred that year.

"He said he looked all over for us when he got home."

I seriously doubt that, Ms. Snark commented internally.

I silently agreed.

"And he was in jail for a while," Nell added. "He said that's where he found God and knew he had to find his kids and make amends."

Ah, so he admitted to at least one of his incarcerations.

Shifting gears, I asked, "Where did he get his merchandise for his stall?"

Nell ducked her head and peered up at me through a veil of blonde bangs. There was a wariness in her eyes that hadn't been there a moment ago. "Estate sales, mostly."

My ex had dragged me to some estate sales when we were furnishing our house, insisting that was the best way to get cheap antiques. I'd found them depressing, with their worn settees and scratched armoires, scattered over unkempt lawns neglected by owners too elderly to garden and mow regularly. Or worse yet, the stuff was still inside the houses, which were often dingy and smelled either medicinal or of incontinence, or both.

Smaller items were usually dumped into box lots—sometimes things that were related like tools or books, and sometimes not so much. I suspected these box lots would have been what Zeke bought.

"What did he do with the stuff he didn't want?"

She looked at me, her eyes wide…too wide.

I added, "The other stuff in a box that he'd bid on, that weren't knives or swords."

She visibly relaxed. "Oh, if it was kitchen stuff, he gave it to me."

"And if it wasn't?"

She tensed again. "Sometimes he sold stuff to Gary, the guy in the stall next to his."

Wait, I thought that guy's name was Denny. "The guy with the baseball caps?"

"No, on the other side."

I paused for effect, then said, "And the things that were disappearing from people's stalls?"

More wide-eyed exaggerated innocence. "What about 'em?"

I lowered and softened my voice. "Who took the stuff, you or Zeke?" I already knew the answer, but I wondered if she would admit to it.

She hung her head and said nothing for several seconds. I'd about given up on an answer, when she whispered, "Me."

She raised her head a little, but didn't quite make eye contact. "Sometimes Zeke put the stuff back, if the person hadn't noticed it was gone yet. Sometimes he took it and sold it and gave me the money."

And sometimes you kept it for your collections.

I shook my head slightly. Nell's collections weren't my concern, but… I hardened my voice some. "Why did you take Derek's dragon-head cane?"

Her head jerked up. "I didn't." Her tone was indignant, as if she hadn't just admitted to being a kleptomaniac.

But for some reason, I believed her.

Derek was still busy when I strolled back by, so I headed down the aisle again to Zeke's bare stall.

I hadn't remembered Gary from the prayer service last Sunday, which now felt like a month ago. But he seemed to remember me. He greeted me with a smile, and we made small talk for a few minutes.

Then I plunged in. "Nell tells me that Zeke used to provide you with some of your merchandise."

Gary nodded. "Sometimes, if he could give me a good price on things, so's I could make a decent profit."

"Were they mostly things from estate sales?" Gary's stall was crammed with lamps and small electronics, with a few odd knick-knacks thrown in. I could see some of the stuff coming from estate sales, but not everything—like the three new flat-screen TVs, still in their boxes.

Gary's face sobered. He glanced around, then leaned toward me.

"Can ya keep a secret?" he said in a low voice.

I hesitated for a moment. The last time I'd glibly agreed to that request I'd ended up in the double bind that I was now trying to extract myself from.

In for a dime, in for a dollar.

Was that my mother's voice—it was certainly a motherism—or was it Ms. Snark?

I stifled the urge to shake my head at the inner voices.

"Sure," I said out loud.

"I think some of the stuff fell off a truck, if you know what I mean."

"Such as?" I said, pumping some incredulity into my voice, even though his pronouncement didn't surprise me a bit.

He pointed to a display of clock radios, in their pristine boxes, a big sign in front of them stating they were only ten dollars. They looked like they were decent quality, would probably retail at Walmart for at least twenty-five. "Ever known a little old lady to have twenty new clocks stashed in her closet?"

Buddy and I returned once again to Derek's stall. No one was there at the moment except him. But it had dawned on me that the information I needed to lay out for him was too complicated to do it betwixt and between customers.

Do you realize, Ms. Snark observed, *how many times you've used that word* complicated *in the last twenty-four hours?*

Yeah, well, it is *complicated.*

I looked at my watch. Twenty after two. It wouldn't be that much longer before Derek closed up for the day.

Buddy and I wandered down the aisle to another stall that sold office supplies. After buying a packet of lined letter-sized pads, we went out to my car.

It was a mild day. I lowered the windows and dug a pencil out of my purse.

Time to get the complicated situation down on paper.

CHAPTER TWELVE

I'd just finished laying out the timeline of Jacob/Zeke's life, when movement in my peripheral vision had me lifting my head. Derek was walking, with his sticks, toward his handicapped parking space.

"I'll be right back, boy," I said to Buddy. I jumped out of my car and trotted over to his white SUV.

He had tossed his walking sticks onto the passenger seat and was holding himself up in the driver's doorframe. "There you are. I thought you wanted to talk to me asap?"

"I did, but I saw that you were busy. I figured it could wait until quitting time." Suddenly my eyes stung. This guy had been dealt so many blows in the last few days, and I was about to throw another one at him.

"Is there somewhere nearby where we can get a cup of coffee? Maybe sit outside. I've got Buddy with me."

He nodded. "Follow me."

We got into our vehicles, and I followed his white truck to the parking lot of a small diner.

They had some rickety wooden picnic tables set up along one

side of the lot, but none were occupied at the moment. Derek rolled his wheelchair up to one end of a table.

I told Buddy to lie down and stay, then dropped my end of the leash next to him, knowing he wouldn't go anywhere.

I went inside and got us two cups of coffee and a couple of donuts.

Once I was settled at the table and we had tested our coffees, I cleared my throat.

"I ran a background check on Zeke. I hate to have to tell you this, but he wasn't in the military, and his real name wasn't Ezekiel Lord. He developed that alias about twenty-four years ago, around the time that he started the flea market."

Derek shook his head. "I figured out that his name wasn't real. My mom referred to him as Jake. But how can you say he wasn't in the military? I have his fatigues."

"I think they were part of the pretense. You can buy fatigues at any military surplus store." I spread the lined sheets of paper out in front of him on the picnic table, showing the timeline I'd constructed.

He stared at it for a full two minutes. At one point, his index finger stabbed one of the spots where I'd written *incarcerated.*

He abruptly pushed back from the table. "I need the men's room," he muttered and wheeled off toward the ramp leading into the diner.

He was gone far longer than even a man in a wheelchair should need to use the facilities. I'd eaten one of the donuts and was eyeing the other, when he finally returned.

His eyes were red-rimmed. He maneuvered his chair back into position and pointed at the timeline. "There's a three-year gap here."

"I know. I've got no idea where he was or what he was doing during that gap. But my best guess is that whatever it was, he ran away from it, back to Florida to establish a new identity."

"Witness Protection maybe?"

"I doubt it. They wouldn't have sent him back to where he'd lived before, where he might be recognized."

"Maybe he was in Witness Protection somewhere else, and he left it for some reason. Maybe because he wanted to find Nell and me."

"Maybe." It was plausible. "I can ask my background check company to see if he testified against somebody dangerous."

Derek's eyes had gone shiny. "His military service was the one thing honorable I could hold onto, and now even that's turned out to be a lie."

I truly hated where I needed to go next. "Derek, I need to tell the sheriff what Nell told you, that Zeke was your father."

His head jerked up. "Why?"

"Because he no doubt hung out with many unsavory types in his criminal career, anyone of whom might have tracked him down and killed him for some reason. But the sheriff may only have the name Ezekiel Lord. He may not have been able to track him back farther. My background check company couldn't, until I…" I caught myself. I didn't want to tell Derek that I'd run a check on him as well. "They couldn't at first," I finished lamely.

He stared off to the side, then slowly nodded.

"But knowing he was your father may bring the sheriff's scrutiny back to you as a suspect," I pointed out, "so I felt the need to talk to you first."

He brought his gaze back to meet mine and nodded again.

"Derek, did you have anything to do with his death?" I had to ask, even though I wasn't sure what I would do if he answered in the affirmative.

He reared back in his chair. "Of course not."

"So, I've got to go talk to the sheriff." I started to push up from the table. "Are you okay?"

"Why did my mother lie about him being in the Army?" His tone had a forlorn edge.

An insight blossomed in my brain. I sank back into my seat. "Maybe she thought it was the truth."

He stared at me, his mouth partway open.

"Think about it. Zeke was a con artist. Maybe he'd lied about being in jail in his youth, said he was in Vietnam. Then he told her he'd been called up again, when he knew he was about to be arrested. When he got out, he got ahold of a set of fatigues and came home in them."

"He had dog tags. He showed them to me. They said Ezekiel Lord."

I pondered that for a moment. "Were they worn down some?"

"Yeah."

"Could they have originally said Ezekiel Ford?"

He closed his eyes. I figured he was bringing up the image of the dog tags.

He opened them again. "Yeah. They were worn around the first letter of the last name."

I told him what Elise had found out regarding an Ezekiel Ford, who had served and died during the Vietnam War.

His eyes went wide and he smacked the table. "Marcia, he was a fence!"

"What?" I said, even though I'd had the same thought.

"It all fits," he said in an excited voice. "The stolen stuff Nell was holding for 'someone else.'" He made air quotes. "And I wasn't the only one he gave or sold things to that he said didn't 'fit in with his merchandise.'" The air quotes again. "He was a fence for stolen goods."

"The guy in the stall next to his," I added. "He said he bought some things from Zeke that he suspected had 'fallen off a truck.'"

I resisted the urge to make my own air quotes. A family had settled at one of the other picnic tables, ice cream cones in hand, and the father was now staring at us.

I lowered my voice. "The dog tags, you think he stole them?"

He shook his head. "Zeke said one time that he used to go to yard sales and flea markets years ago. He liked digging around in the old stuff, particularly the military memorabilia." His voice choked a little on the last two words. "He said that's where he got the idea for startin' his own flea market, when he was goin' to them himself. How much you wanna bet he found those dog tags in a box lot, and that gave him the idea for a new identity?"

"Could be. He might've been using Ezekiel Ford's Social Security number as well." That would explain how he'd managed to lease property and open a bank account. I made a mental note to check the documents Elise had sent me.

I glanced at my watch. Twenty until five. "Look, I gotta try to catch the sheriff before he leaves his office. Let's–"

Derek interrupted. "I'm going to ask around tomorrow, see if any of the other vendors got stuff from him. They'll tell me."

"Okay, but be discreet. We don't know if maybe his killer is someone at the flea market."

He nodded, his expression now grim.

As I pulled into the Crystal County Sheriff's Office parking lot, the sheriff was walking across it toward a light blue pickup truck.

I tooted my horn, then quickly hopped out of my car and waved.

While the sheriff walked my way, I ducked in the backseat and undid Buddy's safety strap. He jumped out and sat beside me, his head leaning against the side of my knee.

He was probably picking up on the butterflies doing the tango in my chest and stomach.

"Ms. Banks…um, Marcia, to what do I owe this pleasure?" There was touch of sarcasm in his voice.

"I have some information for you, Sheriff."

He looked at his watch and frowned.

"It's pretty important information."

He sighed and gestured for me to follow him.

Buddy and I trailed behind as he led the way back into the building and down the hallway to the conference room.

"Um, maybe we could go into your office." The thought of spilling my guts in the glass-sided conference room, where the deputies in the bullpen could see both my body language and the sheriff's, was making me even more nervous.

The sheriff changed directions and led us down a smaller corridor. We entered a somewhat Spartan but roomy office. The sheriff went around and sat behind a wide metal desk. He tented his fingers together over his stomach as he leaned back in his desk chair.

He gestured for me to sit in the rather uncomfortable-looking visitor's chair across from him. I complied and Buddy settled at my feet.

"Now, *Marcia,* what is this info that's so all-fired important?"

I took a deep breath. "May I make an educated guess that you had some difficulty tracking Zeke Lord back more than twenty-four years?"

His eyebrows went up, but then he nodded.

"His real name was Jacob Bradshaw. He was Derek's father." I quickly added, "But Derek didn't know that until after he was dead."

I told the sheriff about Zeke's past, before he became Zeke.

His eyes grew wide a couple of times as I talked, but he didn't interrupt me.

When I stopped talking, he leaned forward. "And when did you learn all this, Ms. Banks-Haines?"

Not a good sign that he was once again using my extended last name.

I took a deep breath. "Recently, but some of it was told to me in confidence. When I realized it might be relevant to your investigation, I asked the person who told me for permission to tell you."

The sheriff's gaze bore into mine. "And that person is?"

"Derek Bradshaw, and he gave permission without hesitation."

He nodded, one quick up and down of his head.

I started to breathe a soft sigh of relief.

"Some of it? Who told you the rest of it?"

My insides clenched anew. "I, um, ran background checks on Zeke and on Derek, and my background check company got a little carried away."

The eyebrows shot up again. "*Your* background check company?"

Heat rose in my cheeks, but for once, I managed to clamp my mouth shut. Anything I said would make things worse.

He sighed. "Is there anything else you would like to add?"

I shook my head.

His mouth twisted for a moment into what might have been a smirk. Then it flat-lined. "Thank you for coming forward with this information, Ms. Banks-Haines. We'll look into it."

Hands on his desk, he pushed himself to a stand. "Now stop poking your nose in my investigation."

I wanted to say that I hadn't meant to butt in—most of what I'd told him had come from Derek.

And the background checks you hadn't meant to order? My inner mom's exasperated voice this time.

I kept my mouth shut.

CHAPTER THIRTEEN

I made it home fifteen minutes before Will arrived. I'd called him on the way, and also Jess, reassuring both of them that I was fine.

My husband brought a pizza home with him, bless his heart.

I pulled a moderately good red from our wine rack. As I wrestled with the cork at the kitchen counter, I asked, "Did you catch your bad guy?"

A deep sigh emanated from the breakfast bar. Will yanked his tie loose and tossed it behind him. It landed on the sofa.

I took the sigh as a *no*. "You're actually off for the rest of the weekend then?"

"Yes," he said in a tired voice. His rugged face drooped with fatigue. "My boss has relegated the file to the cold case pile."

He sighed again. "So, can you tell me now why you had to go gallivanting over to Crystal County?"

I carried napkins, wineglasses and the wine over to where he sat. "It's a long story."

And now that I'd gotten Derek's permission to tell it to the sheriff, I felt okay about telling Will.

"My client found out yesterday that the murder victim was his father. But he swore me to secrecy before he told me that. And you need to keep it to yourself, please."

Will raised an eyebrow but said nothing as he pulled a piece of pizza out of the box. He took a big bite.

My stomach growled, but I needed to get through this before I ate. "I ran a background check on Zeke Lord…" Will's face tightened. I kept talking. "And discovered that he didn't exist before twenty-four years ago."

"Why did you do that," his tone was annoyed, "when the sheriff would have found–"

I held up my hand in a stop gesture. "Of course he'd already found that out, but he wouldn't have found Zeke's real identity anytime soon without the info that he was Derek's father. I also had Elise run a background check on Derek, looking for more info about his father."

"Who's Elise?" Will asked.

"The woman at the background check company. His father's name was Jacob Bradshaw, and he was an ex-con, although Derek had been told that he was in the Army and had been overseas during the times he was in prison." I paused for breath.

Will was staring at me, ignoring the pizza slice drooping from his hand and the tomato sauce pooling on the gray granite top of the breakfast bar.

"Jacob Bradshaw disappeared three years before Zeke Lord materialized out of thin air. When I had all those pieces of the puzzle, I realized I had to tell the sheriff what I knew, but first I had to tell my client that I couldn't keep his secret."

Will dropped the partially-eaten pizza slice back into the box. "Sheriff Burns would have the victim's real I.D. by now anyway. All he had to do was run his prints through the system and any old aliases and old crimes would have come up."

My stomach fell. I hadn't thought of that. Had I just wasted an entire afternoon running around Central Florida telling law enforcement what they already knew?

My cheeks flushed. "Why didn't the sheriff say something about that when I met with him?"

Will shrugged. "Probably being polite, and he doesn't want to discourage you from coming to him with anything else you might find out."

I didn't tell him that the sheriff had warned me off of trying to find out anything else.

The tension in my muscles had relaxed. I'd confessed my secret to the sheriff and to Will, and the worst I'd suffered was some wasted time.

I breathed out a long, slow breath and reached across the breakfast bar to pick up a piece of pizza.

Will suddenly turned his head away. "Marcia, I don't think you get how crazy you make me when you get involved in…" His voice was rough now. "…stuff like this." His pause told me he'd wanted to use a stronger word than *stuff*.

I withdrew my hand, still empty. Apparently the tense conversation wasn't over yet.

His Adam's apple bobbed in his throat as he swallowed hard. "Sometimes I lay awake at night worrying about you, and I get distracted at work."

That last part was said as a throw-away comment, but it struck fear into my heart. Literally, it felt like a knife had pierced my breastbone. A distracted cop could end up a dead cop.

I took a deep breath, which only eased the pain a little. From the intensity of the fear, I got it that I'd been hiding behind a thick wall of denial for a long time. And I also got why Will's ex-wife had nagged him about the dangerous nature of his job.

I had vowed I wouldn't repeat her behavior, so I'd walled off the fear instead.

"Look," I said, struggling hard to shove my fear for him aside for now, "I'm not as impulsive as I used to be. I *have* learned a few things in recent years. But sometimes life throws us a curve ball. And at those times, we may need to make choices about doing what's right or hiding our heads in the sand."

I realized that I was quoting my father this time, right down to the curve ball analogy. He'd also pointed out that doing what's right often took courage, although I think he had standing up against social injustice in mind, not chasing murderers.

"You're not the only one," I said, "who's allowed to be brave and do what's right."

Will was looking at me now, his face unreadable. "And I'm programmed to protect people. *Protect and serve.* It's the motto of pretty much every police department in the country."

He grabbed the wine bottle and poured some into the glasses. Then he picked up his glass, wine sloshing dangerously close to the top edge, and took a big swig. "So, in the interest of honest disclosure, I've got to say that I really don't want you going anywhere near Williston or that flea market until Zeke Lord's—or whoever the heck he is—until his killer is caught."

I opened my mouth, but he held up his hand. "I'm not done. I understand that I can't make that demand on you. You have a job to do, just as I do. But…" He stared at me over the rim of his glass. His face had softened, and his eyes looked shiny.

"But please, please be careful." He tossed back the rest of the glass of wine.

I walked quickly around the end of the breakfast bar and took the empty glass from him. Putting my hands on either side of his stubbled face, I said, "I will be. I always am, now. Honestly, Will, I've scared myself a few times, and that's made me much more careful."

Maybe the *much* in that sentence was stretching the truth a bit, but I *was* more careful these days. I loved my life and I loved Will. I didn't want to lose either.

An echo of my earlier fear jabbed at my heart. And several memories popped into my mind, of moments in the recent past when Will had seemed preoccupied. I'd assumed it was about his recent cases with their lack of leads. But now that I thought about it, the preoccupation had begun before he'd been assigned those cases.

And the intensity of his reactions tonight…that was a little off. I dropped my hands to my sides. "Is something else going on?"

He turned away, poured himself more wine.

I sat down on the stool next to his and picked up my own glass. This was something my former counselor and I had worked on, letting a man keep silent for a while as he processed his feelings. I didn't always catch myself right away, but I was getting better at it.

He picked up his piece of pizza again and finished it in three bites.

I grabbed a piece and ate it, mostly to keep my mouth full so I wouldn't bug him to tell me what was going on.

He took a sip of wine. I followed suit. It was good, full-bodied and fruity. I took another sip.

Without looking at me, Will said, "I had to shoot a man six weeks ago."

I was glad I'd finished swallowing the wine, or I would have surely decorated the breakfast bar with it.

"I had no choice. The perp was going to…" He trailed off.

I swallowed hard. I was pretty sure he'd been about to say that the perp was going to shoot him. Now a dozen tiny knives were poking at my heart from all directions, and pizza-flavored bile rose in the back of my throat. I swallowed again. Trying to ignore my feelings, I concentrated on Will's words.

"Those days off last month, they weren't given to me out of the goodness of my boss's heart. I was on admin leave, and then on desk duty for a while. The incident was being investigated to determine if it was a good shoot. Which it was." He paused, took a deep breath. "A few days after I was cleared for regular duty again, I caught a new case. I thought I could bury myself in work. I guess I assumed it would all fade in time."

I was reeling. *He kept this from me!* A jumble of emotions did battle in my chest—anger, fear, guilt—although I couldn't figure out what I should feel guilty about. Maybe because I hadn't noticed sooner that something was off. And heartache for Will…

He picked up my free hand in his. "The guy I shot, he's had two surgeries, unsuccessful ones. The doctors have determined that he'll never walk again."

Ironically, relief coursed through me. I'd assumed he'd killed the guy. I stared into Will's face. But then again, maybe his guilt wouldn't have been much worse if he had killed him.

I put my wineglass down and reached toward Will to draw him into a hug. "It's not your fault–"

He pulled back a little, but still held onto my hand. "There's more. The times lately that I've stayed at the department, they weren't always because I was working a case. I didn't want to come home. I was having nightmares, and I didn't want to have to explain all this to you."

"Why not?" I blurted out.

He ducked his head and turned it to the side, staring off into space. "I don't know. Shame maybe. I told myself I didn't want to disturb your sleep."

I didn't know what to say. He'd kept all this from me for weeks. Were my loved ones right to be concerned about my marriage?

He faced me again, his eyes red-rimmed. "I'm so sorry, Marcia.

I should've told you right away, but I told myself I didn't want to worry you. Then the longer I went without telling you, the harder it was to bring it up. When you had to go to Williston to train your client, well, I thought maybe I'd be able to pull myself out of this…funk, by the time you got back."

"Don't you ever keep anything like that from me again." I was going for a stern but loving tone. The words came out a little choked instead.

He shook his head. "I won't. I promise."

Insight hit me so hard, it knocked the breath out of me for a second. "Your fussing and worrying about me, it's related to all this, isn't it?"

He stared at me, blinking. "Maybe, I guess so."

I took both of his hands in mine. "Look, I am not your ex. You don't need to keep things from me. Yes, I do worry, but I can handle it. It comes with the territory. And I know you can take care of yourself. Now you need to trust that I can take care of myself as well."

He nodded.

"You said you were having nightmares, past tense. Are you still having them?"

"Not as often." He grimaced. "I've had to draw my gun plenty of times in my career, and shoot it twice. But I've never come that close to killing somebody." He shook his head. "You think it won't bother you, that you'll be able to rationalize that the scumbag brought it on himself by trying to shoot you, but…"

He trailed off, and this time he let me hold him.

~

The weekend went by fast, as weekends are prone to do. Will and I had some quality time on Saturday. We didn't talk again about the shooting, other than my suggestion that he needed to get some counseling. He hadn't argued the point. "The department's got somebody they refer to. I'll get their name and number."

That evening, we grilled steaks on our back deck for supper. Will seemed more relaxed than he had in weeks.

On Sunday afternoon, my new assistant, Carla Cummings, brought over our new mutual trainee. She'd spent the last two weeks reinforcing the basics—such as sit, come, and stay—with this new dog, a big and incredibly furry Chow-Siberian Husky mix.

This recently recognized designer breed, dubbed Chuskies or Husky-Chows, was popular right now. But sometimes those cute fluff balls people had acquired as puppies became too overwhelming when they grew into fifty to seventy-pound adults. Some of them were ending up in rescue shelters.

This gal was one of those rescues. Her soon-to-be veteran owner had named her Bear.

Neither Huskies nor Chow-Chows normally make good service dogs. They both tend to be too independent. Chows also bond strongly to their owners, which could be good or bad from a service dog standpoint.

But both were incredibly smart, and when the two breeds mixed, you could end up with a more mellow blend of both. Bear seemed to be one of those dogs.

Mattie Jones, the director of the agency I train for, had made my position as a trainer of other trainers official. She'd even talked the board of trustees into an hourly rate. It was barely above minimum wage, but it was nice to have my efforts recognized.

Plus, having a trainer-in-training assistant meant I could concentrate on one dog at a time, putting the final touches on the training and working with the veterans, while said assistant handled the more basic, and more boring, stuff with the next dog.

This particular service dog trainer-in-training, was already an experienced dog trainer, so my job was mainly to show her the ropes regarding the specific tasks that service dogs perform. Carla was also several years older than me. I wasn't real sure how she felt about receiving instruction from someone younger.

Today, in the backyard of my training center, she was showing me what Bear could already do. The dog seemed to be well-behaved, with a heart almost as big as her body. Things went smoothly, until I pointed out that a non-verbal gesture needed to be paired with each verbal command.

"Why?" Carla demanded.

"For flexibility. In public, the veteran may not want to be too obvious about his or her signals to the dog, so a subtle gesture may be better."

"Then why don't we train the dogs to just respond to the nonverbal commands? Wouldn't that be easier than the veteran having to remember both?"

I counted to five. Asking questions was good when you were learning something new, but I wasn't crazy about her tone.

"What if the veteran's hands are full?" I said. "The sergeant I'm working with now either walks with two canes or is in a wheelchair. He needs the option of verbal–"

"How can he walk if he needs a wheelchair?"

This time, I counted to ten. Eventually, Carla would need to learn about the mental and physical injuries our veteran clients were dealing with, but I really didn't want to go there today. "He's only partially paralyzed," I said, and left it at that.

But a thought niggled in the back of my brain, that maybe I'd overlooked something regarding Derek.

I shook my head slightly and refocused on the task at hand. "The gesture commands are almost always natural ones, easy to remember, like…" I looked over to where my dog snoozed under our magnolia tree. "Buddy."

His head came up. I patted my thigh, and he came running.

Unfortunately, Bear also responded, only she thought I was playing with her. She jumped up, her massive paws coming down on my shoulders.

I braced myself to keep from falling over, giggling in spite of myself as she licked my face.

"No, Bear. Get down!" Carla said sternly. "Sorry, I've been trying to break her of that."

I took a long backward step, ducking out from under Bear's front paws. She landed on the ground and bunched to jump up again.

I quickly turned around. "Sit, stay," I said with my back to her.

I glanced over my shoulder. She had obeyed. I turned back and gave her an ear scratch. "Good girl."

To Carla, I said, "It's better to find a way to get the dog to do the desired behavior, like I did by turning around and telling her to sit. And then reward that—rather than scolding her for the bad behavior. It's all attention to them, so scolding may not be seen as punishment."

Carla frowned.

Oops. Had I stepped on her toes by pointing out a rather basic concept of behavior modification?

"Unfortunately, when we use rescue dogs," I said in my best

conciliatory tone, "they sometimes have bad habits we have to train out of them. It's not the same as training a dog from puppyhood."

Carla shook her head slightly and pasted on a small smile. "I've had rescues as pets before. Often breaking the bad habits is the hardest part."

I nodded, grateful that she was making an effort to get along. "Unlearning is harder than learning," I said.

I leaned down and petted Bear again. "But this one's a bright girl, and she's eager to please. Two of the most important qualities in a service dog."

Carla's face relaxed into a more natural smile.

"Thanks for bringing her over," I said. "I can start working with you soon after Thanksgiving, hopefully." Which meant I really needed to get the training done with Derek and Fred as soon as possible, so I could concentrate on Bear and Carla.

The dog would probably be easy to train. Carla, maybe not so much.

I walked them out to her car in front of my house and waved as they drove away.

I turned and froze on the sidewalk. My earlier niggling thought had exploded into a full-blown insight.

I'd been assuming from the get-go that Derek couldn't have killed Zeke because of his disability. From his wheelchair, he might be able to stab someone in the abdomen, but not in the heart. And he couldn't stand without support.

How could he thrust a sword into a man's chest hard enough to kill without throwing himself horribly off balance? He would risk falling down, something he tried hard to avoid.

Or at least that's what he's led you to believe, Ms. Snark observed.

Those assumptions, combined with the fact that he seemed to be such a nice guy, had led to other assumptions, such as nice people weren't very good liars.

But I really didn't know the guy. What if he was a better actor than I'd given him credit for, and what if his abilities weren't as limited as he'd described?

Could he have stabbed the father he'd hated since his teens?

I shook my head to clear it. I was letting my imagination run wild.

CHAPTER FOURTEEN

By Sunday evening, I had mostly banished my paranoia about Derek from my mind. He just didn't have it in him to be a cold-blooded murderer.

But in a fit of rage… Ms. Snark trailed off. I ignored her.

My best course of action, I'd decided, was to get the training over with as quickly as possible, while keeping a low profile. I definitely would not be doing any more investigating.

I felt a twinge of guilt because I'd told Derek I'd have Elise look into some things about Zeke—his Social Security number and whether or not he might have been in Witness Protection during those missing three years.

But that was before the sheriff had warned me again to butt out. And honestly, I'd lost the urge to investigate. Maybe I was afraid I'd find out Derek wasn't what he seemed to be.

At dinner, Will was not thrilled when I told him I was going back to Williston the next morning and would stay there through Tuesday as planned, although at the bed and breakfast rather than Becky's house.

"Nothing else has happened," I said, "since the sheriff held that news conference. The killer must've gotten it that the evidence he was trying to find is already in the hands of law enforcement."

Or Derek's been pretending that someone was looking for something, Ms. Snark pointed out. *Maybe Mr. Green Shirt is his partner in crime.*

Why have you decided to torture me with unfounded paranoia? I asked her internally.

She chortled. *Because it's fun.*

I made a mental note to make an appointment with my former counselor, when all this was over. And to ask my mother if there was any schizophrenia in my family tree.

Will glanced up. "Maybe," he said, and went back to shoveling food into his mouth. I had roasted a chicken, along with new potatoes and baby carrots. It was one of the few cooking lessons my Mom had given me that had actually stuck in my long-term memory. It was also Will's favorite meal.

"Andy's gonna have a Williston police cruiser swing by the B&B regularly," I told him. "I might even stay over until Wednesday, depending on how things go."

He glanced up from his food again, without commenting.

I reached over and took his hand—the one that wasn't wielding a fork full of potato. "Why are you acting like this? You know it's not that dangerous now."

He sighed and put his fork down. "Yeah, I know. And yes, I know you're more careful these days. But I also know that once you're over there, you won't be able to resist poking around again. And it isn't your home turf. You don't know where the hornets' nests might be."

"I will not *poke around*, as you call it." I tried to sound indignant but couldn't quite pull it off. It wasn't an unreasonable thing for him to assume, based on my track record.

"Bottom line," I said, "I've got no reason to investigate now, and I have every confidence that the sheriff will get his man, or woman."

"Mm-hmm. Pass the bread, please."

~

I rose early the next day, despite a restless night. I needed to feed my horse and the other residents of the Mayfair Riding Stables. Susanna Mayfair, Edna's niece, usually took turns with me, feeding and mucking the stalls. She'd had to carry more than her share of the load lately, with me being away.

It was a lovely cool morning, and I couldn't resist taking Niña out for a short ride. Thus, I got off to a somewhat delayed start.

Once I was on the road, with Buddy and Fred in the backseat, I called Derek. I got voicemail and left a short message.

The little dribble of traffic that constitutes rush hour in rural Florida had already diminished to the occasional pickup truck. I made up some for lost time and was only ten minutes late when I got to Derek's house.

He was in his driveway, loading one of two cardboard boxes into the backseat of his SUV. "Hey," he called over, when I climbed out of my car. "When you said you'd be late, I thought you meant a lot late. I was going to run some new stuff over to the flea market, get it set up for Wednesday."

I shoved down the thought that Derek seemed to be handling the bulky boxes just fine, telling myself that was because he was hanging onto the doorframe of the truck for balance.

"Not a problem." I stuck my head into the backseat of my car and unhooked the dogs. Releasing Fred's safety strap from the seatbelt latch, I took it with me as we walked over to Derek's truck.

"How about we check out how easy, or not so easy, it will be for you to load Fred into the backseat?"

"Okay." Derek shoved the box over farther on the seat, then stepped aside and settled into his wheelchair.

I attached the safety strap and stepped back myself, sweeping my arm in an after-you gesture. "Jump in, Fred."

He scrambled over the high threshold of the SUV and up onto the backseat.

I stepped back farther and gestured again, letting Derek figure out the best logistics for the process himself.

He rolled his chair close to the opening, but he had to lean pretty far forward to grope around for the end of the safety strap, which Fred was sitting on.

"Hmm," I said, "you got any string?"

He looked up at me and nodded. "We can tie the strap to the

seatbelt shoulder piece. String's in the junk drawer in the kitchen, left of the sink."

Buddy followed me as I jogged to the house.

When we returned, a roll of twine in my hand, a Williston PD cruiser was parked at the curb behind my car. Derek was chatting with Andy Matthews next to the SUV.

Buddy and I trotted over to them. "Hey, stranger," I said to Andy.

"Hey, yourself. I see Will wasn't able to keep you down on the farm."

"Nope." I might have said more, but not in front of Derek.

"Well, I was stopping by to see how things were going," Andy said, trying to sound casual. But of course, he wouldn't just be "stopping by" when on duty. This was one of those stepped-up patrols the Williston police chief had promised.

"Becky wants you to come over after you're done training this afternoon," he added.

I tilted my head at him, confused, but again not wanting to say too much in front of Derek.

"Walk me to my car," Andy said.

I handed Derek the string and walked with Andy toward his cruiser.

In a low voice, he said, "The Crystal County sheriff called my boss this morning. He said he's close to an arrest. But he doesn't think the person he suspects is a danger to any of us at this point. Our police chief still wants us to keep the added patrols going though, until the person is arrested."

Excitement bubbled in my chest, but a brick of dread had taken up residence in my stomach. Talk about mixed emotions. It would be great to be able to stop looking over my shoulder. But what if the person about to be arrested was Derek?

"Who does he suspect?" I whispered.

Andy shook his head. "He wouldn't say. Said he needed to gather more evidence before making an arrest."

The dread cancelled out the excitement. Had the information that Zeke was Derek's father, whom he'd hated most of his life, tipped the scales of suspicion in his direction?

I swallowed hard. "Thanks for coming by, Andy. I'll call Becky later with an ETA."

"She wants you to stay with us again, rather than spending money on that B&B."

"What do you want?"

He smiled. "I want you to come too. The danger seems to be over now."

I returned the smile. "See ya later then."

When I got back to his SUV, Derek had already rigged the string to the loose shoulder strap of the seatbelt, with a small extra loop hanging down.

I fished the hook end of the safety strap out from under Fred's butt and handed it to Derek.

He tried it out, hooking it to the loop of string. "All I gotta do is remember to hook it up there when I get Fred out of the truck."

I nodded. "Turn, Fred."

The dog, who'd been sitting straight on in the seat, turned away from us, making the metal ring on his service vest readily accessible.

Derek gave me a lopsided grin. "You think of everything, don't you?" He leaned forward and hooked the safety strap to the ring. "Will that strap actually keep him from getting hurt in an accident?"

"Depends on the accident. What it will do is keep him from being thrown out of the vehicle or through the windshield. Both of which would likely be fatal for a dog."

With Fred secured in the backseat and the wheelchair stowed in the very back of the truck, Derek led the way to the flea market. I followed with Buddy in my car.

The parking lot contained only a smattering of cars, probably other vendors who had come in to restock. I spotted the clunker that Nell drove. It's presence reinforced my suspicion that she lived in her trailer.

Buddy and I walked over to Derek's truck as he was making his way to its rear, holding onto the door handles to steady himself.

When he reached into the back and slung the wheelchair out and onto the ground, I got it why he used such a lightweight one, made of aluminum and barely big enough to hold his large frame. It was a chair he could handle one-handed.

I watched him reverse the process of getting Fred into the truck, telling him to turn, unhooking the strap, and hooking it within easy reach through the string loop. He was already making it look second-nature.

Good, one hurdle easily surmounted.

Derek piled the cardboard boxes onto his lap, then led the way to his building.

At his stall, he transferred himself from the chair to his motorized cart. I backed out of the way, as he began rearranging things on the tables, making room for the new items.

"Good crowds this past weekend," he called out as he worked. "We're getting into the Christmas season."

Standing out in the aisle, a dog sitting on either side of me, I said, "Before Thanksgiving?"

"Yeah, although it'll get even busier after Black Friday. This time of year, it's when I make most of my money. All the old folks down here in Florida, wantin' something different for their grandkids."

He rolled his cart over to the bigger of the boxes he'd brought and pulled out a small wooden stool. He held it up so I could see the animals painted on it. They were brushing their teeth.

I grinned, making a mental note to remember them when it was time to buy presents for the twins' birthday.

Derek pulled out more stools and stacked them beside a table.

Fred stood and started pacing. It dawned on me that it had been a long time since the dogs' last bathroom break. "I'm going to take these guys outside for a bit, okay?"

"Sure," he said in a distracted tone, as he put wooden toys from the smaller box out onto a table.

I left him to his work and led the dogs down the aisle to the back of the building.

The sight of the house trailer church with its lopsided steeple brought a lump to my throat. Would someone else take up the mantle and keep the Sunday prayer services going?

A stiff breeze blew, making me shiver in my long-sleeved tee shirt. It was the precursor of the cold front that was predicted to come through and cause the temperature to plummet into the low forties tonight.

Fred tugged slightly on his leash, reminding me of the urgency of our mission. I let go of both dogs' leashes.

Fred ran over to the grassy area nearby and only sniffed around a little before lifting his leg. His expression of relief was priceless. Then he began sniffing in greater earnest.

Dang, I should've brought a plastic bag.

I glanced over at Buddy. His need didn't seem to be as great, but he was taking advantage of the opportunity. I smiled at my boy attempting to remain dignified as he lifted his leg.

"Stay close," I called to both the dogs. I stuck my head back inside the building, looking for something to use to pick up after Fred.

I spotted a large trash can farther down the aisle and jogged to it. Someone had tossed the wax-paper wrapper from a breakfast sandwich into it. I leaned down and fished it out.

As I headed outside, my fickle mind wandered to my worries about Derek. I kept waffling—one minute thinking that maybe he had killed Zeke in a moment of passion, then coming around again to believing his innocence and fearing he'd be blamed for a crime he didn't commit.

Out back, Buddy trotted over. I looked around.

Fred was nowhere in sight.

Butterflies danced in my chest. *Crapola, where could he be?*

"Fred! Come here, boy," I yelled.

No response.

Heart in my throat, I ran toward the strip of woods beyond the grass. "Buddy, come." He bolted after me.

We fought our way through the underbrush. I repeatedly called Fred's name, while praying we wouldn't trip over a snake or alligator.

The butterflies had invaded my stomach.

A breeze blew in my face. Not a good thing. My scent, and probably my words as well, were being blown away.

I stopped, frantically scanning the woods. *Where could he have gone?*

To my right, I spotted some red threads, caught on a frond of a saw palmetto. They could be from his vest. I took off in that direction.

The large leaf of a giant philodendron whacked me in the face. I stumbled a little, wrinkling my nose as I almost stepped on a decaying armadillo carcass.

I kept running and calling Fred's name. Fear for him clogged my throat. My mind had jumped ahead to the most ominous outcome.

And one corner of it was desperately trying to calculate how I would pay for the expensive animal I seemed to have lost. If he ended up a gator's lunch, I'd be running in the red for a very long time. Crass thoughts, I know, but also realistic.

Buddy and I blundered our way out of the other side of the woods, and I faltered. An empty field stretched out in front of us, the weeds and grass thick and waist high. My dislike of snakes stopped me. The underbrush in the woods had been bad enough, but in this field, I wouldn't be able to see my feet or the ground at all.

I called Buddy back to me, then screamed Fred's name. My chest heaved.

A sob escaped, just as the scruffy dog emerged from the weeds, a big stick in his mouth.

Relief washed through me, leaving my muscles weak. "Come here, boy," I managed to croak out. He came to me, and I gingerly took the stick from him.

Wait! This stick was way too straight.

Mouth hanging open, I stared at the object in my hand—the cane sheath of the dragonhead sword.

CHAPTER FIFTEEN

Twigs and pine needles adorned Fred's leash. I was surprised it hadn't snagged on something bigger, like one of the many roots or large branches lying about on the floor of the woods.

As we made our way back toward the flea market, I tried to piece together what had happened here. Had Fred picked up on Derek's scent, which would be all over the cane, and followed it?

If so, that meant Derek had carried it through the woods and the tall grass of the field. No way could he do that, either in his chair or with his walking sticks. The ground was too uneven and cluttered with debris. And I'd seen no signs of a crushed path through the underbrush or the grass in the field, which a wheelchair would surely make.

Fred must have wandered away, gotten disoriented in the woods, and as he got closer to the cane sheath, maybe picked up Derek's scent on it?

Buddy paused, sniffing at something on the ground. The food wrapper I'd dropped. I picked it up and stuffed it in my pocket.

We emerged from the woods near the flea market, me holding the cane by its tip—the spot least likely to have the fingerprints of those who'd handled it before me.

A piercing shriek. My head jerked up.

Nell was running toward us. "Gimme that!" she yelled.

Buddy and Fred inserted themselves between me and the approaching person, as they had been trained to do. It was a maneuver normally meant to give an anxiety-prone veteran some additional personal space.

But Nell was still coming strong.

"Protect, Buddy!"

He barked loudly, the hair along his backbone straight up.

Only Will and I knew he wouldn't bite, even if I was physically attacked. Although he was also trained to grab and hold someone's arm, without biting down.

But the sight of a large black dog, now ferociously barking at her, did finally stop Nell.

"It's okay, Buddy." He sat down beside me.

"Nell! Marcia!" Derek's voice. His cart shot out of the end of the building. He brought it to a halt behind Nell. "Y'all okay?" He leaned to the side to see past her.

I struggled to control my ragged breathing. "Yes, but I found something."

Awkwardly juggling both dogs' leashes, plus the tip of the cane, I managed to get my phone out of my pocket. Fortunately, I had already entered the sheriff's cell number into my contacts.

When he answered, I said without preamble, "Sheriff, you need to come to the flea market right away. I found some important evidence. And I'm afraid to put it down for fear of smudging prints."

At the word *prints*, Nell's face blanched. She burst into tears, hands covering her face. "You don't know what you've done," she wailed.

Derek scooted to her side on his cart. Looking helpless, he patted her elbow.

I returned my phone to my pocket and passed the handle of Fred's leash to Derek. "Take Nell inside, and send the sheriff back here when he arrives."

His eyes were wide. "Is that what I think it is?"

I nodded. "Fred found it."

~

I was once again sitting in the Crystal County Sheriff's Department's conference room. Detective Rick Young sat across from me, and the sheriff was at the end of the table, arms crossed over his chest.

"Tell us again," the detective said, "where you found the cane."

I slowly blew out air, trying to disguise my sigh. "I didn't find it. The dog did. He came out of the tall grass in that field behind the woods, with it in his mouth."

"You said before that he found it in that field."

This time I let the sigh out. "I assumed he found it there. He really didn't have time to get much farther than that field. As soon as I saw he was gone–" I stopped abruptly, swallowed hard at the thought that my carelessness could have... "I started calling and looking for him right away."

Now the sheriff sighed. "My deputies were told to search a mile radius. That field is within that circle."

"Yes, sir, but the grass is really thick. They could have missed the cane, or maybe it was under some leaves. Fred might've smelled Derek's scent on it and dug for it."

"So he followed the scent into the woods?" the detective said.

Detective Rick here needs to get his hearing checked, Ms. Snark observed internally.

I shook my head. I understood the need for the repeated questions, but it was getting old. "I doubt it." I repeated my observations that Derek couldn't have made it through the woods or the thick grass, and if he'd somehow managed it, he would have left a visible trail.

"Something with his scent on it," I said yet again, "being carried by someone else, wouldn't leave a sufficient trail for a dog to follow."

"So why'd the dog run off?" Detective Rick asked.

"I don't know. I thought his training to stay close, even without the leash, was more solid than that." It was something we would be working on back home this weekend.

"What would've been attractive enough to lure him away?"

"I don't know," I repeated, trying to keep the frustration out of my voice. Did this detective enjoy making me admit over and over that I was a less-than-perfect dog trainer?

Nobody's perfect, my inner mom offered as comfort.

"Wait, the armadillo!" I blurted out.

Detective Rick leaned forward. "What armadillo?"

I glanced at the sheriff, who had an inscrutable expression on his face.

"I just remembered. There was one in the woods, a corpse of one, that is." My words tumbled out. "A little before we got to the field. It was pretty far gone decay-wise. Fred might have picked up that scent and that lured him into the woods."

The detective frowned, looking skeptical.

The sheriff made a slight noise. "But why couldn't he follow his nose back?"

I turned toward him. "Most likely because it's breezy today. The wind has to be blowing in the right direction for a dog to pick up a scent."

"Why didn't he come when you called him?" the sheriff asked. "Don't dogs have good hearing?"

I perked up some. This was a new line of questioning—it broke up the boring repetition—and it was a subject I knew something about.

"They do have good hearing, and good eyesight, but not quite the same as humans. They're red-green color blind, for example." I plucked at my red, long-sleeved tee shirt. "Fred would see this as dull green or brown. I'd blend right into the background in the woods."

I warmed to the topic. "As for hearing, it's better in some ways. For one thing, the dog's ears act as funnels for sound, so they can hear the sounds in front of them better than a human might. But behind them and from a distance, the sound would be more muffled."

Sitting forward in my chair, I added, "The breeze would've also made it hard for him to determine where my voice was coming from. He might've thought he was running toward me, when he was actually going farther into the woods."

Again, Detective Rick looked skeptical. "But what about all these dogs you hear about who find their way home over hundreds of miles?"

"They're the rare exception, which is why they get so much press. Sadly, most dogs that get lost, stay lost, unless somebody sees a poster the owner put up, or the dog has a tag on their collar or is microchipped." I let out a soft snort. "If dogs could readily find their way home, we could close half the animal shelters."

The sheriff nodded and put his palms on the table. "Thank you, Ms.…um, Marcia. Call us if you think of anything else."

"Uh, Sheriff, I wanted to apologize."

He paused halfway to a stand. "For what?"

"For wasting your time the other day when I was telling you about Derek's father. You were very patient with me, when you must have known all about him already, from running his fingerprints."

He sank back into his chair. He and the detective exchanged a glance.

The sheriff cleared his throat. "Actually, your information was valuable. We hadn't gotten anything from his fingerprints." He held his left hand palm up, fingers splayed. "There was too much scar tissue," he said, running his right index finger across his fingertips. "We're not sure what it's from."

My hand flew to my mouth. "I know."

"Know what?" the sheriff said, sounding confused.

"I know where the scar tissue came from." I told them about Zeke touching his "lucky sword" each day, and sometimes drawing blood.

Detective Rick scowled. "It was lucky alright. He was keeping his prints from being traceable."

~

It was well past noon by the time Derek and I finally had a chance to do any training.

"Let's tackle the anger training," I said. "Hopefully, Fred will pick up on your anger the first time or two, and we won't have to keep repeating the process."

Derek nodded, his expression glum.

I had another agenda as well. I wanted to see how well he controlled his anger, when he put his mind to it.

This we could do inside, away from neighbors' prying eyes.

I told Buddy to stay in the kitchen, and we settled in the small living room, Fred lying beside his master's wheelchair.

"I know this is a stupid question," I said, "but can you think of a time when you were really pissed?"

Derek let out a bark of humorless laughter. Then he settled back into his chair. Without prompting, he closed his eyes. I could tell when the emotions were starting to build by the increased tension in his face.

I held my breath.

Fred lifted his chin from his paws.

Come on, boy, you can do this, I mentally prompted. I breathed slowly through my mouth, trying to keep my own tension level down so it wouldn't distract the dog.

Derek's hands tightened on the wheelchair arms. His left leg jiggled slightly.

Fred stood up and touched his nose to the side of Derek's hand.

Derek opened one eye.

"Stay with the emotions a little longer," I said softly.

Derek nodded.

Fred walked around in front of the chair and put his chin on one knee. He whined.

Derek opened both eyes. The dog put a paw on the other knee and nudged his head forward, giving his master easy access.

Derek obliged and stroked his head. "Should I give him a treat?"

"You can, some of the time. But usually the attention is reward enough."

"Good boy," Derek said, continuing to pet his dog.

And Fred was his dog now. The connection between them was almost palpable.

I smiled to myself. "We should repeat that one more time, but not today."

I had them practice a couple other simple tasks, mostly to distract Derek from the anger-provoking memories. Then I called for a break.

We sat at his kitchen table, with iced tea at hand. I'd brought my own thermos of unsweetened—I'd never get used to Southern sweet tea. It made my teeth hurt.

"I asked around some over the weekend," Derek said, "during the few lulls between customers. A couple of other vendors bought stuff dirt cheap from Zeke. I'm convinced now that he was a fence."

"You need to tell the sheriff that."

But he was already shaking his head before I got all the words out. "I don't want to get these guys in trouble for accepting stolen goods."

Here we go again, my inner mom commented.

I chose my words carefully. "What's more important, protecting them or catching Zeke's killer?"

I was expecting him to say the latter, but he was silent, his expression thoughtful.

After a moment, he said, "I'm not sure I care all that much who killed him. It was probably some lowlife he was dealin' with, who thought Zeke had cheated him." Derek voice was mildly bitter. "Heck, maybe Zeke did cheat him. A man who runs out on two women and their kids isn't exactly a model citizen." The bitterness was more than mild now.

I understood his reaction, but it did nothing to solve my dilemma. Maybe an anonymous tip to the sheriff's department was in order.

When we were ready to get started again, I suggested we move to the backyard. "I want to see how well he heels without the leash."

Derek nodded. "I'll be out in a minute. I need to use the bathroom."

"We'll meet you out back." The dogs and I went out into the yard. I told Buddy to lie down in the shade of a live oak. Then I let Fred off his leash, gave him the release signal, and said, "Stay close."

I strolled around the yard, acting as if I wasn't paying a bit of attention to the dog. Fred walked alongside. Occasionally I'd say, "Good boy. Stay close."

He sniffed a nearby bush and cocked his leg. I walked a little farther and stopped, giving him time to finish his business.

He trotted right up to me without prompting. "Good boy!" I gave him a treat.

We walked around for a while longer, me periodically repeating, "Good boy. Stay close."

Nose in the air, he caught a scent and began to move away from me.

"Fred!" He turned and looked at me. "Stay close."

He immediately came back to me, and I gave him a treat. I wondered if he had some hound in him. That's a breed I try to avoid using as service dogs, because they are so bent on chasing down every scent they pick up, which makes them easily distracted.

I made a mental note to change Fred's microchip registration over to Derek's name and contact info, but I would ask them to keep mine on there as well. If this dog got away from him in the future, I wanted to know about it.

At the end of the yard, I turned back toward the house. Fred stuck with me without prompting. I smiled.

The back screen door banged open. Derek burst onto the porch in his chair. I thought he was going to run right off the edge, but he stopped a few inches short of it.

Heart pounding, I ran toward the house. Obviously, something was wrong.

"Marcia," he yelled, "I gotta go."

"Go where? What's happened?"

Closer now, I could see that his face was twisted in a grimace of pain. Had he hurt himself?

"Nell called. She's been arrested."

My heart sank. "I'll follow you," came out of my mouth before I'd had a chance to think about it.

~

It had been less than twenty-four hours since I'd promised Will, and myself, that I wouldn't "poke around" in Zeke's murder case. And yet here I was, sitting in the Crystal County Sheriff's Department waiting area—for the *second* time today.

I'd brought the dogs this time, unwilling to leave them at Derek's house, just in case our anonymous searcher was still active. They were in their service vests to justify bringing them inside.

I certainly couldn't leave them in the car. In late November—heck, even in January—the Florida sun was intense enough to turn a car into an oven in minutes.

Derek had called his defense attorney. The man had apparently pointed out that it was a conflict of interest to represent two potential suspects of the same crime.

"Fine," Derek had said angrily into the phone, "I'm firing you, and then rehiring you to help Nell."

Now, the attorney was in the interrogation room with Nell, the sheriff, and Detective Young.

And we were cooling our heels out here in the waiting area.

Derek sat in his wheelchair, his face in his hands. Fred, sensing his distress, did as he'd been trained and tried to get the man to pet him in order to calm down. Derek ignored him.

Under other circumstances, I would have gently chastised the veteran for ignoring his dog's signals, but I couldn't bring myself to do it. Fred whined and looked at me, confusion on his doggy face.

I patted my thigh. He came over to me, and I petted him, eyeing the tear in his red vest, made by the saw palmetto in the woods. Maybe I could darn it, although I wasn't the greatest with needle and thread.

"Are you okay?" I said gently to Derek.

He jerked his head up, then shook it. "I'm supposed to take care of her," he whispered.

"You got her a lawyer. That's all you can do right now."

He turned his head without responding and stared off into space.

More and more, I suspected that Derek was in love with Nell. Hadn't Zeke seen the signs? Why hadn't he told Derek that she was his half-sister, and nipped the whole thing in the bud?

I got it that Zeke had been afraid to reveal his true identity, once he found out how much Derek hated his father. But how could he selfishly continue to keep that information secret, even after he realized his son had romantic feelings for his own sister? Or had Zeke not realized what was going on?

I shook my head slightly. No, Zeke was a con artist. He understood psychology and no doubt watched those around him carefully to read their feelings, so he could use that information to his advantage. He hadn't missed the signs, but still he hadn't told Derek his identity.

Despite his claim to have found God, Zeke Lord, or rather Jacob Bradshaw, was not a good man.

My reverie was interrupted by the lawyer coming through the door between the back offices and the waiting area. He walked over and sat in the chair on the other side of Derek. "Nell's being arraigned in the morning," he said in a low voice.

"Her fingerprints were all over the cane sheath of the murder weapon. Before I got here, she told the sheriff she had found the body, with the cane next to it. She threw it in that field, behind the woods. On the way back, she found the sword. It was stuck in a drainage grate in the parking lot."

The lawyer glanced from Derek's face to mine and back again. "She thought she had wiped it clean when she put it back in the display. But she never turned on the overhead lights in the flea market. She was afraid of drawing the attention of the killer, she said, in case he was still around. She just used her flashlight, so she didn't notice that she'd missed some of the blood."

"Why'd she mess with it?" Derek asked.

The lawyer blinked. "She didn't tell the sheriff the answer to that question, thank God, but she told me privately. She thought the sword implicated you, that Zeke had told you he was your father, and you had killed him."

Derek and I sucked in air in unison.

"They're charging her with the murder?" I asked.

"No, for now, only with theft and tampering with evidence. But she's still under suspicion for the murder." The lawyer gave Derek a sharp look. "As are you. Your fingerprints are all over that cane sheath too."

"Of course, they are," I said. "It was his cane."

The lawyer glanced at me. "Which his *new* lawyer will point out if he's arrested." Then his face softened and he patted Derek's shoulder. "I'll find somebody to take over your case. Someone good. I'll call you. Now the two of you should go home. There's nothing more you can do for Nell today."

Derek was staring into space again, as the attorney left.

I stood. "You gonna be okay?"

He looked up at me, his eyes dull, but he nodded.

The dogs and I followed as he wheeled himself out of the building. I dawdled at my car, dragging out the process of hooking the dogs to their safety straps.

Finally, Derek's SUV pulled away, and I let out pent-up air. Unhooking the dogs, I headed back inside the building, with them in tow.

Time to talk to the sheriff, again.

CHAPTER SIXTEEN

The receptionist tried to get rid of me, telling me the sheriff was very busy right now. But I insisted I had important information for him. I was about to call his cell number, when he came out of the inner sanctum and gestured for me to follow him.

"Conference room's in use," he said over his shoulder, his voice neutral. "Come back to my office."

As we passed through the bullpen of gray metal desks, most empty—some occupied by deputies or plain-clothes detectives—the sheriff gestured to one of the latter. The man jumped up and began turning a portable whiteboard around.

Before it's plain back came into view, I caught a glimpse of the gruesome crime scene photos the sheriff hadn't wanted me to see. A man on a bed, looked like it was a hotel room. Dark pants, light green shirt, dark hair, his face a bloody pulp.

I turned my head away and swallowed hard.

"Sorry," the sheriff said, "I should have gotten that out of sight before I came out to get you."

"It's okay. Um, I've seen worse on TV." Only this wasn't a TV show. This was a real murder scene.

"Two murders in the same month," I said, more to distract myself from what I'd seen than anything else. "Isn't that unusual for such a rural county?"

The sheriff snorted. "Two murders in the same year used to be extraordinary."

"Where was..." suddenly my throat was clogged with a large lump. I cleared it. "Where was that...where was he found?"

The sheriff gestured with his left hand. "Motel down the road apiece." He glanced sideways at me as he ushered me into his office. "It tends to rent by the hour, if you get my drift."

I nodded and stopped asking questions about that corpse. I didn't want to use up all of the sheriff's goodwill on a case other than the one that truly concerned me.

"So, what can I do for you, Ms. Ban–"

I raised my hand in a stop gesture. "Marcia."

He gave me a small smile. "Marcia, what can I do for you?"

"I have some more information, although I can't tell you how I came by it. It was purely accidental though. I'm not trying to investigate, but sometimes I hear things."

The sheriff remained quiet, his expression impassive.

I took a deep breath. "You maybe should look into the possibility that Zeke Lord was the recipient of stolen goods, a fence to be exact."

"Why do you think that?"

I shook my head. "I can't say, but the evidence should not be hard to find if you ask around at the flea market."

"I see."

"Um, by the way, did you find out what was in the little vial?"

"Dried blood."

I already knew that but didn't say so. Instead I raised an eyebrow, as if I were a bit surprised and just curious, that's all. Ha, who was I fooling?

"Whose blood?" I asked, not really expecting an answer.

The sheriff stared at me for a long minute. Then he made a harumphing sound. "Belonged to a woman who died in New Jersey twenty-five years ago."

"Wow, you found that out this quickly?"

"DNA testing doesn't take as long as it used to. And I was curious enough, I sent it to the fire marshal's lab."

"Huh?"

He sighed. "Normally, smaller jurisdictions like ours have to send our stuff to the FDLE lab in Jacksonville."

I knew from Will that FDLE stood for the Florida Department of Law Enforcement. It was the state's version of the FBI.

"But sometimes," the sheriff said, "if we need results in a hurry, we send it to the Tallahassee Office of the Fire Marshal. Their lab's the best in the state. They'll usually help us out, if we don't abuse the privilege by sendin' stuff too often."

He sighed again. "Unfortunately, this time the results don't tell us much worth knowin'."

"Did they even have DNA testing twenty-five years ago?"

"Yeah, and the FBI's database was established around then."

"So why are the results not worth much?" I asked.

The sheriff let out a small snort. "I don't know what Zeke Lord thought he had with that old blood sample. Most likely, that sword's killed multiple people in its day. An antiques appraiser has taken a look at it. Lord was a ways off about its age. It dates back to pre-Civil War times."

My mouth fell open. Then something clicked in my brain. "The provenance, it was a fake?"

The sheriff nodded. "The sword's worth more than fifteen thousand too. More like twice that. We'll return it to Sergeant Bradshaw eventually…" He trailed off.

The words *if he isn't convicted of Zeke Lord's murder* hung in the air between us.

"Wait a minute," I said. "We were talking about the blood in the vial, and now suddenly you're talking about the sword."

The sheriff's cheeks turned pink under his tan. He scrubbed a big hand over his face.

Aha! He'd let something slip he hadn't intended to share.

Finally, he said, "If you got nothin' else to tell me, I've got work to do." He rose from his chair. "Good day, Ms. Ba–"

I held up a hand as I stood. "Marcia."

He rolled his eyes. "Good day, Marcia."

It was high time I checked in with the director of the agency I train for and brought her up to speed on the situation with our client. It wasn't a conversation I was looking forward to.

Although I'm technically an independent contractor, Mattie Jones is essentially my boss. She's one of the most no-nonsense people I've ever known, and even after years of working for her, I find her a little intimidating.

I bit the bullet and called her from my car on the way to Becky's. I filled her in, feeling myself choking up some as I described Derek's despondency. "I, um, considered leaving Fred with him, but it seemed premature." I opted not to mention his anger issues. They were mentioned in his file, so it's not like I was withholding anything. "But I'm worried about him, that he might–" My throat tightened, strangling my words.

A pause. I had no idea how Mattie might respond. She wasn't much into emotions.

"Marcia, Sergeant Bradshaw is not your responsibility." Her voice, coming from the Bluetooth speaker, was surprisingly gentle.

I swallowed and forced my voice to cooperate. "I know. I'm just…worried," I said again, rather lamely.

Another pause. "He's not the one in jail, and he's got his sister to look out for." Then she shocked me completely. "He's not Jimmy Garrett."

My stomach clenched. My eyes burned. Blindly, I pulled off onto the rough gravel of the country road's shoulder and jammed my car into park. The dogs rustled around in the backseat. One of them whined softly, probably Fred.

"What do you mean?" I managed to choke out.

Mattie cleared her throat. "You tend to take on a little too much responsibility for the veterans we serve. Your job is to train the dogs," her usual matter-of-fact tone was back, "and then to train the veterans how to utilize their dogs. You're *not* their counselor. You don't need to fix them."

"Okay." My voice sounded feeble. "I, um, wanted to let you know what was going on."

"Duly noted." And with that, Mattie disconnected.

I drove the rest of the way to Becky's on autopilot, my mind trying to process what Mattie had said.

Jimmy Garrett was the first veteran client for whom I'd trained a dog—Buddy, to be exact. And two years later, his was the first legal mess I had gotten myself sucked into. It had not ended well, which was why Buddy was now in my possession.

Was Mattie right? Was I compensating for that failure by trying to fix other messes I stumbled onto in my clients' lives? If they were in trouble, I was drawn to that trouble like a moth to the light.

Or was that why I'd gotten a degree in psychology in the first place? Even though I'd never actually practiced as a counselor. Had I always had this need to help people? Although I had to admit, sometimes I went beyond normal limits of helping. It was almost a compulsion.

I didn't recall being like that, when I'd lived in Maryland. I hadn't gotten involved in other people's problems up there.

Then again, I'd lived a rather sheltered life, first as a pastor's kid and then as a musician's wife. Ted and I had socialized mainly with other members of the Baltimore Symphony and their spouses.

The gossip in that crowd had been about who was wearing last year's fashions and whose husband was sleeping with whose wife. I'd tried to hold myself above all that, until my own husband turned out to be one of the philanderers.

Am I just more engaged now in real life? My chest warmed some. *That's a good thing, right?*

I had no answers by the time I turned onto Becky's street. And I found myself driving past her house.

I called her. "Uh, I'm not feeling too good. I may be coming down with something." I faked a cough. "I don't want to make you or the babies sick, so I'm gonna go back to the B&B and crash."

Becky made appropriate sympathetic noises, ending with, "Call me in the morning. Or before then, if you need anything. Anything at all."

She sounded so concerned.

Great, I could now add guilt over lying to my best friend to my generalized angst.

~

My room at the B&B was dripping with pink chintz. I flopped on the high antique bed, fully clothed, and groaned when I realized I'd have to go out to get some dinner.

The last thing in the world I wanted to do was get in my car again this evening.

I checked in with my stomach. It was one big knot. I rolled over on my side and hugged one of the down pillows against me.

A cold nose, followed by a deep woof, woke me.

For a heart-pounding moment, I was totally disoriented in a pitch black space—when just a second ago, a dark-haired man in a pale green polo shirt had been chasing me through the woods behind the flea market.

Slowly, my brain registered that I was in the B&B in Williston, the man chasing me had been a dream, and the sun had set while I'd been napping.

I sat up and fumbled for the switch on the bedside lamp. When the light came on, my first sight was of Buddy's face and paws on the edge of the mattress. His eyes looked worried.

Fred was beside him, paws also on the bed, a matching expression on his face. I must have been moaning or thrashing some in my sleep. Both dogs had reacted, as they'd been trained to do, by waking me up.

"It's okay, guys. Thanks." I patted their heads.

My stomach rumbled, but I had even less desire to go out now that it was dark.

I dug through my purse and found a packet of crackers, filched from some restaurant. They were more crumbs than actual crackers at this point. I dumped the packet into my mouth. The cracker remnants were stale.

I got up and went in the bathroom to perform my evening toilette.

Teeth brushed, face washed, jammies on, I crawled under the covers with my ereader. But I couldn't focus on the story I was trying to read.

Why had I been dreaming about Sheriff Burns's other murder case? I yanked my mind away from that question and back to the cozy mystery on my screen.

Finally, my eyelids grew heavy and I turned out the lamp.

I woke up gasping. It must have been hours later, because a faint light showed through the chintz curtains over the room's sole window.

My unconscious mind had put the pieces together as I'd slept.

The sheriff's two cases *were* related. The man in the pale green shirt was the one I'd seen hanging around the flea market, and he was probably the man Buddy had chased away from Derek's stall.

CHAPTER SEVENTEEN

I sat on the side of the bed and grabbed my phone off the nightstand. Sanity prevailed when I glanced at the old-fashioned clock on said nightstand. It was only five-forty in the morning.

I showered and got dressed, went downstairs and grabbed a bagel from the breakfast buffet, which opened at six. Finally, I couldn't make myself wait any longer. At six-thirty, I called the sheriff's cell phone.

Three rings, then, "This better be good." His voice was groggy.

"Sir, I am so sorry to disturb you this early, but I have some more information."

"Harumph."

I opted to interpret that as "Go ahead, Marcia. Tell me what you found out."

I explained the connection between the flea market and the dead man in the hotel room.

"Wait," the sheriff said. "What man hanging around Sergeant Bradshaw's stall?"

"Um, I told Detective Young about him later. When I first saw the guy, I assumed he was also a detective, but I'm pretty sure he was the one who searched Derek's stall, before Buddy chased him away."

A beat of silence. "Oh yeah. I remember now seeing something about that in Young's report."

"I noticed the guy," I continued, "because he seemed out of place, and instead of strolling along, he hung out in front of the stall next door, acting like he was really interested in the vendor's camping gear. I remember thinking at the time that he didn't look like he'd ever camped a day in his life."

"Can you describe him?"

"Big guy, not all that tall, maybe five-ten or eleven, but beefy. He wore dark slacks and a pale green knit polo shirt. The clothes were what first caught my eye. The shirt looked like it had been ironed. Who irons polo shirts? And the slacks were dress ones, like from a suit." I paused, closed my eyes. "Dark hair, well groomed. I didn't get close enough to see his facial features that well, but his face was broad, kind of jowly. I'd say he was in his fifties."

Another pause, this one stretching out a bit.

"You still there, Sheriff?"

"Yes, I'm here. That certainly could be the hotel vic."

"Uh, have you been able to identify him? Were his fingerprints in the system?"

Again, a brief pause. "Don't know. Couldn't get good prints off of him."

"Why not?"

The sound of air being blown out slowly. The sheriff was running out of patience. "His fingertips were surgically altered to disguise his prints. We'll have to go by DNA instead, but no matches yet."

A day ago, before I'd realized Zeke intentionally messed up his fingerprints on that sword blade, I wouldn't have understood what all that meant. And I was a little surprised the sheriff had told me so much. Maybe he figured he should stay on my good side, since I had given him some good info so far.

"Ma'am, would you be willing to look at the corpse, see if you can definitely identify him as the man you saw that day at the flea market?"

Hmm, that's why he's still answering your questions, Ms. Snark commented. *He wants something from you.*

My stomach roiled, threatening to give back my breakfast bagel.

"Uh, it might be more helpful if I saw his clothes. You said his face… it's um, gone, correct?"

"Yes. We can have you look at some of the photos first. See what you can tell us from those."

"That would be better, I think. Do you want me come to your office now?"

"Make it in an hour. *After* I've had my coffee."

"Okay."

On the way to the sheriff's department, I called Derek to tell him I might be late getting to his house to train.

"Can't say that I'm really up for trainin' today," he said in a glum voice. "I'm going to Nell's arraignment in a while."

"Uh…" I realized I'd been saying that a lot this morning. "Okay, well, I'll touch base later."

"Okay." Derek disconnected without saying goodbye.

~

The sheriff slid a couple of pictures, printed out on plain white paper, across the conference room table to me. He'd digitally doctored the crime scene photos, cropping off the victim's head.

Trying valiantly to ignore the dark red stains on the green shirt, I examined the photos. "I couldn't swear to it in court, but yes, that's him. That's the guy who was hanging around Derek's stall, and who Buddy later chased away."

"But you don't know that last part yourself," the sheriff said.

"No, when the other vendor brought Buddy to me and told me my dog had been chasing a guy in a green shirt, I assumed it was the guy I'd seen earlier."

Ms. Snark slipped past my guard. "Mr. Green Shirt," she said, in a sugary, just-trying-to-be-helpful voice. Then she snickered inside my head, as my cheeks heated up.

The sheriff tapped the point of his pen on the pad in front of him. "What's this vendor's name?"

"I never got his name." I closed my eyes, recalling the layout of the flea market. "But I think he's in the other building."

He jotted a note on his pad. "Do you think that looking at any of the other crime scene photos would help solidify your identification?"

I shook my head vehemently, the nauseous reaction in my stomach canceling out my usual curiosity-killed-the-cat nosiness.

The sheriff shrugged. "That's okay. Right now I'm more concerned with figuring out who he is and how he's connected to the case, than worrying about what we can prove in court."

My *feline-fatale* curiosity reasserted itself. "You still don't have any idea regarding his identity? Did he have a car?"

Duh, of course he'd had a car. There was no public transportation in this rural part of Florida.

"A rental," the sheriff said. "The driver's license he showed to rent it had to have been forged. Same fake name that he gave the motel clerk."

"I assume the rental car place didn't make a photocopy of his license."

The sheriff shook his head. "I'd give next month's salary for a picture of this guy, before he got his face blown off. Then we could ask around if people saw him, get a better feel for what he was up to."

"Wait!" I dug out my phone and located the photos I'd taken of Derek and Fred, in front of his stall.

Sure enough, the guy in the green shirt was at the edge of two of them. The first one I'd snapped had apparently caught him by surprise. Only about two-thirds of his face was showing, but his eyes were wide, his mouth hanging slightly open. In the next shot, he had turned away, the back of his dark head at the edge of the photo, some random piece of camping gear in his hand.

I handed the phone over to the sheriff. "I didn't actually notice him until a few minutes later, when he neither bought any of the camping gear nor moved on."

"May I send these to myself?"

"Of course."

His big fingers moved over my phone screen far faster than I would have thought possible in a guy his age. My mom was a hunt-and-peck texter, and most of her friends didn't text at all.

My phone pinged in the sheriff's hands. He stared at it, chuckled, and then handed it to me.

Speak of the devil, Ms. Snark commented internally.

Mom had texted, *You still alive down there?*

I let out a self-conscious laugh. "That's my mom's way of saying I haven't called her recently."

"My mother texts me if she hasn't heard from me for two days." The sheriff flashed a quick grin. "You'd better answer her, or she'll be on the next plane."

"Your mother texts?" I blurted out.

"Yep, she's eighty-four, and she thinks cell phones are the neatest thing since sliced bread."

I grinned back at him, then pressed my advantage while he was in a good mood. "Would you let me know when you find out who this guy is? It's kind of nerve-wracking not knowing *why* he was hanging around and searching my client's stall." As well as my car and Becky's house.

The sheriff's face sobered. "I thought you were assuming he was looking for the vial of dried blood."

You were assuming, not *we* or *I*. Did the sheriff know something he wasn't telling me?

Ms. Snark snorted. *There's probably lots he knows that he's not telling you.*

"Well, yeah," I said out loud. "I guess that's what he was looking for, but how did he know it was there. Derek said he hadn't told anyone he had it, and he hadn't even told Zeke where he'd hid it."

The sheriff sat back and ran a hand through his gray-sandy hair. "How likely is it that Zeke Lord told anyone else about that vial?"

I gave that a moment's thought. "Pretty unlikely, I'd say, considering how many other secrets he kept close to his chest."

The sheriff nodded very slowly, his eyes slightly out of focus. He was putting some pieces together.

"What are you thinking?" I asked.

"I'm thinking that if this green-shirt dude knew about that vial, Zeke must've been the one to tell him."

"But I thought that *you* thought that the blood in the vial wasn't related to this case?"

The sheriff's face closed down.

Before he could invoke the "I can't comment on an ongoing investigation" line, I changed tacks. "Have you found out anything about the possibility that Zeke may be a fence?"

"My detective will be asking some discreet questions, when the flea market opens on Thursday."

I recalled the change in schedule. "It opens on Wednesday this week, because of Thanksgiving."

"Oh, right. I'd forgotten all about the holiday."

"Um, will Derek and Nell eventually be able to get Zeke's merchandise back? There were some expensive items among his stuff."

Sheriff Burns gave me a confused look. "What are you talking about?"

"The stuff from Zeke's stall at the market. We assumed you all had confiscated it."

He shook his head. "We searched the stall, but we only took a few things, like the provenance for the sword."

"Well, then who took the rest of his stuff? It was gone the next day."

The sheriff scratched his cheek with a beefy finger. "A very good question."

~

Once outside the sheriff's department, I texted my mother back. *I'm fine. I'll call you soon.*

Then I pondered the last part of my conversation with Sheriff Burns, as I drove to Derek's house. I'd opted not to call ahead. If he wasn't home yet, I'd wait. But I didn't want to give him the chance to back out of training today.

Why was the good sheriff thinking that Zeke had told Mr. Green Shirt about the vial? And who had taken all of Zeke's merchandise from his stall? And *why*?

I had no answers by the time I pulled up in front of Derek's house. His white SUV was in the driveway.

Derek was as shocked as I'd been when I told him the sheriff's department had not taken Zeke's things from his stall. Sitting at his kitchen table, he'd been about to take a sip of his iced tea. He put the glass back down with a loud thud. "Then who did?"

"Good question," I said. "Could Nell have taken it?"

"I doubt it, but let's ask her." He pulled out his cell phone.

"Wait. She's out of jail? Did they release her on her own recognizance?"

"No." His cheeks pinked a little. "I posted her bail. I put up the house as collateral, through a bail bondsman."

I realized my mouth was hanging open.

"She's my sister," he answered the unasked question. "I've gotta look out for her."

I clamped my mouth shut, then opened it again to say, "If she runs, she might not be better off than in jail."

Not to mention he would lose his house. I shuddered to think about Nell on the streets, homeless.

"She won't run. She promised me." He gave me a determined look, his mouth set in a grim line. "And I promised *her* that I'd find out who really killed Zeke."

I digested that while Derek placed the call. He apparently got her voicemail. "Hey Nell, call me as soon as you can." He disconnected. "She was going to her lawyer's office. Guess she has her phone off while she's meetin' with him."

I pointed out that we really needed to do some training.

He let out a long sigh. "Might as well. Hopefully, it'll get my mind off all of this."

Derek tried and we did accomplish some training, but his head wasn't in the game. Although I understood, I was getting a bit frustrated with having to repeat myself.

I had his full attention, though, when we took our next break, and I brought up the subject of his anger. "You need to realize that this animal will be totally dependent on you." I was trying for the right tone of voice, firm but not scolding schoolmarm. "If you drive your truck crazy, for example, when you're mad, you'll be throwing him all over the backseat. There's only so much that safety strap can do. He could be hurt or, at the very least, scared out of his wits."

Derek nodded, his expression serious. "I get it. I promise I will not let the anger take over like that again."

I hid a small smile. Ironically, one of the ways that service dogs helped with the anger in PTSD sufferers was by putting them in this very position, where they couldn't indulge in out-of-control rage, because of their responsibility to the dog.

We practiced the dog responding to his anger again, and that went well, I thought.

Afterwards, he confessed that he wasn't as mad at Zeke as he had been—which struck me as a good thing.

"And I was kind of distracted," he admitted, ducking his head, "worryin' about Nell."

"That's okay," I said. "The dog responds the same way to anxiety or anger, to help you calm down. The physiological reactions are pretty much the same—increased heart rate, muscles all tensed up, and such. And it's not unusual for us to feel both of those feelings at the same time. We humans are complicated when it comes to emotions."

Derek gave me a lopsided smile. "Ain't that the truth."

We went out to his backyard to resume training. But half an hour later, he was totally distracted again, and I was back to repeating myself.

"Sorry," he said for the umpteenth time. "I just keep goin' over in my head about all of Zeke's stuff disappearin'. And this havin' to wait for the flea market to open tomorrow, before I can even ask questions, it's makin' me nuts."

It was making me a bit nuts too.

Derek shook his head. "I can't imagine how anyone could've taken everything like that. Swipe a few of his more valuable pieces, yeah, I can see that. But clean out the whole stall. That was a major operation."

"If Nell didn't take it herself, maybe she heard something that night?"

He shook his head again. "She wasn't there. She said she got spooked being by herself at the flea market—with a killer maybe still hangin' around. So she went to a motel for the night. If she'd said something to me at the time, I would've invited her to stay here."

Uh huh, Nell might be a little slow, but she was still a woman. She knew that would have been a very bad idea, especially since Derek hadn't known at that point that she was his half-sister. But she had known.

"Hey, do you mind if we call it a day?" Derek sank into his wheelchair. "I'm kinda tired, and I need to work on some toys this evening." He laid his walking sticks across his lap. "See ya next week?"

"Actually…" I'd been debating all day whether to go home this afternoon as planned or stay through tomorrow.

Yesterday, I couldn't wait to get home. I was worried about Will's mental state.

But this morning, he'd texted to say he was on another new case. I'd be going home to a mostly empty house, since a man slipping into your bed at two a.m. and leaving it again at six didn't really qualify as much company.

"I think I'm going to stay over," I said, "and help you ask around at the flea market tomorrow. But we need to be careful that we don't run afoul of the sheriff's people. They'll be there too."

"Why?"

Crapola. I didn't want to admit to Derek that I'd passed on the Zeke-may-have-been-a-fence lead to the sheriff.

I shrugged, implying that I didn't know. Did a gesture count as a lie? I crossed my fingers behind my back. "He said his detectives would be asking more questions this week."

Derek nodded and gave Fred the release signal in a way that said it was becoming second-nature.

I smiled. Despite all the interruptions and distractions, the training was coming along nicely.

"I think I'm going to leave Fred with you tonight." I was satisfied that Derek had sufficient control over his anger to keep the dog safe.

He enthusiastically rubbed Fred's head. "You hear that, boy?"

"Hey," I said, "tomorrow let's pretend that we're training at the flea market, that we're taking Fred around to make sure he doesn't get distracted by all the hubbub." We already knew that the dog did fine in the noisy setting, but the flea market vendors didn't know that. It would make a good cover story.

"See you at the flea market in the morning, bright and early." Derek flashed me a mischievous grin. In our short acquaintance, he'd already figured out that I was *not* a morning person.

I groaned theatrically.

~

I was bleary-eyed the next morning, as I drove myself and Buddy to the flea market.

My phone rang. *Will* showed on the dashboard screen.

I'd emailed him last night, filling him in on Mr. Green-Shirt's demise and telling him I was staying for another day of training and to call when he could.

I ignored the lump of guilt in my stomach and answered the call. "Hey there, how's the case going?"

"I'd rather not talk about it."

Not going well at all then.

"If you're training again today," Will said, in a tired voice, "does that mean you'll be at the flea market?"

"Um, yes, but since Mr. Green Shirt got killed, I think it's safe enough. We're pretty sure he was the one who was searching everywhere for something, most likely the little vial Derek had, but that's with the sheriff now." I realized I was babbling and clamped my mouth shut.

The sound of air being blown out in a sigh. "Just be careful, okay?"

"Yes, of course," I said quickly. "I am, I will be. You sound…" I stopped myself before saying *depressed.* Will wouldn't admit to that. "…discouraged."

"That's because I am. See you at home eventually?"

"Of course. I'll be home this evening. Are you going to be able to take tomorrow off?"

More air being blown out. "Probably, at the rate things are going."

"You be careful too. Love you."

"Always. Love you too." Will disconnected.

I chewed on my lower lip, back to worrying about his mental state. Being a law enforcement officer was stressful enough when things went well. Add in guilt for having to shoot someone and leaving them paralyzed, plus two cases in a row that didn't go well. I shuddered.

Pressure from my own guilt filled my chest. I hadn't exactly lied to Will. Then again, I hadn't told him the whole truth either.

But I wasn't investigating the murder—murders, actually. Derek and I were only going to ask around about Zeke's stuff.

Yeah, Ms. Snark scoffed internally. *As if you don't know that the two things are likely related.*

"I don't know that," I answered out loud.

Buddy, lying on the backseat, raised his head from his paws and cocked it to one side.

I shook my head and pulled into a shopping center that had a Starbucks' drive-thru. I needed caffeine.

CHAPTER EIGHTEEN

Derek already had his stall open. He greeted me in front of it, on his cart. "Nell will text me if any serious customers come around, but there isn't usually much action this early on weekdays."

"What'd she say about Zeke's stuff going missing?"

"She's as clueless as we are about it."

I nodded, distracted by the end of Fred's leash looped loosely over the cart's handlebars.

I was somewhat concerned about the leash getting tangled in the wheels when the cart was moving. Hmm, having Fred practice heeling beside the cart without the leash might be a good thing to be doing today.

You're just rationalizing. My inner mom this time.

I ignored her and relayed my concerns to Derek and the possible solution.

He shook his head. "It's not crowded this early, but these aisles can get pretty packed at times. It'd be too easy for Fred and me to get separated if he's not on a leash." He ran a hand over his buzz cut. "I've got another idea. Come here, boy." He patted his thigh.

Fred cocked his head, then took two steps and scrambled up to drape himself across the man's legs. He was a lot of dog, but Derek had a big lap.

I smiled. This was part of the training of the veteran—discovering what worked best for the vet's particular circumstances and needs.

"But what about your numb leg. It might have the blood cut off from his weight and you won't know it."

"Good point." He shifted Fred some, so most of the dog's weight was on his other leg. "I won't leave him up here too long either. Only to get to where I'm goin'."

"Let's give it a try. You can have him get down whenever we stop."

Derek nodded and we set out, headed for the vendors nearest Zeke's stall first.

We tried to sound casual, pretending we were just stopping to chat as we got Fred used to the flea market. Then, with each vendor, we would bring up our curiosity about how Zeke's stock had disappeared. Derek was also keeping his eyes open for anything among the vendor's merchandise that looked like it had come from Zeke's stall.

We'd chatted up three vendors, the dogs sitting patiently beside us, before we hit pay dirt. Although it wasn't the kind of dirt we'd been expecting to find.

Denny, the Vietnam veteran, had been busy with a customer when we'd made our first pass. Now he was free and we stopped to say hi, ostensibly. He also denied any knowledge of what had happened to Zeke's stuff.

On impulse, I pointed to his baseball cap. "Did you know that Zeke wasn't in 'Nam?"

Denny's pleasant expression morphed into a disgusted scowl. "Yeah, I knew. The valor-stealin' s.o.–" He caught himself, then touched the bill of his cap. "Sorry, ma'am."

"You knew he wasn't in the military?" Derek asked in a low voice.

Denny nodded and spat on the concrete of the building's wide aisle.

"How did you find out?" I asked.

Denny took off his hat and pointed to the multicolored bar running horizontally between the words *Vietnam* and *Veteran*. "I asked him one time if he'd gotten any of these. The different colors represent the medals given to the troops that were in certain operations in 'Nam." He spat on the floor again, a little less vehemently. "He tried to cover it up, but it was obvious he didn't know what I was talkin' about."

"What did you call it a minute ago?" I asked.

"Valor-stealin'. It's what we call it when somebody pretends they was in the military when they wasn't." He puckered up as if to spit again.

"But you went to his prayer services," I said quickly. All the spitting was actually getting to my sensibilities more than his almost cussing had.

"That was the wife's doin'. She didn't like it that we couldn't go to church 'cause of the flea market openin' so early on Sundays."

"How long ago," Derek asked, his voice casual, "did you find out about Zeke's valor-stealin'? 'Cause I didn't know until recently."

Denny shrugged. "Not that long ago." He rubbed his chin. "Couple a weeks, I guess. Kinda felt guilty some for bein' angry with him, after he got himself kilt."

We chatted with him for another minute, then wandered on down through the building. Once out of earshot, Derek muttered, "Yet another person who might've been mad enough to kill Zeke."

"For yet another reason," I said in a low voice.

~

The crowd was growing, so we headed back to check on Derek's stall.

My inner voices were arguing over the fact that Derek seemed to be a pretty darn good actor. If I hadn't known better, I would've thought he truly was merely making idle chit-chat with the vendors.

As we entered the end of his building, his phone pinged. He slowed the cart and reached across Fred's back to pluck the phone out of the front basket. "Nell says there's a guy hangin' around my stall."

He sped up a little. Buddy and I broke into a slow jog to keep up.

Buddy growled, a deep rumble, and ran faster.

I followed his line of vision and saw a man just inside Derek's stall—dark-haired, slightly overweight, in a blue shirt and black slacks. His head was turned away, and he held one of Derek's painted walking sticks in one hand and a piece of cloth in the other.

I was about to signal Buddy that it was okay—it was only a customer—when the guy glanced our way.

He froze for half a beat, then took off, still holding the cloth and walking stick.

"Buddy, protect. Grab arm." I let go of his leash.

Buddy sprinted off, barking. I ran after.

The man ducked into the cross-aisle between the buildings, Buddy hard on his heels.

When I got to the cross-aisle, neither dog nor man were in sight. I ran full-tilt to the next building, stopped and looked both ways.

A moment of déjà vu, as the same vendor as before brought Buddy toward me. "He was chasin' that guy again."

"What guy?" I said, between huffing and puffing to catch my breath.

"That guy in the fancy clothes. He sure can run fast for a hefty guy."

It dawned on me that Mr. Green Shirt's death might not be general knowledge. "The one with the green polo shirt?"

"Yup, only this time his shirt was blue. Did he steal somethin'?"

"I don't know." I asked his name to give to the sheriff, then thanked him for stopping Buddy, even though I wished he hadn't. If the dog had caught the guy, we might have found out why strangers kept searching Derek's stall.

The vendor tipped his baseball cap and wandered off.

Derek pulled up beside me in his cart. "What happened? Who was that guy Buddy was chasin'?"

"A dead man," I said. "Come on."

CHAPTER NINETEEN

We found the walking stick halfway back to his stall. I hadn't even realized the guy had dropped it.

Derek was the only one who could definitively say if something was missing from his stall. But I needed to do something—I was so antsy, I felt like I was jumping out of my skin—so I offered to help search.

Telling Buddy to stay out in the stall, I went behind the curtain. The steamer trunk was closed, but there was no padlock on it.

"Derek," I called out. "Did you put a new lock on the trunk?"

"Sure did." He nosed the front of his cart through the opening in the curtain.

I pointed to the trunk. "Well, it's gone now."

Pulling the ends of my tee shirt's long sleeves down over my hands, I opened the trunk. "Your cashbox is here." I fumbled a bit, with my fingers covered by sleeve, but got the cashbox's latch to release. "There's money in it. Doesn't look like much."

"It wouldn't be. I start the day with only a few ones and coins to make change."

I lifted the cashbox out and visually searched the rest of the contents of the trunk. It was mostly tools. "Hey wait. Where are the fatigues?"

Derek nudged his cart forward some. "Zeke's fatigues? I'd forgotten they were in there."

He's got a very convenient memory, Ms. Snark pointed out.

"You didn't think of them when you remembered the little vial?" My voice held more skepticism than I'd meant to let slip out.

He shook his head slightly. "Zeke gave them to me at the same time, but he was much more focused on the vial. Said to hide it good, and not in the same place as the fatigues."

"Why?"

"I asked him the same question. He refused to say, just asked me to do it as a favor. I could hardly say no, after all he'd done for me. I assumed they had some sentimental value, although I didn't understand why he hadn't washed them after the last time he wore them. And he specifically told me *not* to wash them."

Derek leaned forward, trying to peer into the trunk. "Is his tee shirt gone too?"

"You had a tee shirt of his?"

"Yeah. It was covered with paint stains. Again, no clue why he wanted me to keep it for him."

I shook my head, looking down at the open trunk. "I don't see a tee shirt, and that makes even less sense than the fatigues. The deputy who searched the trunk must've assumed the clothes were yours." I recalled it had been Deputy Harrison, not the most competent LEO I'd ever met. But still… "Why didn't he confiscated them?"

Buddy barked as a voice from behind us said, "Yes, that was pretty careless of him."

I jumped and jerked around, almost tripping over Derek's cart, which he was trying to turn around in the tight space.

Detective Rick Young stood just outside the opening of the curtain. "I've been talking to folks. Hear you've been doing the same."

Doesn't this guy ever knock? Ms. Snark said internally.

"Uh." I rubbed my hands on my jeans-clad thighs. "We were wondering what happened to Zeke's stuff, um, from his stall. We thought maybe someone had taken it for safekeeping."

"Uh-huh, so then you wouldn't be interfering with the investigation of a crime, if you didn't believe the stuff was stolen, right?"

I nodded feebly. It was pretty lame.

But the detective changed tacks. "I heard somebody was poking around your stall again, Sergeant. Anything missing?"

Derek tilted his head toward the trunk. "A set of fatigues that Zeke Lord asked me to hold for him. I'd forgotten they were even in there."

I pointed to the walking stick that I'd put down on a shelf. "He had that in his hand but he dropped it."

The detective pulled on a latex glove and picked up the stick. "Anything else missing?"

"Oh, yeah," Derek said. "An old tee shirt. It was also Zeke's."

The detective's expression was inscrutable, a little too inscrutable.

"You all have the tee shirt, don't you?" I was guessing.

Young looked like he was debating with himself for a moment. Finally, he said, "Yes. I'll call this in. In the meantime, lock your gate. You're closed until a crime scene crew can go over your stall."

He turned away, then glanced back over his shoulder. "And you can stop asking about Lord's missing merchandise. It's been found."

"Where?" we blurted out in unison. "And when?" I added.

The detective seemed to hesitate for a moment, maybe weighing if it would matter to the case if we knew the answer. "This morning, about five blocks from here, in a vacant field. Some kids found a large charred area, with a big blob of metal in the middle, some blades sticking out of it. Somebody'd built a bonfire. Everything that wasn't steel melted."

Derek groaned softly. "There were some antique pieces in there."

"I'm sure there *were*." The detective came down hard on the *were,* and his tone wasn't the least bit sympathetic.

~

We took the dogs back to Derek's house while the sheriff's department processed his stall as a crime scene. But neither of us had the motivation to do any training.

We settled at his kitchen table, dogs at our feet, glasses of iced tea at our elbows. In other parts of the country, someone might offer coffee, but in Florida it was almost always iced tea mentioned first when offering refreshments to guests. And that offer was almost always accepted—summer, spring, fall and what passes for winter down here.

Derek had brought a blank legal pad and pen to the table. "I need to figure this out, clear Nell's name." He began to write furiously.

I added a teaspoon of sugar to my unsweetened tea. Derek's had come from a separate pitcher and no doubt would cause a sugar high if I drank some of it. But being from Florida, he was used to it. I appreciated that he'd made the effort to make two separate batches of tea.

Derek scribbled for a good fifteen minutes, during which my antsy feeling from earlier returned.

Finally, he sat back and stared at the two sheets of paper he had covered with writing. After a moment, he flung them on the table. "I can't make any sense out of this."

I picked up the pages and read through his list of things we knew or speculated.

Then I slid the pad over in front of me and turned it sideways, landscape-style. I made four columns and labeled the first one *Zeke*. The third one I titled *Green Shirt* and the column in between *Intersection*. The last column was *Questions*.

I plugged Derek's items into the appropriate columns, putting them in chronological order and adding a few.

Surprisingly, most things had some intersection noted. Among the few that didn't were Zeke's murder itself, Green Shirt being found in a motel room without his face, and Zeke's stuff being taken and melted in a bonfire in some field.

Although come to think of it, possibly Green Shirt had done that before he was killed. I added that thought to the intersection column with a question mark next to it.

I laid the chart down between us, and we both leaned forward to scan over it.

My eyes stopped on the question *Who took it?* next to *Sword/cane stolen from Derek's trunk*. "Are we absolutely sure that Nell didn't take the sword initially, the day before Zeke was killed?"

"She says she didn't."

"Do you believe her?" I asked gently. She denied taking it to me as well, and I'd believed her at the time, but now…

Derek shrugged. "I want to, but I'm probably not the best judge of that, at this point. I'm still gettin' used to the idea that she stole all that little stuff from people's stalls, when it was only her and Zeke there at night."

Hmmmm... my inner voices said in unison.

Still keeping my tone gentle, I said, "I kinda got the impression that you suspected her, before all this hit the fan."

He shrugged again. "Maybe, on some level. Yeah, I guess I did. What with the locked room in her trailer and her vague references to her 'collections.'" He made air quotes. "Even the other day when I went to ask her about them, she ducked the question and then started talkin' about Zeke bein' my dad."

I tapped the chart. "Why do you think Zeke gave the sword to you?"

"I don't know, but looking back, he wasn't happy that I wasn't really trying to sell it."

"So he wanted it gone, but not the fatigues and vial. Why?"

Derek put a hand up, rubbed his forehead. "No clue."

But I had a theory. "I think Zeke was blackmailing someone."

He jerked his head up, eyes a bit wide. "What makes you think that?"

I tapped the chart again. "What if all three of these items were related to that blackmail, evidence of something? Why would Zeke want to hide two of them and get rid of the third?"

Derek sat up straighter. "I just thought of somethin'. Zeke asked me about five months ago how attached I was to that dragonhead cane. I told him, very. That I was thinkin' about takin' it out of my stall completely and usin' it myself. He turned white as a ghost, and then he convinced me that was a bad idea, that the cane might get damaged, or I might get mugged by somebody wantin' to steal it."

He sighed. "That last argument won me over. I didn't particularly want to get beat up over a fancy cane."

"When did he give you the fatigues and vial for safekeeping?"

"Lemme think." He rubbed his forehead again.

I was really starting to suspect he had memory deficits, maybe from the IED blast, but now was not the time to bring that up.

"About a week after that," Derek finally said.

I sat quietly for a moment, trying to put the pieces together. Most wouldn't fit. "Again, why try to get rid of the sword but keep the other two things?"

Derek slapped the edge of the table, startling me a little. "Because the sword was too conspicuous and too hard to hide."

A couple more pieces slid into place. "So he gave it to you. If you were the one to sell it, that would make it harder for it to be traced back to him. But why didn't he give you the fake provenance?"

"Fake?" Derek said.

"Yes. The sheriff had it checked out. It's a forgery. Maybe Zeke had planned to sell it himself at first so he developed the fake provenance, then realized that would leave a paper trail. But he didn't count on you becoming sentimentally attached to it."

"Why didn't he just destroy it?"

"Hmm." My mind flashed on the detective's comment earlier, that steel blades were sticking out of the metal blob in the field. I used my phone to ask Siri at what temperature steel melts. She answered, "Steel melts at around 1370 degrees Centigrade or 2500 degrees Farenheit."

"Would a sword that old be made of steel?" Derek said.

I was scrolling through the article Siri had brought up. I clicked on an embedded link attached to the word *steel*. It took me to another article, about the history of the metal. "It seems steel was first invented, eons ago, by the Chinese and the Indians, as in from India."

"Huh," Derek said. "Learn somethin' new every day."

I smiled. He'd used another motherism.

"Hey," I said, "what did Nell tell you about the night Zeke died?"

"Not much. She said it was too upsetting to talk about. The short version was she heard a noise, went to investigate, heard a scream, ran back there and found him."

I sat up straighter. "First I've heard of noises and a scream. Her lawyer didn't mention that. I think we need to hear her long version. She may have seen or heard something that will tie all this together." I hesitated for a moment, guilt once again raising its ugly head. I had promised Will to leave this alone.

But what could it hurt to talk to Nell. The woman couldn't weigh more than a hundred pounds. And Derek would be there.

He was looking at his watch. "It's noon now. It'd probably be better to wait until the market closes at three, so we have her undivided attention."

"And so no one will overhear us," I added. "We could do some training in the meantime."

That would ease my conscience some. I wasn't here today mainly to investigate; I was here to train.

Yeah, right, Ms. Snark commented.

CHAPTER TWENTY

The cold front had been short-lived and today was sunny, already in the mid-seventies. I shoved my tee-shirt's long sleeves to my elbows as we drove in Derek's SUV to downtown Williston. The goal was to get Derek and Fred used to being out in public together, some place other than the flea market.

Plus, I needed to find Will an anniversary present. But Williston offered few quaint shops in which to find unique gifts.

When I expressed my disappointment about that, Derek said, "We've got quaint restaurants, like The Ivy House." He pointed across the street to a large white, cracker-style house, with a wide brick walkway, leading up to a welcoming, old-fashioned front porch. "Best fried chicken anywhere. But for today…" He flashed a grin at me, as he made a U-turn. "You like barbeque?"

"Yeah, sure."

He swung the SUV into a parking lot on the left. The sign above the building's red metal roof sported a caricature of a pig and the word *BubbaQue's®*.

I laughed out loud. "You're kidding."

"Nope. I never kid about barbeque."

We got out and released the dogs from their safety straps in the backseat. Fred jumped to the pavement, his leash dangling, as Derek moved to the back of the truck to get his wheelchair.

"Considering how he ran off the other day," I said, "you should specifically tell him to sit and stay until you can pick up his leash." Fred had been off duty when he'd followed his nose. I doubted he would wander off when on duty, but to be on the safe side.

Derek had settled into his chair.

"Fred, get leash," I said.

The dog picked up the end of his own leash in his teeth and extended it toward Derek.

He took it and chuckled. "You really do think of everything."

Inside, the staff seemed to know Derek. A cute, young waitress showed us to a table.

She reached toward Fred. "Is this your new dog?"

I opened my mouth, but Derek was ahead of me.

He held up a hand. "Sorry, you can't pet him now. He's workin'." He leaned toward the girl and winked. "This lady here, she's the dog's trainer, and she'll yell at me if I don't get this right."

I gave him a mock frown. "Since when have I yelled at you?"

He grinned and slapped a hand on the menus the girl had dropped on the table. "Two pulled pork sandwiches with fries and baked beans."

I grimaced as I imagined the calories gluing themselves to my already ample hips.

"Or," Derek swept an arm toward one end of the room, "they've got a great salad bar."

"I'll take that, with my pork sandwich."

"Comin' up." The girl bounced off.

I looked around. The walls were bare brick or light wood paneling and were covered with memorabilia—pictures of wilderness scenes, old tools, posters, a black metal silhouette of a pig, and a mounted buck's head.

"You've never been to a BubbaQue's?" Derek asked.

I shook my head. "Is it a chain?"

"Yup, there's a whole mess of them, all around this part of the state."

"Hunh. I've never heard of them before."

"Obviously, you haven't been hangin' out in the right parts of the state." Derek's grin was huge.

I smiled back, delighted that his normal cheerful mood was resurfacing.

I went to the salad bar. By the time I returned with a loaded plate, our sandwiches had arrived.

The barbequed pork *was* delicious.

Derek insisted on picking up the check. I let him. I wasn't about to do anything to dim his good mood.

Out on the ramp to the parking lot, I scanned Noble Avenue, one of the major streets of the town. On the other side and down a few blocks was a low brown building with yet another red metal roof. Some local roofer must've had a special going at some point on red metal.

The driftwood sign above the building's door read *Dixie's Antiques*. I pointed. "Let's go over there."

"Dixie's? Sure." Derek turned his chair in that direction.

I hung back some, observing, as we headed down the sidewalk toward the crosswalk at Main Street. Fred was now used to staying on Derek's right, but that put him on the side nearest the traffic. That made me a bit anxious, until I noticed that Derek had taken in his leash some.

I smiled to myself, and *at* myself. Becky was right. I really was a mama bear, so protective of my charges. But I could stop worrying about Fred's well-being. He was as safe with Derek as he would be in my care.

Dixie's was divided up into booths, crammed full of antiques and collectibles. Not all of them were manned, but when we came to one that was all about clocks, a fiftyish woman greeted Derek by name. He introduced us.

Hmm! Hadn't I read somewhere that clocks were the more modern gift for first anniversaries? And Will had insisted on a fireplace in the central room of our new house, even though it was rarely cold enough to merit a fire.

Gwen, the saleswoman said, "Can I help you find something?"

"A first anniversary gift, for my husband. I'm thinking maybe a mantel clock."

"I have just the thing." She turned and headed for the other end of her double-sized booth. We followed, the dogs trailing along.

"What does he do for a living?" she asked over her shoulder.

That struck me as an odd question. "He's in law enforcement," I answered hesitantly.

Then it registered that we were now standing in front of a shelf of wooden clocks of various sizes, many of them adorned with symbols of different professions. One had a clock face shaped like a chef's hat.

One of the tallest of the mantel clocks had a brass police badge at the top. "It also comes with a sheriff's department star or a detective's shield," Gwen said.

"Detective's shield," was out of my mouth before I'd spotted the title of the poem engraved on a brass plate below the clock face—*A Hero Is….*

I grimaced. Will would hate being called a hero, especially right now.

Gwen quickly said, "You can get something else engraved on it."

"I know what would be perfect." Excitement bubbling in my chest, I dug out my phone, grateful now for my tendency to procrastinate about taking photos off of it.

Will had been given a merit award a few months ago, for cracking a particularly tough case. I found the snapshot I'd taken of the commendation plaque. "Can you engrave this on it?"

"Sure. I can have it for you by the middle of next week."

The bubbles burst. My throat closed. "Our anniversary is Sunday."

"Hmm, the engraver has a rush service. It might be tricky, with tomorrow being Thanksgiving, but I think I can get it for you by Saturday afternoon."

It meant an extra trip over to Williston, but… I had to resist the urge to jump up and down and squeal. It was the perfect gift!

Derek was beaming at me.

I gulped a little when I saw the final bill. With the rush service, the clock was almost two-hundred dollars.

Will is worth it, inner Mom pointed out.

Yes, he is. I signed the credit card slip.

~

Back at Derek's, we gave the dogs some water. Then Buddy and I followed his SUV in my car.

At the flea market, Derek drove through the deserted parking lot and around to the side of Building A. He pulled in on the far side of Nell's trailer. I pulled in beside him, nudging my front bumper almost against the building to get most of my car in its shadow. The pursuit of shade is pretty much second nature once one has lived in Florida for a while.

Buddy and I walked around the end of my car. I glanced past the back of Nell's trailer and noticed a black SUV pulling off the road. It stopped at the far edge of the large parking lot. Probably some lost tourist trying to figure out how his GPS had led him astray.

Derek had remembered to tell Fred to sit and stay. The dog waited obediently as Derek extracted his wheelchair from the back of the truck and settled into it. Then he rolled up alongside the two small steps of Nell's trailer, leaned over and knocked on the flimsy metal door.

Nell's china-doll face lit up when she saw him. She bounded down the steps and gave him a hug. Leaning down, she pulled something out from under the trailer.

It was a small ramp, which fit over the steps like a glove, most likely custom-made by Derek.

"I'll leave the dogs out here," I said. The trailer would be cramped enough with three people.

Derek nodded, as Nell pushed his chair up the ramp.

I tied Fred's leash to one of the supports under the steps, but Buddy's I left loose. Otherwise, the leashes would get tangled. I told both dogs to lie down and stay. They dropped to the cement pad in front of the trailer, under a small awning that created some shade.

Nell walked gingerly down the ramp, carefully carrying a bowl of water. "Will they do okay sharing a water bowl?"

"Sure. Thanks." My heart warmed toward her. I hadn't particularly liked her initially, seeing her as a complication in my client's life that he didn't need. Which hadn't been very fair of me.

Or maybe you were just jealous 'cause she's gorgeous, Ms. Snark pointed out, not all that helpfully.

I imagined sticking my tongue out at Ms. Snark, while I gave Nell a warm smile.

In the trailer, she and I sat on the tiny benches across from each other and Derek rolled his chair up to the table's edge. "Can I get y'all something?" Nell said. "Sweet tea? Coffee? I'm afraid all I've got is instant."

I shook my head, as Derek said, "No, I'm fine. Nell, we need to ask you some questions."

"'Bout what?" Her sky-blue eyes shone as she looked at him.

Shame they're siblings, Ms. Snark commented internally.

Crapola. She'd picked up on it sooner than I had. Nell adored Derek. But was that because he was her half-brother, or because she loved him in a different way?

"There's a few things that've been happenin'," Derek was saying, "that are kind of confusin'. Like what happened to the stuff from Zeke's stall."

"Did you see or hear anything out of place," I asked, "that Monday night or the next morning? Maybe when you were going back and forth to the motel."

"No. Why?"

Derek's face was grim. "Because whoever took Zeke's things hauled them a few blocks away and lit them on fire."

Nell's chin dropped and her eyes went wide. "Why'd they do that?"

Her surprise seemed genuine enough. I answered, "Probably to destroy anything he had that might be incriminating."

"Marcia thinks Zeke was blackmailin' somebody," Derek said.

I hid a wince. I hadn't really wanted her to know that quite yet.

"Nell," I said. "I know it might be upsetting, but can you tell us exactly what happened the night Zeke died?"

Her eyes shiny with unshed tears, she nodded. "I don't always sleep real well. I heard noises that night, around midnight. I stepped outside and listened, and thought they was comin' from the back of the market."

She paused, sucked in a deep breath. "I snuck back there. I can be real light on my feet when I wanna be."

Does that go with being light-fingered? Ms. Snark commented.

I mentally shushed her.

"I listened from the corner of the buildin' back there," Nell continued, "Zeke said somethin' about havin' some extra insurance. At first I thought he must be talkin' to his insurance man, but why would he be doin' that in the middle of the night?"

She stopped, sniffed, and cleared her throat. "Then I heard mumblin' for a while, then somebody cried out, like they was in pain. Without thinkin', I called Zeke's name. Then I heard rustlin' and metal clankin' against metal. I ran around the corner, but nobody was there."

She covered her face with her hands. "Except Zeke was there, lyin' on the ground, bleedin' and not breathin'. I checked for a pulse, like they do on TV, but couldn't find one."

She pulled her hands away and looked intensely at Derek. "When I saw the cane, I thought it was you, that Zeke finally got up the nerve to tell ya that you're his son, and you got mad and…" She covered her face again and burst into tears.

Derek leaned over and tried to put an arm around her shoulders, but he couldn't quite reach. He patted her back instead. "It's okay, Nell. I might've thought the same thing, in your shoes."

I dug in my purse for a tissue.

Nell used it to wipe her wet cheeks and blow her nose. "I grabbed the cane. I didn't even see, in the dark, that the dragon was gone from the end. I ran through the woods to the edge of that field. Then I threw it as hard as I could. When I came back I saw the moonlight glintin' off the dragon. It was lyin' on top of the drainage grate in the pavement back there." She waved a hand in the general direction of the back of the flea market.

"I tried to pick it up but it was stuck. When I finally got it loose and I saw that sword, I almost fainted." She hung her head. "I thought I'd gotten all the fingerprints and blood off of it, before I put it back in your stall, but I missed some."

She started crying again. "If only I'd gotten it completely clean…" Her voice hitched. "Then neither of us would be suspects now."

While Derek attempted again to comfort her, I was distracted by another spurt of envy. Nell didn't even get ugly when she cried—no swollen eyes, no blotchy red skin. It really wasn't fair.

I shook my head a little to clear my mind. "How many voices did you hear, before the outcry?"

Nell closed her eyes. A stray tear dripped off her long lashes and rolled down her pale cheek. "I think it was only Zeke and one other person, but it could've been two people with him. Male, I'm pretty sure."

"This is really helpful," I said, trying to cheer her up. "Do you remember any more of what either of them said?"

She swiped at her cheek with the wadded-up tissue. "The other voice was a low rumble. I never made out any words, except Zeke's." Her head jerked up. "Wait. He said he had more evidence and it was in a really safe place."

I nodded, but couldn't help wondering if her mind was making that up, now that the seed of a possible blackmail scenario had been planted.

"Do you remember seeing a guy hanging around last week? Heavyset, dark hair, looked kind of out of place." I intentionally left the description vague.

She thought for a moment. "Yeah, now that you mention it, there was this guy who kept moving back and forth from my stall to the one next to Derek's. I wondered if he was killin' time, waitin' for his wife or somethin'."

"How was he dressed?" I asked.

She gave a wan smile. "Real nice. I remember thinkin' his wife was a lucky lady. I mean he was overweight, but you could tell he had money. He smelled good too. Some woodsy cologne that I thought must be pretty expensive."

"His clothes?" I prompted.

"Oh, yeah. He had on a light green shirt, pressed real nice, and dark pants. Dark shiny dress shoes too." She sat up straighter. "He looked a lot like that guy today, the one hangin' around Derek's stall."

I nodded again. "The green-shirt guy, do you think you'd recognize his clothes if you saw them again?"

"Oh, yeah, and I got a good look at his face too," she said eagerly. "I'd be able to pick him out of a crowd."

Not anymore, Ms. Snark said in my head. *That face is gone!*

I winced a little. "Just a couple more questions. How did you get into Derek's stall to put the sword back in the display?"

Nell's cheeks pinked some. She was even more gorgeous with the touch of color. It was so not fair!

"Zeke had one of those gizmos, like yours," she turned to Derek, "to open the gate to your stall. I got it from his trailer."

Derek nodded. "The gate had two controls." he said to me, "He kept one, in case I ever lost mine."

I'll bet Zeke kept keys to other stalls too, Ms. Snark commented internally. *And Ms. Light-fingers here used them to do her stealing.*

She was probably right.

Again, I kept my voice gentle. "Nell, I know I already asked you this before, but I gotta ask again, to be absolutely sure. Saturday night, you didn't take the dragonhead cane from Derek's trunk, did you?"

She scowled at me. "No!"

Derek was staring at me, a knowing glint in his eyes. He'd figured it out. "Who do *you* think took it?" he asked anyway.

"Zeke."

He gave a small nod.

I glanced out the tiny window next to the table, while I tried to put the remaining pieces together. The image of a man walking away from the distant SUV blurred, as my eyes went out of focus.

A small part of my brain registered that the guy had run out of gas.

"Penny for your thoughts," Derek said.

I let out a humorless chuckle. "For once, they're worth a bit more than that. I think I know what happened, but I'm not sure. Not everything fits."

"Well?" Derek's eyes had gone wide. "Don't keep us in suspense."

I took a deep breath. "I think the dragonhead cane-slash-sword was evidence of some crime. Mr. Green Shirt was most likely the other guy Nell heard. Zeke was blackmailing him. Green Shirt had come here to pay up and get the sword, but something went wrong, and for some reason, Green Shirt killed Zeke. Unless there was a third person there too. But then he dropped the sword, and it got caught in the grate. He heard Nell coming and had to take off without it."

I paused, thinking again. No, that part still didn't make sense.

"Green Shirt came back Monday night, searching for the sword and the, quote, 'extra insurance' Zeke had mentioned. He couldn't find either so he took all of Zeke's stuff and burned it."

Derek nodded. "He might have seen the dragonhead in my display at some point, so he watched for an opportunity to search my stall."

I turned to Nell. "Did you tell all this to the sheriff? Including everything you heard Zeke say?"

She shook her head, but then said, "Yeah, most of it. But I didn't remember that part about the 'more evidence' until just now."

I put my hands on the table and pushed myself to a stand. Derek moved his chair back to let me out of the tiny booth. "I need to call the sheriff." I looked at Nell. "He's probably gonna want to hear it all again from you, though."

She didn't seem thrilled, but she nodded.

The walls of the small trailer were starting to close in on me. I opened the door and walked down the ramp.

Buddy stood and gave me his cocked-head, *what's-up* look. I patted my thigh, and he followed as I stepped away from the trailer, pulling my phone from my pocket.

Fred stood up, as if to follow. I held up my hand to him in the *Stay* gesture. He sat back down and watched us.

"Sheriff Burns, please," I said into the phone. "Marcia Banks-Haines calling."

Surprisingly, the receptionist didn't resist putting me through.

"Burns," the sheriff said in my ear, in the same crisp way that Will answered his cell phone.

Suddenly, I was blindsided by a spurt of longing for my husband. It made it hard to talk.

"Um, I have some info for you," I managed to get out. "But first I have a question. The DNA of the fresh blood on the sword handle was Zeke's, right? But it was contaminated with someone else's DNA, wasn't it?"

"How'd you know that?" His tone was sharp, but, in an odd way, also resigned.

"Could they tell whose DNA it was?"

"No, there was enough to muddy the waters, or blood in this case. But not enough to identify the other person."

"I can make an educated guess," I said. *The dead woman from twenty-five years ago.*

"I already did," the sheriff replied, his voice friendlier.

"I think I know what happened, except for one piece that doesn't fit." I told him about Zeke's words that Nell had just remembered.

"Hmm, so Mr. Lord was blackmailing our green-shirted vic," the sheriff said, "and the vic was probably the one who stabbed him."

I nodded, even though he couldn't see me. "Yes. But he dropped the sword and couldn't get it loose from the grate. Nell's presence meant he had to come back later to try to find it, plus the 'other insurance' Zeke had mentioned. Um, you might focus on New Jersey to identify Mr. Green Shirt."

Now the sheriff chuckled. "One step ahead of you there, young lady. I've got a call in to the gang unit of their state police."

"Gang unit?"

"Yep, I suspect he's a made man."

"Made of what?"

The sheriff laughed. "Made man as in mobster."

"They've still got those?"

"In New Jersey, they do. Their gang unit keeps track of what's left of the mob families up there."

"But why do you think the mob's involved?"

"Because the young woman who was killed twenty-five years ago was the mistress of a mob boss. And keep that under your hat, please."

"Okay," I said, vaguely aware of a rumbling sound behind me. "So the DNA from the blood in the vial wasn't so irrelevant after all." Too late, I realized I probably shouldn't have rubbed the sheriff's nose in that earlier assumption.

But he chuckled. "If we're right about Mr. Green Shirt, as you call him, there's only one question left."

"Who killed *him* and why?"

"That's the question. Take care, Ms. Banks-Haines." He disconnected before I could tell him again to call me Marcia.

The rumbling had grown louder. I turned around.

Buddy was growling low in his throat, the hair along his back standing at attention.

I followed his line of vision. A dark-haired, slightly heavyset man had rounded the front corner of the building, about fifteen feet away. He looked like a younger, somewhat thinner version of Mr. Green Shirt.

Buddy growled louder.

The man stood perfectly still for a beat, then bolted off across the empty parking lot. He jumped into the passenger seat of the black SUV, and it sped away.

Unfortunately, I couldn't make out the license plate from this distance, nor could I see the driver. The vehicle's windows were heavily tinted.

I'd gotten a good look at the man, however, before he'd taken off.

I hadn't been close enough to the guy in Derek's stall earlier to make out his facial features.

But I doubted that two different men just happened to be hanging around here today—both wearing pressed light-blue polo shirts and dark dress slacks with a crisp crease.

CHAPTER TWENTY-ONE

The sheriff's department had dispatched two deputies—fortunately neither was Deputy Harrison. They had searched the premises and had found something quite disturbing.

A gas can, empty, and gas splashed against the far wall of the flea market building, near the back door of Derek's stall.

Apparently Mr. Blue Shirt had been in the process of setting the place on fire. The driver of the black SUV must've seen me walking around with my phone to my ear and signaled the would-be arsonist.

Two firefighters from the local volunteer fire department were coating the gas-soaked area with something to neutralize its combustibility. The deputies were interviewing Derek and Nell, and I was once again on the phone with the sheriff.

"Sorry I couldn't come over there myself," he was saying. "I've got a county commissioners' meeting in a little while."

I recalled Will's issues with his flaky commissioners when he was sheriff of Collins County. "My condolences," I said.

"What?" Then he chuckled. "They can be a challenge at times. So, tell me what happened."

By the time I had finished filling him in, Derek and Nell were at my elbow.

"She's coming to my house," Derek said.

One of the deputies gestured to Nell. "I'll go with you while you pack some things."

Meanwhile, the sheriff was saying in my ear, "It's not safe for Ms. Benson to be there by herself."

It took my brain a second to compute that everyone was on the same page, especially since I had long since forgotten that Benson was Nell's last name.

"She's getting some things from her trailer now," I told the sheriff. "She'll be staying at Derek's for the time being."

"Good. Let us know if you think of anything else." He disconnected.

I turned to Derek. "Do you think that's a good idea, having Nell at your place?"

His expression became shuttered, as closed down as I'd ever seen him. "I've gotta look out for her."

Mattie's words echoed in my head. *You're not responsible for your clients' lives.*

Suddenly, I was exhausted. This day had been a total roller coaster. "I'm gonna head home. Hopefully by Monday, the sheriff will have this figured out, and we can train in peace."

Derek nodded glumly.

"You got everything you need for Fred?"

His face brightened some. "You're leaving him with me?"

"Sure. But be careful that he doesn't get away from you."

"Don't worry. I'll take good care of him," Derek promised, "and yes, I have food and everything."

I smiled. "See you Monday."

~

I glanced at my watch as I loaded Buddy into the backseat of my car. It was almost five-thirty. I groaned. I'd planned to leave earlier than this, since I needed to stop in Belleview for groceries for our Thanksgiving meal tomorrow.

Will had asked if we could have a quiet meal at home, just the two of us, so I'd turned down Sherie Wells's invitation to dinner at her house, with her large clan of children and grandchildren, plus Edna, Susanna and Dexter Mayfair.

Was it too late to accept that invitation after all?

I pointed my car toward home, then pushed the button on my steering wheel to call Will. My phone rang, making me jump a little.

And Will's name flashed up on the dashboard screen.

I grinned. Great minds, and all that jazz. "Hey there, I was about to call you. I'm headed home."

"Uh, well, I was calling you because I'm headed *your* way." He sounded unnaturally cheerful. "Or I should say, we're headed your way."

"What? Why? And who's we?"

"Me and your mother."

Good thing I had the country road to myself. I was all over the place before I got my wits about me and my car settled back into my own lane.

"She's *with* you?"

"Yup, you're on speaker, by the way."

"I didn't hear from you," Mom said, "so I decided to come on down and surprise you."

"But I texted you that I'd call soon."

"I never got a text back."

I picked up my phone and flipped over to my messages. Sure enough, I'd neglected to hit send.

"Sorry, Mom. I typed the text but didn't send it."

"Well, I'm here now, for the holiday."

"I called Becky first," Will said, "to see if you were there, and she invited all of us to join them for Thanksgiving tomorrow. She's planning a feast."

"But I've been avoiding there, because… you know."

"She figures with a mob there and two lawmen, we should be okay."

I winced at the word *mob*, but I couldn't fill Will in right now on the latest developments. My mom would have a heart attack if she thought the Mafia was after me.

"Becky's got a point," I said. "But she also only has one guest room."

"She said your mom can stay on the sun porch." His voice was still cheerful. "They have a daybed out there."

Was this a new, more spontaneous side of Will I was seeing, or had my mom twisted his arm to go along with all this? Best guess, it was the latter.

My mother had gone suspiciously quiet.

"You do realize that this feast will be vegetarian," I pointed out.

"I've got that covered," Mom said.

Aha! My vague suspicion blossomed into a full-blown theory. "You and Becky cooked this up ahead of time, didn't you, Mom?"

"Well, maybe, but only a couple of days ago. I figured I'd surprise you two, and I wanted to see the twins. And Becky and Andy, of course," she hastily added.

I smiled. My godchildren had stolen another heart.

"Your brother's wife won some contest at her work," Mom was saying, "a long weekend at some ski resort in Colorado. Her parents are watching the kids. Sooo, I was at loose ends…" She trailed off, trying to sound forlorn.

But I knew she didn't care for my sister-in-law. She almost never called her by name if she could avoid it. Getting out of having Thanksgiving at their house would be heaven for my mom.

"Okay then, I'll turn around and meet you all at Becky's."

I made a U-turn at the next wide place in the road and headed back to Williston.

About a quarter mile down the road I passed a vehicle going the other way—the first I'd seen on this lonely stretch.

It was a black SUV with heavily tinted windows.

~

My right tire went off onto the gravel shoulder yet again, as I stared in my rearview mirror. But the road behind me was empty. No black SUV.

I told myself I was being paranoid—while black isn't a popular vehicle color in hot Florida, there are still a few black SUVs around. I hit the accelerator, speeding a bit to get back to the somewhat busier streets near Williston.

I was almost to Becky and Andy's when my phone rang. *Sheriff Burns* flashed on my dashboard screen. I answered the call.

"Where are you at the moment?" his voice boomed through my

dashboard speaker.

"Almost to Officer Matthews's house. My husband, mother and I are spending Thanksgiving with them."

A beat of silence. "Not the world's best idea. They in the car with you?"

"No, they're coming over from Mayfair."

"Heard back from the New Jersey gang unit. I got possible identities on our polo-shirt-wearin' fellas. Blue shirt is probably Antonio Allessi, Jr., thirty-eight years old, son of the head of the Allessi family. Green shirt is probably his uncle, Paolo, youngest brother of that same head of the family. The woman who died twenty-five years ago was Antonio, Sr.'s live-in mistress. The Jersey City PD suspected young Tony, who was thirteen at the time and was known for poor impulse control and a hot temper. But they couldn't find any physical evidence. Twenty some years ago, the FBI managed to break up the illegal operations of the family. Antonio, Sr. went to prison, and his brother, Paolo invested their laundered ill-gotten gains in legit investments. The family's been living off of those investments ever since. In more recent years, Paolo's main job has been cleaning up Tony, Jr.'s messes. Apparently he's still got poor impulse control."

I pulled up in front of Becky's house but didn't turn off the engine. "Was the woman, the mistress, stabbed?"

"Nope, bludgeoned to death."

I winced.

"The report said she had some weird patterns of bruises, kind of swirly. If I was a bettin' man I'd plunk down a fair amount on that cane's dragonhead handle being the murder weapon." The sheriff let out a humorless chuckle. "Do you think you could identify the guy you saw earlier today from a photo?"

"Yes," I said, distracted as I stared at the house. How could I go in there when I had the Mafia after me, or at least the remnants of a Mafia family?

"How about the guy in the green shirt?" Sheriff Burns asked. "Did you get a good enough look at his face?"

"No, but Nell said she did, when he was hanging around Derek's stall."

"Okay, I'll send a deputy with a photo array over to the sergeant's house, and I'm bringing one myself to you. Stay put."

"Sheriff," I said quickly before he could disconnect. "How much danger are we in?"

Another beat of silence. "I'd feel better if you'd gone home."

"Not sure I'd be safer there." I told him about the black SUV that had been headed in the general direction of Mayfair.

The sheriff sighed. "Allessi knows you can identify him now. He came down here to clean up an old mess and now he's got an even bigger new mess." A slight pause. "Okay, I'm gonna coordinate with the Williston's Police Chief and get some protection for you and the sergeant and Ms. Benson, until we catch up with Tony boy. I'll give the Marion County sheriff a heads up as well, so he can send a cruiser over to Mayfair."

That was a good idea. I felt guilty for not thinking of it myself. I shuddered as I imagined Edna Mayfair or Sherie Wells confronting the strangers in a black SUV.

"I'll be there soon," the sheriff was saying. "Marcia, try not to worry." He disconnected.

The sheriff likes you, Ms. Snark pointed out with a soft snicker.

Ignoring her, I turned off the ignition. I looked at the house again and sighed. Time to go tell Becky that I was once more putting her family at risk.

~

We all sat around the large kitchen table. Becky had put an extra leaf in it.

We had glasses of iced tea in front of us, but she'd turned down the oven to warm, rather than dishing up the casserole she'd made for our dinner. None of us, except the babies, had any appetite right now.

Andy had apparently been brought up to speed by his chief. He and I took turns filling everyone in.

My mother hadn't said much, but there was an unhealthy greenish tinge to her face. I prayed her heart could handle all this.

Will too was quiet, a grim expression on his face.

I turned to Becky, who was spooning something purple and pureed into the twins' mouths. "Beck, we should leave. We can't put all of you at risk."

She had the most conflicted look on her face, but Andy was shaking his head. "I agree with Becky's earlier assessment. There's strength in numbers. Just because you're not here, doesn't mean this guy won't come looking for you here. Better that we're all able to watch each others' backs, especially if we're going to have a cruiser sitting out front. That's a pretty good deterrent."

The front doorbell rang. Andy and Will rose to answer it together. "You and Buddy keep an eye on the back door," Will whispered to me as he went past.

We followed them out to the living room, and I quickly checked that the back door was locked.

Andy peered out the peephole and opened the front door. We all visibly relaxed when Sheriff Burns stepped into the house.

"Come into the kitchen," Andy said.

I introduced the sheriff to those who didn't know him. He nodded and murmured, "Pleased to meet ya." Until I got to my mom.

Then he smiled. "Nice to finally meet the lovely lady who produced this spunky gal."

Mom's cheeks turned pink.

I could feel my own face heating up, but I ignored the sensation. "I'll remind you that I'm a 'spunky gal,'" I made air quotes, "the next time I'm annoying you."

Will gave me a small smirk. "Probably won't have to wait long for that."

I resisted the urge to stick my tongue out at him.

"Sit, Sheriff." Becky jumped up and pointed to her chair. "Let me get you some tea." She headed for a cabinet to get out a glass.

The sheriff sat in the vacated chair. He glanced at the twins and reared back, eyes wide in mock horror. "Officer Matthews, did you know your children are purple?"

We all looked at the toddlers. Both had some of their dinner smeared across their faces. Winston even had some purple goo in his soft dark curls.

Chuckles and smiles around the table. The twins stared back at us, and then broke into grins. They weren't sure what was going on but they knew when they were the center of attention. And that's all they cared about.

Becky handed the sheriff a glass of sweet tea. Wet rag in hand, she tackled the purple-faced munchkins. After a few moments of spluttering—and Jasmine pretending to cry, which Becky ignored—they were cleaned up. She gave them each a cookie.

Sheriff Burns took a long swig of tea and smacked his lips. "That hits the spot." He put his glass down and his expression turned serious. "Now then, if y'all would not say anything for a few minutes, I need to show Ms.–"

I raised my hand in a stop motion.

"…Marcia here a photo array." He spread out six head-shots of dark-haired white men in their late thirties.

The face of the man in the parking lot jumped out at me. Number five. I pointed to him. "That's him. No doubt about it."

"You're sure he's the one you saw at the flea market, just before we found the gasoline and matches?"

"Absolutely. I got a good look at him."

"Which means he got a good look at you." My mother's voice started out sharp but ended a little shaky.

"Which is why we're taking precautions," I said gently. I didn't like how pale her face had gone, framed by her fluffy white curls.

And it looked like she'd lost some weight since the last time I'd seen her. Had she been sick?

"Williston Police is kind of short-handed," the sheriff was saying, "'cause of the holiday and officers like Matthews here takin' off to be with family. Since this is my county's mess that has spilled over into their jurisdiction, I offered some of my men to help with protection duty. So you'll see either a Williston or a Crystal County cruiser out front this evening and all day tomorrow."

He pushed himself to a stand. "I'll touch base with y'all tomorrow."

"Stay for supper, Sheriff?" Becky said. She now had oven mitts on her hands and was pulling an eggplant parmesan casserole out of the oven.

Sheriff Burns eyed the purple and cheesy mass and did his best to hide a frown. "Thanks for the invite, but I gotta get back. Some other time."

I swallowed a snicker. I'd had similar reactions to some of Becky's dishes, but they always turned out to be delicious, once I got past the lack of curb appeal.

My mother was staring at the sheriff's hands. She cleared her throat. "How about dinner tomorrow? Becky's making all the traditional sides and I brought the turkey." She pointed to a blue cooler that Will had lugged in earlier from his car. "And the makings for my cornbread stuffing."

The sheriff looked around at all of us, the strangest expression on his face.

"Did you have other plans?" Mom asked sweetly.

"Well, no, ma'am." He wiped his palms on his uniform pants.

"Come on," I said, "some of us may be tangentially related to one of your cases, but we're not suspects. And there'll be two other law enforcement officers at the table." I'd made a wild guess that this was what was bothering him. He wasn't sure how to classify us as a group—witnesses in a case or fellow LEOs or just plain folks.

He broke into an almost shy smile. "Well, I think then that I will join you."

You nailed it, Ms. Snark said internally, in a rare complimentary mood.

"Excellent," Mom said.

We all stood and walked with him to the door in a loose group, Becky stopping in the kitchen doorway to keep an eye on the twins, still in their highchairs. She called out a cheery goodbye.

"Until tomorrow." Mom extended her hand. "Dinner's at four."

He took it between both of his, the left one on top. "Looking forward to it."

Duh, that's what she was staring at. He had an indentation around his left ring finger, that indicated he'd worn a wedding band for many years, but there was no white line on his tanned finger. He hadn't worn that ring recently.

He was either divorced or a widower.

"I gotta ask," the sheriff said to Mom, his tone teasing. "You didn't bring that turkey down on a plane, did you?"

A giggling sound.

Did that just come from my *mother?*

"No, I bought it and the cooler at a store called Publix." She pronounced it *Poob-licks*.

We all chuckled. "It's Publix, Mom, as in *public* with an apostrophe *s*."

She laughed self-consciously. "Oh, that makes more sense." She ducked her head, then looked up at the sheriff with a coy expression on her face.

I resisted the urge to roll my eyes and turned back to Burns. "See you tomorrow, Sheriff."

He smiled at me. "Mar-see-a," he exaggerated the syllables of my name, "if I'm gonna have Thanksgivin' supper with you and your family, I guess you should call me Clint, in private at least."

I grinned back at him and opened my mouth to say goodnight. Then something else occurred to me. "Sheriff…Clint, Detective Young said that you all had a tee shirt from Derek's trunk."

His cheerful expression shut down. "Yes. It should've been on the inventory sheet that was given to the sergeant."

Hmm, Derek had acted like it had gone missing that morning. Maybe he'd forgotten it was on the sheet.

"Derek said it had paint stains on it. Did you get them tested?" I was wondering if some of those stains were blood, not paint.

The sheriff shook his head, but he wasn't making eye contact.

"Were the stains too degraded to test?" I asked.

He took a deep breath. "Maybe. We'll never know. The shirt disappeared before we could send it to the lab."

My mouth fell open. I gaped at him. Then I remembered who had searched Derek's stall that first day, and had no doubt confiscated the tee shirt in the first place.

The incompetent Deputy Harrison strikes again. He probably lost the darn thing.

"Well, goodnight, y'all," the sheriff said. "See you tomorrow."

I gave him a warm smile, by way of an apology for putting him on the spot. "Goodnight, *Clint*."

CHAPTER TWENTY-TWO

The next day, Becky, Mom and I cooked, while Andy watched the twins and Will hung out with him.

Well, I didn't cook so much as follow directions when I was told to chop, fetch, or get out of the way. The latter instructions usually came from my mom, who harbored no slouches in her kitchen. Or in this case, her surrogate kitchen in Becky's house.

Will dared to wander in, sniffing the now fragrant air. He poured a cup of coffee and sat at the table. I plopped into a chair next to him.

"Andy's putting the kids down for their nap," Will said.

Becky looked up at the kitchen wall clock, which read two-thirty. "Hopefully they'll wake up before or after the meal, not during it."

Mom yawned.

"Are you okay, Mom?" I asked.

At the same time, Becky said, "Didn't you sleep well last night?"

"Oh yes, I slept fine. I just get a little tired, the day after I travel. As somebody once said, 'Getting old ain't for sissies.'"

"I think it was Bette Davis," Will said.

I gave him a curious glance.

"What?" he said. "My mom loves her. She quotes her all the time."

"Miz Banks," Becky said. "Why don't you rest for a bit too. Everything's under control here."

"It's Claire, and I think I'll do that."

Buddy and I followed Mom into the living room, with Will behind us. Mom headed on into the sunroom.

"Wanna catch some of the New Orleans-Atlanta game?" Will asked.

Buddy had gone into the mud room and stood by the back door, signaling that he needed to go out.

I shook my head and pointed at the dog. "Football will have to wait. Under the circumstances, I'm not letting him out by himself."

Will sighed softly. "I'll go with you."

I wasn't about to argue.

We went out to the fenced backyard, a quarter acre of heaven as far as Buddy was concerned, full of new and tantalizing smells.

Will settled on the back stoop, stretching his long legs out in front of him. I lowered myself beside him. We sat in comfortable silence, the warm sun offsetting a cool breeze.

I loved autumn in Florida, when the heat let up and most days were sunny and warm. Whereas I'd disliked it in Maryland, only because it was the harbinger of a long, dreary winter.

I took a deep breath and let it out slowly.

Buddy was methodically sniffing along every inch of the fence, lifting his leg to mark each bush and tree he came to. Will chuckled at his antics.

Then his face sobered. "We need to talk."

"Uh oh, the dreaded 'we need to talk.'" I was joking.

Apparently he wasn't. His expression remained serious. "I really wanted to wait until your training here was done, and we could get back to normal at home."

I went from pleasantly relaxed to totally tense in a nanosecond. This did not sound good.

Will shook his head. "I'm not sure I can do this anymore."

My heart ricocheted around my chest. *He's leaving me!*

I swallowed hard. "Do what?" I tried to sound casual, like someone who did not have a rock in her stomach.

"Law enforcement."

My insides relaxed. A relieved laugh escaped from my lips.

"What's funny?" Will said, frowning.

"Uh, nothing. It's…"

Go on, Mom's voice encouraged, *you need to be honest with him.*

It felt kind of weird to have my inner mom talking to me in my head while my real mom was just inside the screen door behind us.

"I had a flash of insecurity, that's all. For a second, I thought you were going to…" I couldn't bring myself to use the words *ask for a divorce*, "um, say that there was something seriously wrong with our relationship."

"Marcia, when are you–" He stopped himself and sighed.

I took his hand. "I trust you, and I trust that you love me." Although I still couldn't quite figure out why. "It's only a knee-jerk reaction. So, you were saying?"

He squeezed my hand. "I think I want to change careers."

"Is this about that shooting?"

"Not completely. I think I've been burning out for a while. Maybe even before I came to Florida. I was getting cynical, seeing everyone as a potential perp. That's why I went for sheriff of a rural county. I figured that drunk and disorderlies would be the worst crimes I'd have to deal with."

"And instead you ended up with a complex murder and corruption investigation." The investigation that had brought us together.

"Yeah, and I realized I'd missed the tougher cases. But now I'm feeling the cynicism coming back." He stared at the toes of his sneakers.

Crapola, the clock! My throat tightened. So much for finding the perfect anniversary gift.

I yanked my mind back to Will. He was the priority, not my disappointment.

"The problem is I have no idea what else I'd want to do," he was saying.

I looked around. Buddy was still inspecting bushes, probably to make sure that he had marked every last one of them. "Maybe you should wait a little while," I said, "until the impact of that shooting wears off more. You may feel differently down the road some."

He gave me a quick sideways glance, then went back to contemplating his sneakers. "Well, there's something else in the mix now, as a result of the shooting. I'm afraid I'll hesitate in the future, in a similar situation."

That had my insides tightening up all over again. I tried to stay calm, focused on him. I didn't want my worries about his safety to sway such an important decision.

He pulled his feet in, let go of my hand and rubbed both palms on his jeans. He didn't let his emotions show much, but I'd learned that was a tell. When he rubbed his hands on his thighs, he was fairly anxious about something.

"We don't have to come up with solutions today," he said. "I just wanted you to know where my thoughts have been going lately."

I opened my mouth to reassure him that I was with him, no matter what. Instead, I froze.

A low rumble in the background had escalated into a full-blown growl.

I held up my hand in a stop gesture. Scanning the yard, I finally spotted my big black dog in the shade of a small tree, next to the fence.

He was staring past the corner of the house, toward the street out front, the hair standing straight up along his back.

Will and I jumped up and jogged to him. I put a hand on Buddy's head, reassuring him, and followed his line of vision.

Beyond some camellia bushes along the side of the house, I could make out our sheriff's deputy guard standing beside his cruiser at the curb, talking to someone.

I groaned softly. The guard was Deputy Harrison, which did not instill confidence.

The guy he was talking to was a little husky. He had his broad back to us and wore a well-cut black business suit.

Maybe he was Harrison's replacement.

One can hope, Ms. Snark commented. *This guy sure is a snappy dresser.*

Mr. Suit handed Harrison something, and they shook hands. Yup, he was relieving the deputy from duty.

My inner mom made a tut-tut sound. *I hope the poor man got to eat Thanksgiving dinner with his family first.*

The two men started up the sidewalk toward the house, Harrison in front, Mr. Suit following.

Did Harrison feel the need to introduce him to us? That would be way more dedicated than the deputy usually seemed to be.

Mr. Suit was staying behind Harrison. But just before they disappeared behind the camellias, I caught a glimpse of his profile.

I gasped softly. It was Tony Allessi.

CHAPTER TWENTY-THREE

Will apparently didn't need an explanation. My gasp was enough. "Stay out here," he whispered and bolted for the back door.

"The heck I will," I muttered, running right behind him.

This guy was here for me. I wasn't about to let him hurt any of the people I loved. My chest felt like it was in a vice. My stomach roiled.

Will was inside by the time I got to the porch. Grabbing Buddy's collar, so he wouldn't run past me, I caught the screen door on the rebound with my shoulder. We entered the mud room. Still holding Buddy back, I peeked into the living room around the edge of the doorframe.

"Stop!" Will yelled. "Don't open that!"

He was a second too late. Andy's face was still at the peephole, but his hand was already unlocking the door.

It burst open, knocking him backward. Harrison and Tony Allessi sprang into the house. Harrison slammed the door behind them.

Tony had a small, nasty looking pistol in his hand. The deputy's weapon was holstered.

But because of the kids, Will and Andy weren't armed. Their pistols were locked in the gun safe.

My heart did a nosedive into my stomach. Tony Allessi wanted me out of the way because I could identify him. And now Andy and Will had seen him too.

He had no intention of letting anyone in this house live.

Will! My brain screamed. *Mom!*

Another thought slammed into me. *Becky and the babies!* Would he at least spare the little ones?

I struggled for breath against the pressure in my chest and blinked away the sting of tears.

"What are you doing?" Andy was yelling at Harrison.

The deputy grinned. "Makin' myself rich."

I tried to scan the living room to locate anybody else in there. But without sticking my head out farther, I couldn't see everywhere. I mentally went through where everyone should be. The twins had been napping in the nursery when we'd gone outside. And Mom had gone to the sun porch to rest. No doubt all the yelling had woken her, but hopefully she'd have the good sense to stay out there.

And hopefully Becky would stay in the kitchen, preferably behind a large appliance. If the gun went off in some random direction, Will, Andy and I would probably be the only ones at risk.

Swallowing hard, I crouched down next to Buddy's ear, my index finger on my lips. The low rumble in his throat ceased, but his gaze never left Tony Allessi.

Up close, the suit looked tailored and expensive. Under it he wore a black shirt and a gray tie.

He's been watching too many gangster movies, Ms. Snark commented.

"Where's the girl?" Tony said, waving his gun hand in an arc.

"What girl?" Will asked.

He narrowed his eyes. "Who are you?"

"A Marion County detective. You'd better think about what you're doing here. You're holding a gun on two police officers."

Which was why Harrison didn't have his gun drawn. Did he think that would protect him from being charged with assault of a police officer? If things went south for Tony, would Harrison later claim that he was trying to protect us?

Tony took a step toward Will, his gun hand extended.

My heart ricocheted around my chest, but a small, calm corner of my brain cheered inside. He was now standing at a much better angle for what I had in mind.

"Yeah, I'm holding the gun, so answer my question. Where's the girl?"

"Again," Will said, "what girl?"

Surely they could hear my pounding heart from across the room, but no one looked my way.

"You know who I mean," Tony snarled. "Harrison said she's in here." He gestured again with his gun hand.

Best opening we're likely to get. "Protect" I whispered fiercely in Buddy's ear. "Grab–"

"What the heck's going on?" A gruff voice from the sunroom—my mother trying to sound like a man.

Harrison and Tony whirled around, the deputy reaching for his holster.

"Grab arm!" I yelled. Buddy rocketed across the floor, growling loudly.

Will tackled Harrison, as Buddy jumped up and sank his teeth into the lovely black fabric of Tony's sleeve.

I held my breath, waiting for the gunshot that didn't happen. The pistol hadn't gone off as I'd feared it would.

Tony was trying to shake Buddy from his arm. "Get this dog off of me!" He batted at Buddy with his other hand, but the dog hung on.

Andy jumped behind Tony and grabbed his elbows. "Drop the gun." He yanked his arms backward.

"Get the dog off," the man shrieked.

I stepped into the room. "Not until you drop the gun."

He tried to aim the pistol in my direction, but Buddy's weight hanging from his arm kept him from raising it very far.

Will had disarmed Harrison. Now he brought the butt of the deputy's weapon down on Tony's wrist.

"Yow!" He dropped the gun, and Will scooped it up.

I ran across the room. "Down, Buddy." The dog let go and dropped to his belly.

My mother raced out of the sunroom and grabbed me in a bear hug.

Andy yanked Tony's arms back harder. "Keep struggling and I'll dislocate your shoulder. You ever had that happen? Hurts like crazy." The last part was said in a casual voice. Andy was enjoying his small revenge.

I gave Mom a quick squeeze back, then disentangled myself. "Where's Harrison?"

Will and Andy looked around. The front door was hanging open.

"Don't worry, he won't get far." Becky stepped out of the kitchen, holding up her cell phone. Sirens wailed in the distance.

~

My knees were still pretty much jelly when Harrison's real replacement careened into the Matthews's driveway a few minutes later.

By the time he'd raced into the house, Andy and Will had their prisoner trussed up like a Thanksgiving turkey, plastic restraints on his wrists and a rope holding him to a kitchen chair.

Tony was yammering for his lawyer, despite Becky telling him to shush or he'd wake the babies. He kept talking in a loud voice, threatening all of us with lawsuits for illegal detention.

Becky walked over and jammed the end of a dish towel into his mouth."Sorry to have to do that," she said in her sweet Carolina drawl. The smirk on her face belied both her words and her tone.

The newly arrived deputy—Stockton, his nametag read—told us that more backup was on the way. "Harrison won't get away," he said, the hint of a smirk on his own face.

It was amazing how universally disliked Harrison was.

The sheriff arrived and quickly reiterated the reassurance, while standing in the middle of the living room.

I think they doth protest too much, Ms. Snark commented inside my head.

Probably embarrassed that one of their own is a dirty cop, I answered her internally.

Mom came into the room from the bedroom area. She and Becky had gone to check on the twins "The little lambs slept right through it," Mom said.

I hid a small grin. Mom had only experienced the kids under contained circumstances so far, either in their high chairs or cribs. *We'll see if they're still 'little lambs' when she sees them in action.*

The sheriff reached out a hand toward her. "Are you sure you're okay, Miz Banks?"

She took his hand briefly. She might've even given it a little squeeze—I couldn't tell for sure.

"Yes, I'm fine, and call me Claire."

Deputy Stockton's radio emitted staticky noise, but he seemed to be able to decipher it. "They caught Harrison, Sheriff."

Clint Burns sighed and sniffed the fragrant air. "Unfortunately, I'll have to take a rain check on supper. I need to go interrogate him, and this fella." He pointed to Tony, who was still struggling against his bonds in his chair.

"I'd love to be a fly on that wall," I said, with a chuckle.

He actually shot me a quick grin. "And then there will be the inevitable paperwork."

Mom's face had fallen. "Oh, no!"

"I can process 'em, Sheriff," Stockton said eagerly, "when you're finished questionin' 'em."

"And we can wait supper awhile." Becky had a mischievous twinkle in her eye. She'd caught the interactions yesterday as well—Mom staring at the sheriff's ring finger and his smiles and over-the-top compliments.

"You gotta eat sometime," I said.

Stockton nodded vigorously. No doubt he was just looking to score points with his boss, but I was glad to have him as an ally.

I wasn't sure how I felt about whatever was going on between the sheriff and my mother, but I wanted the chance to pump him for information once he'd talked to Harrison and Tony Allessi.

"Might be helpful to let them stew some," Will said, "after your initial interrogation."

"Good point." The sheriff glanced at his watch. "How 'bout I give y'all a call around four and let you know how close I am to done?"

"That would be great," Mom said. "Let me give you my cell number."

Becky snorted, then quickly pretended to be coughing.

CHAPTER TWENTY-FOUR

The sheriff made it back by six.

Becky had fed us some salad to tide us over, but I was still more than ready for turkey and its trimmings. We sat down around the big kitchen table, and I picked up my fork.

Mom scowled at me.

Oops!

"Marcia," she said sweetly, "why don't you say grace?"

The words had grown unfamiliar with disuse, but I stumbled along. Finally, we were able to dig in.

Everything was delicious. I thought I might swoon.

When I was partially satiated, I said, "So, Sheriff…I mean Clint. What did Tony Allessi and Harrison have to say for themselves?"

The sheriff sat back in his chair and contemplated the remaining tidbits of meat, potatoes and gravy on his plate. Then he stared at me for a beat.

"I *should* give you the I-can't-discuss-an-ongoing-case line, but I guess that ship's already sailed."

Will covered his mouth with his napkin, but I could see the corner of his lips twitching behind it. His knee was bouncing under the table. He was trying hard not to laugh out loud.

"So here's what I'll do," the sheriff continued. "You tell everybody what you've figured out, while I have me some more of that delicious cornbread dressing. And if I can add anythin' to it when you're done—that won't jeopardize the investigation, that is—then I will."

My mother quickly passed him the dressing bowl. They exchanged smiles.

I struggled to keep my face expressionless and launched into my summary of the events surrounding Zeke's death. Everybody but my mother already knew parts of it.

"It looks like Zeke was blackmailing Tony Allessi," I concluded, "with the sword as evidence of his murder of his father's mistress years ago. Tony probably sent his uncle Paolo to get the sword. What I don't get is what happened to Paolo. Did Tony kill him in a fit of rage because he didn't get all the evidence?"

Clint Burns took a swig of sweet tea to wash down a of dressing. "That's what I think happened, but he's denying it. Also says he wasn't the one who was about to set fire to the flea market, that he saw the gas can and ran over to make sure no one was in the building. Beyond that he clammed up and demanded his lawyer."

I snorted. "Yeah, not what happened. And I saw him with the gas can. I thought he was a tourist who'd run out of gas."

The sheriff arched his shaggy eyebrows at me.

Yikes, I'd forgotten to mention that at the time.

But Andy spoke up before I could say anything. "No point in him holding out on his uncle's murder, since they've got him dead to rights for that older murder of the mistress."

"Yes, there is," the sheriff...Clint said. "New Jersey ain't got the death penalty anymore."

"Oh," several of us said in unison. The State of Florida did have the death penalty and wasn't afraid to use it.

"So, if you've got nothing tying him to Paolo's death," I said, "then he goes back to New Jersey, because murder trumps arson?"

Clint paused in the act of sopping up gravy with a roll. "State's Attorney probably wouldn't even fight extradition."

I was secretly relieved. That meant I wouldn't have to testify.

"But Tony boy may or may not be convicted of that old murder," Clint continued, "even with the new physical evidence."

"His lawyer will scream bloody murder," Will said, "about lack of chain of evidence, for one thing."

I paused to contemplate how often death makes it into casual conversation—dead to rights, scream bloody murder....

Becky was shaking her head. "How could this Tony guy kill his own uncle?"

I thought about how he would've killed all of us if his plan had succeeded, and shuddered. "I'm pretty sure he'd qualify for the diagnosis of antisocial personality disorder."

"What's that?" Mom asked.

"It means he's a psychopath," I clarified. "I doubt family affection and loyalty is more than an intellectual exercise for him. So when his uncle screwed up royally, not only didn't get the sword–"

"But killed the guy who had it," Becky said, "thus drawing attention to it."

"And didn't get the rest of the evidence either," I said, "and now the guy who knows where it's hidden is dead."

"Paolo tries to make it right," Will said. "Takes all the stuff from Zeke's stall and destroys it, and searches Derek's stall."

"How'd he know to look there?" I asked.

"Maybe he'd been watching for a while," Clint said. "He knew that Zeke and Derek interacted a lot. Or maybe he'd spotted the dragonhead in the sergeant's display of walking sticks."

I nodded. "But he couldn't get it because Derek never left it out unless he was right there. He probably searched Nell's trailer and stall at some point too, but the sheriff's people had already confiscated the stuff from her storage room."

"Speakin' of which," Clint said, "can y'all keep somethin' under your hats?"

Everyone nodded, me perhaps a little too enthusiastically.

He pointed to me, his napkin in his hand. "Your speculation that Zeke Lord was a fence was spot on. My detectives had already gotten a few of the vendors to admit that they thought stolen goods were passin' through the flea market, and something Harrison let slip also points in that direction."

"What'd he say?" I asked.

"Somethin' along the lines that Lord wasn't payin' him enough to look the other way."

I shook my head. "So that's why he never gave you Andy's

phone message."

"And why he was looking for an excuse to shoot Derek Bradshaw," Andy said.

I turned to him in horror. "What? You think that's what was happening that day?"

"Um…Harrison has a bad rep among law enforcement around here." Andy paused and cleared his throat, glancing sideways at the sheriff.

"Not news to me, son," Clint said, leaning forward.

Andy gave a small nod. "But when he drew on Bradshaw in his own backyard, when all we were supposed to do was bring him to the flea market to answer some questions and open his stall. While I can kind of get how he initially thought the sergeant's walking sticks were potential weapons, he should've stood down a lot sooner. That whole scene was a little over the top, even for Harrison."

A chill ran through me. "You think he was trying to kill Derek?"

At the same time, Clint said, "First I'm hearin' of all this."

Andy's cheeks flushed to a deeper copper tone. "In retrospect, I should've told you, but, well, he's your man–"

"Not anymore he ain't," Clint said emphatically. He turned to me. "I think I see where Matthews is goin' here. If Harrison had gone there on his own, which would normally be the case. Stoppin' by to notify the Williston Police was more a formality, a courtesy really. Normally, the local jurisdiction wouldn't send their own man along."

"But they did," I said, "and I was there."

"Right." Clint nodded. "Harrison was expectin' to find the sergeant home by himself, and he could…" He paused, glanced at Becky and my mom. I guess he'd long since realized I did not have a high level of sensitivity to such topics. "Let's just say that he could claim young Bradshaw came at him with a weapon, and there'd be no one to refute that."

"Then Bradshaw would've been blamed for Lord's murder," Will said, "since he resisted arrest. And if the case was closed quickly, without any more looking into the flea market or the vic's business dealings, Harrison could've quietly taken over the fencing operation."

"And no one the wiser," I added.

Clint tapped his index finger against his lips. There was a strange glint in his eyes. "Hmm, have to give some thought to how I'm gonna approach Harrison on that."

"He didn't lawyer up?" Will asked.

"Nope, he's playing all innocent. Even claims I misheard him when he made that little slip. Said he didn't realize that Tony Allessi was the guy he was supposed to be protecting y'all from. That Tony'd said he was a family member, and Harrison was bringing him to the door to ask y'all if that was true, when he pushed past him and drew a gun."

Becky let out a small snort. "Not even close to what happened."

Clint chuckled. "Joe Harrison is not the brightest bulb in the package. I am tickled pink that I don't have to keep him on my payroll anymore. Indeed, I think I'm gonna enjoy the next county commissioners' meetin', when I announce I'm searchin' for a new deputy and why."

"It sounds like this Tony isn't the brightest bulb either," Becky said. "Did he really think he could come down here and run around killing people and lighting fires and such and nobody would catch on to who he was?"

I shook my head. "Especially since his appearance pretty much screamed Northerner."

"In Miami he might've blended in," Becky said. "Around here, not so much."

"First thing you learn in law enforcement…" Will made eye contact with Andy and Clint.

In unison, they said, "Most criminals are dumb."

Chuckles around the table. "And what smarts they do have," Andy added, "they don't use to think through what they're doing. They made a choice early on, or maybe life pushed them in that direction, to focus on what they want or need right now, and how they can get it the easiest way possible."

Will nodded. "It's a different mindset. The average law-abiding person views the world as a place where you work for what you need and want. Criminals view it as a place where you grab what you want when nobody's looking."

Clint leaned back in his chair, his fingers laced over his now bulging stomach. "In my experience, criminals are either fairly dumb and relatively easy to catch, or they're quite smart. Not much in between. And the smart ones are usually psychopaths, or at least on that continuum. They get away with stuff for a while, but even they slip up eventually."

"They slip up because they're too narcissistic to believe they'll get caught," I added. "Thank God Tony Allessi is a dumb psychopath."

"Marcia," Mom frowned at me, "do not take the Lord's name in vain."

"What *in vain*? I am truly grateful to whoever is running this universe that I had a not-so-bright one chasing me."

The furrow in her forehead deepened. "It would be better if you had no criminals chasing you in the future."

"Amen to that," Will said.

"Ya know," Clint scratched his cheek, "to cut that boy Tony some slack, he never was brought into the criminal aspects of the Allessi family. They'd gone legit, were livin' off of investments, by the time he was full grown. So I guess we shouldn't be too surprised that he wasn't very good at gettin' away with stuff."

"I'm curious–"

"Naw," everyone said in unison and then laughed.

My cheeks warmed, but I ignored the teasing chortles. "The tee-shirt. Do you think Harrison got rid of it? And what's the significance of the fatigues?"

Clint thought for a moment, staring into space. "Okay, this is pure speculation, but that shirt disappeared around the time that Tony probably got to town, around the time of Paolo's death. I think Harrison was bein' paid off to help protect Lord's fencin' operation, and when Lord got killed, he connected up with Tony somehow and started workin' for him. Tony paid him for the tee-shirt—which had blood stains on it, by the way, as well as paint stains. My techs had determined that much."

"Oh, so he did initially turn it in as evidence," I said.

Andy shifted in his seat. "Of course he would've, when he saw the blood stains. He wanted someone to be arrested quickly."

Clint gave a slight nod. "But before we could send it off for testin' at the state lab like we'd planned, Harrison had hooked up with Tony Allessi, who paid him to swipe it from the evidence room."

"And the fatigues?" I asked.

The sheriff shook his head. "Girl, you are like a dog with a bone." But his tone was good-natured.

"Last thing I did, before I came on back here, was look again at the file that the Jersey City PD sent me. Antonio, Sr. had his mistress move in not all that long after his wife passed away. People they'd interviewed said that didn't sit well with young Tony, who was thirteen at the time. His alibi for the mistress's murder was that he was playin' paint ball with his friends. Said friends confirmed he had been there, but they were a little vague about when he left. But one of them did remember the kid takin' off his fatigue shirt and playin' in his tee-shirt. He said his father's 'stupid, blankety-blank mistress…'" the sheriff made air quotes, although I doubted that *blankety-blank* was a direct quote, "She'd been raggin' on him about gettin' paint stains on them that the maid had a hard time gettin' out when she did the wash."

My brain put some more pieces together. "So he goes home and she starts into him again, he loses it and kills her. Where'd he get the cane?"

"There was an umbrella stand in the house's foyer," Clint said. "You can see it in some of the crime scene photos. It had other fancy canes in it that belonged to his father, but none of them matched the pattern of bruises. Young Tony wasn't there when the police arrived. Antonio Sr. claimed he'd come home and found his mistress dead in the foyer. They searched the house but found no fatigues."

Clint actually winked at me. "Oh, and I forgot to mention… The lead detective on the case—he's retired now—he told me that Daddy Allessi had someone workin' for him around the time the mistress died. This guy's description matches Zeke Lord's, and he disappeared right after the murder."

"How much you wanna bet," Will said, "that Zeke or Jacob, or whatever he was calling himself then, stole the evidence and took off?"

"I think," Sheriff Clint said, "that Daddy Allessi may have charged Zeke with the task of gettin' rid of the evidence, and instead, he got out of there, probably because murderin' was more than he'd bargained on. He'd never done anything violent up to that point. He was a thief and a con man, but maybe he drew the line at killin'."

"So he came back to Florida," I said, "and established a new identity."

Everyone was quiet for a moment, digesting our theories along with our Thanksgiving dinner.

Mom slapped the table. "Enough grim talk." She pushed herself to a stand. "Who's ready for pie?"

EPILOGUE

On the eleventh of December, I went to Derek's house for his final training session.

For our anniversary, Will and I had taken a spontaneous three-day trip to the Keys. It had been too late to cancel the order for the clock, so I'd decided to go ahead and give it to him.

He'd seemed to like it. Stroking the brass plate memorializing his commendation, he'd said, "It's a nice momento, no matter what I decide to do about my career."

He hadn't made that decision yet, but he seemed more like his old self.

I'd returned to Williston two days ago to finish Derek's training, which was coming to an end today. We'd spent the day at the flea market.

Fred seemed to be totally acclimated now to the setting. He stayed in the back on his bed, unless Derek called him to assist with something. Usually to pick up a dropped object, so he didn't have to go through the energy-consuming process of getting off and back on his cart.

Nell stopped by a couple of times, ostensibly to say hi. They worried me some. Did they realize they acted more like shy lovers than brother and sister?

Back at Derek's house after the market closed, I put the dog and his new owner through their paces one more time.

"I think you two are ready to fly on your own," I said, trying to ignore the familiar ache in my heart I always feel when parting with a dog.

Grinning, Derek said, "Want some tea, before you head for home?"

I only hesitated a second. A casual chat wasn't a bad idea. I wanted to make sure Derek was okay in other areas as well.

And you're curious as all get out, Ms. Snark pointed out.

Well, that too.

Once settled at the kitchen table with glasses of iced tea, I said, "So, Nell's looking like she's doing okay?"

His cheeks pinked and he ducked his head. "Yeah, she's fine."

I almost blurted out, *You're in love with her, aren't you?* But I caught myself in time.

"Can you keep a secret?" he asked.

"Sure, as long as it isn't about anything illegal." I wasn't about to start another round of I've-got-info-the-police-should-have-but-I-can't-tell-them.

"I'm not so sure I'm her half brother after all."

"What?"

"A few months ago, Zeke came to me with some DNA kits, an off-brand I'd never heard of. He said he got 'em super cheap. He did that a lot, came up with stuff that was expensive but he said he got cheap."

He blushed again. "Can't believe it never dawned on me before that he was a fence. Anyway, he said something about wouldn't it be fun to find out about our ancestors. I went along mainly to humor him." He stopped to suck in air. "But later he said the results never came back, that the company must've been bogus and no wonder the kits were that cheap."

"You think he did get the results back and found out you weren't his son?"

He nodded, then lowered his gaze to the table. He fiddled with his tea glass. "I called my aunt last week. She confirmed what I'd suspected. I was born ten and a half months after my father left, supposedly to fight in Desert Storm. My aunt told me that Mom laughed it off at the time, said I was all cozy in her womb and didn't wanna come out."

Not likely. Doctors didn't allow babies to just hang out in the womb. His mom's doc would've induced labor long before ten and a half months.

"Marcia, I think my mom had an affair." He didn't say it but his hangdog expression told me he was disappointed in his mother.

"Derek, what if she did know that he was in jail, not off to war. Can you really blame her for finding comfort elsewhere?…Not that I condone infidelity, mind you," I quickly added, "but in this case, I can understand it."

"I guess. When he came home, she did try to make it work. I was old enough to remember bits and pieces. We went on picnics…" His voice trailed off and he shook his head slightly. "It was around then—a few months ago, I mean, after we sent off those DNA kits—that Zeke changed some. I don't think I really noticed at first. But he got more distant."

He made eye contact. "That's around the time he hinted that he wanted the cane back, and when he gave me the other stuff to hide for him. He didn't really care that he might be siccing a mobster on me."

I took a deep breath. "I think Zeke was a narcissist."

"Is that like a psychopath?"

I shook my head. "They're similar, but narcissists do have a conscience, although sometimes it's buried pretty deep. They can care about people, but their main focus is on number one."

He narrowed his eyes some. "That sounds like Zeke. He really liked people feelin' grateful to him. He'd act all modest on the surface, but I could tell he was gettin' off on it."

My next thought I kept to myself. A narcissist might very well get pissed at the kid he had thought was his, when he learned otherwise, even though it wasn't the kid's fault.

"So, I ordered two DNA kits," Derek said. "I'm gonna get me and Nell tested. But I gotta figure out how to trick her into spittin' in a tube." He chuckled self-consciously.

"I've got a better idea. Sheriff Burns has access to Zeke's DNA info. Just get the test done on yourself and ask him to compare it to Zeke's."

"You think he'd do that?"

"Probably. He's a good guy."

After a pause, I said, "How are you going to feel if Zeke isn't your dad? I mean, other than relief that you're not Nell's brother."

He stared at his almost-empty tea glass. "Not sure. It's been such a roller coaster. I used to feel so close to him, looked up to him. I've had pretty mixed feelings about believing he was my real dad, but I guess I'd kinda gotten used to the idea…But if I'm not his biologically, at least the mystery will be solved about why he ran off."

"How so?"

"He must've found out about my mother's affair."

Maybe, maybe not. I kept that thought to myself as well. If that's what Derek needed to believe to justify Zeke's desertion back then, so be it.

"Why do you think he didn't tell Nell that you really weren't his son?"

"Don't know. Maybe he didn't think about it, or maybe he didn't want her to become involved with me, so he let her continue to believe I'm her half brother."

"Would you like me to ask Sheriff Burns about getting Zeke's DNA? I think he likes me."

I know he likes Mom, Ms. Snark said inside my head.

"Yeah, that'd be great. If you don't mind?" His smile wasn't quite as cheery as it had been before all this heartache began, but it was getting closer.

"Not at all. I'd better get going."

He walked me to the door.

"Call me if you have any questions or problems." I gave him a gentle hug, not wanting to throw him off balance.

"Thanks for everything, Marcia."

"Happy to help."

I crouched down to give Fred a farewell scratch behind his ears. Despite the fact that he wasn't the cutest dog I'd ever trained, it tugged at my heartstrings to let him go. He was such a bright boy.

I swallowed the lump in my throat and headed for my car.

On my way home, I called the 'good guy,' aka Sheriff Clint Burns. "Hey, this is Marcia. How ya doin'?"

"Harumph. I've been better." He sighed. "Our State's Attorney's office has decided to let New Jersey have Tony Allessi. Can't prove he killed his uncle down here and the evidence of the attempted arson is not conclusive. So he figures let New Jersey take back their own."

I slowly blew out air. I wouldn't have to testify. To the sheriff, I said, "Might be for the best. They've got a better shot at convicting him."

"There's a slim chance they'll subpoena you to go up there."

I groaned. "They can do that?"

"Yes, but it's a hassle. They have to go through the Florida court system. Depends on whether they decide to bring up the crimes that occurred down here, as evidence of Allessi's efforts to cover up his original crime. I'd say there's a better chance that they'll offer him a plea deal, since the case is so old, and the chain of evidence is shaky."

Something else occurred to me. "Am I in danger from the Allessi family?"

"Probably not. Paolo was the last enforcer they had. On a brighter note, the charges against Nell Benson have been dropped."

"Really?"

"None of the flea market vendors were willing to press charges. She did store stolen goods for Zeke Lord, but she seemed a little vague about whether or not she knew the stuff was hot. And since he's dead, that didn't seem worth pursuing."

"She's a bit mentally impaired. She has fetal alcohol effects. Not as bad as full blown fetal alcohol syndrome, but…"

"Yeah, I'd figured that out. I told the State's Attorney that she might not be deemed mentally competent to stand trial."

I smiled at my dashboard screen. "Thanks for going to bat for her. You *are* a good guy, Clint Burns."

A low chuckle. "Tell your mom that."

"What?"

"Nothin'. So, what else can I do for you today, Mar-see-a?" My name was said with another chuckle in his voice, but this time I was pretty sure he was trying to distract from his slip about Mom.

"Can I ask a favor, for Derek Bradshaw? He's questioning now whether he really is Zeke Lord's son. If he gets his own DNA tested, could you get him Zeke's DNA info so he can compare them?"

"Hmm, I might be able to go one better than that, for the sergeant's sake. One of my crime techs can read the DNA reports and tell him whether or not that old reprobate was his old man."

"That would be great."

"I like to help veterans out whenever I can."

"Thanks so much." Then Ms. Snark snuck past me and blurted out, "So, have you talked to Mom lately?"

"Um, yeah, we've chatted a few times."

"A *few* times?" It had been less than two weeks since she'd left for home.

"Uh, she's a very nice lady. Did she tell you her news?"

"What news?"

"Oh, guess not. I shouldn't have said anything."

"Come on, you can't dangle that out there and then not tell me." My heart squeezed in my chest at another thought. "She's not sick, is she?"

"No, no, nothin' like that."

My insides relaxed. "Come on, Clint. Spill it."

Another chuckle, more genuine but also a little nervous. "You sound just like her."

My hands tightened on my steering wheel. "Grrr."

"Okay, but act surprised when she tells you. She's comin' down again for Christmas…"

I let out a small gasp, jerking the wheel. Good thing I was on a mostly deserted country road. I quickly got the car straight in my lane again.

Then the rest of what the sheriff was saying registered in my brain. "…and she's thinkin' about movin' down here."

I almost drove off the road entirely.

~

AUTHOR'S NOTES

If you enjoyed this book, please take a moment to leave a short review on the book retailer of your choice. Reviews help with sales and sales keep the stories coming. You can readily find the links to these retailers by clicking on bookstore at https://misteriopress.com.

I have plans for at least two more books in this series. One is a holiday novella, *My Funny Mayfair Valentine,* and the other is a full-length book tentatively titled *One Flew Over the Chow-Chow Nest*, starring Bear who was introduced in this book.

I hope to have one or both out in 2020 or early 2021 at the latest. (All the stories in this series are listed in order, as well as the rest of my books, at the front of this book.)

This book was proofread by multiple sets of eyes, but proofreaders are human. If you noticed any errors, please email me at lambkassandra3@gmail.com so I can have them corrected.

Heck, email me anyway. I love hearing from readers!!

And you may want to sign up for my newsletter at https://kassandralamb.com to get a heads up about new releases, plus special offers and bonuses for subscribers. You will also receive a free novella, *Sweet Sanctuary*, the prequel to my other series, the Kate Huntington Mysteries.

Hang in there with me for a bit as I express my gratitude to the folks who helped make this book happen, and then I will reward you with some interesting background tidbits.

A huge thank you to my cohorts at *misterio press*, Shannon Esposito and Kirsten Weiss, for their thorough critiquing and proofreading, and to my daughter-in-law, romance and women's fiction writer, GG Andrew, for her read-through and helpful remarks. As always, much gratitude to my editor, Marcy Kennedy, from whom I have learned so much and who continues to challenge me to up my game. Also, all my love and gratitude to my patient husband who puts up with my crazy writer's hours and does the final proofread. (Any errors you might have noticed are not his fault. I can't help myself; I tweak things right up until publication day.)

Plus, I have a special thank you this time for three people. One is to my good friend Mary who suggested the flea market idea. (More on that in a moment.) And also a very special thank you to Clay and Rosie Connolly of Williston, Florida. Clay recently retired from the position of Deputy Police Chief in Williston, and bless him, he volunteered to give me a tour of the town and the surrounding area and fill me in on the workings of the Williston PD and also of Florida sheriff's departments in general.

And then he and his lovely wife, Rosie, took me out to dinner at The Ivy House.

So yes, Williston is a real town, with a real BubbaQue's® and Dixie's Antiques on Noble Avenue.

I only include real towns and counties in my stories when I don't intend to say anything negative about them. If the story requires an inept or corrupt law enforcement officer or government official or unfriendly residents, then I create a fictional town or county. So Crystal County is not a real place (although Crystal City is). I carved the county off of the lower corner of Levy County and gave it a fictitious sheriff's department. ALL of the members of that agency are completely fictitious.

I was afraid that I had made Deputy Harrison a little too over the top, but Clay reassured me that sadly there are sometimes LEOs who are not the brightest or the best.

I have a great deal of respect and gratitude to those who protect and serve, so I hope my portrayal of Sheriff Clint Burns, Detective Rick Young, and of Andy and Will, as dedicated and intelligent officers of the law counterbalances the "bad apple" that is Deputy Harrison.

Oh, and I should have included the Facebook group, Cops and Writers, in my gratitude list above. I asked in that group if LEOs really do believe that most criminals are dumb. The answers I received, from several current and former LEOs, were very enlightening. I rewrote that part of the after-dinner conversation to include many of their thoughts.

The idea for this story came from several different sources. Since all the book titles are take-offs on classic literature, movies, or well-known songs, I sometimes do a search for such classic titles, to see if any of them inspire me. That was what I was doing when I first came up with the title, *Lord of the Fleas*.

Then I tried to create a storyline that would at least partially relate to the story of *Lord of the Flies*. But everything I came up with seemed too dark for a cozy mystery.

I was discussing this dilemma with my good friend Mary one day and she said, "Why don't you make it about a flea market?"

That was the perfect solution! And of course she would think of that, as there is a large flea market in her town, and one of our favorite things to do when I visit her is to take a stroll through there to see what's new and different. The flea market in this book is basically patterned after that one, in Surfside Beach, South Carolina.

Next I needed to decide what wounds, physical and/or emotional, Marcia's veteran client would have in this story. One of my goals with this series is to raise awareness of the ways that combat can leave an undesirable legacy in a veteran's life.

While stumbling around the internet, I came across a series of videos describing a phenomenon I had known little about before—an incomplete spinal cord injury. The young man who makes these videos is great. He is very informative and personable. Check out his videos on his YouTube channel, Wheels2Walking. They are well worth a watch.

One other quick note. I try to research (i.e., Google) the names of major players in stories, especially the bad guys. Even though all the characters are fictitious and any similarity to the name of a real person is coincidental, I still want to avoid using a name that happens to belong to someone famous, or perhaps infamous.

So I did the search on Ezekiel Lord's name that I attribute to Elise, the background check lady, in the story. Indeed, it was hard to research because Ezekiel from the Bible dominated the search. But I did stumble over the obituary for an Ezekiel Ford from the Vietnam War era.

I had been looking for ways that Zeke could shore up his lies about his history, and this fit the bill perfectly. So my apologies to any remaining family of Ezekiel Ford for fictitiously commandeering his dog tags.

And God bless Ezekiel Ford, along with so many other brave members of my generation who lost their lives, at far too young an age, in the Vietnam War.

The Vietnam Veteran baseball cap would have been easy for Zeke to get his hands on. And the colorful horizontal line between the words *Vietnam* and *Veteran* does represent various medals for the different battles fought in that war and for the different branches of service. During the time that I was writing the first draft of this book, my husband and I were on a road trip to visit our son and family for Christmas. At a rest stop in Louisiana, a retired Marine was raising money for a veterans' organization by selling baseball caps from the various service branches. I bought a Vietnam Veteran's cap from him, and he explained about the meaning of the colors in that line.

I told him the gist of the story I was writing, and he explained to me the concept of *valor stealing*. We gave him an additional donation.

I love it when the universe hands me little gifts like that!

To see a picture of the hat, go to my Pinterest page (https: //www.pinterest.com/kassandralamb/) and look on the Marcia Banks and Buddy Series board.

I don't have a full synopsis yet for the next story in this series, *My Funny Mayfair Valentine*; it's still percolating in my brain. But I can say that, in addition to the spark of interest between Sheriff Clint Burns and Marcia's mom, there will be at least one other romance hatching in town, when a charming, silver-haired gentleman by the name of Samuel Truman decides to retire to Mayfair. Stay tuned!

I can offer an excerpt from the first book in a new series I'm considering—a police procedural starring Judith Anderson from the Kate Huntington series. But I'm moving her to North Florida, to a fictional small city just south of Jacksonville.

I don't have a title for the series yet, but this book is tentatively titled *A Pearl Before Swine*. If you have a good idea for a series title, please email me at lambkassandra3@gmail.com

~

Excerpt:

And here I was, at my first homicide scene as a resident of Florida.

I stared down at the body of a twenty-something woman who had once been pretty, before someone had gone after her with the proverbial blunt instrument. Her little black dress was rucked up to her waist. I looked away.

Of course it was the middle of the night, and of course it was raining. Spritzing really, drizzle with some umph behind it.

I swiped the moisture impatiently from my face, while pointing at the area around the vic. "Any murder weapon?"

Both my detective and the uniform who'd been first on the scene shook their heads—the detective resigned, the uniform forlorn.

I made a note of the latter's name badge—Connors. He might have potential.

"So what've we got?" I directed this to the detective, Nate Jacobs.

"No ID. Could be a working girl. Blunt force trauma, it looks like. M.E.'s on the way."

I stared at him.

"No witnesses." He paused, stared back. "Yet. Uniforms are canvassing."

Yeah, good luck with that at two in the morning.

I looked around, saw no way that I could be useful without getting in the way. "Keep me posted," I said to Jacobs.

I turned away, and then intentionally looked back over my shoulder. "And don't be jumping to any conclusions, Detective. For all we know she's a UNF sorority sister who went out with friends for a night on the town."

Both the detective and the uniform bowed their heads. You would've thought I'd said the vic was a nun.

I chuckled inside my head but maintained my cop face.

As the new police chief of Starling, Florida, population roughly eighteen thousand souls, it wasn't really necessary for me to go to crime scenes. But I'd told my detectives and officers that I wanted to be called if it was a major crime.

While Starling is a small city—or medium-sized town, depending on your perspective—it's located just outside of I-295 around Jacksonville, which has all the big-city problems as my home town of Baltimore.

I wanted to get a feel for the types of crimes my department encountered. And besides, one of the many reasons I'd taken this job was because I wanted to get back into the field some. I'd considered it providence when I'd seen the recruitment ad for a new police chief of a town big enough to match my salary but small enough to allow me to be fairly hands-on.

Of course, that salary in Baltimore County had been for a

homicide lieutenant, whereas here it was for the chief, but adjusted for the difference in cost of living, it wasn't a bad deal.

I once again contemplated my feelings about providence—fate, or whatever you wanted to call it—as I drove out of Starling's minuscule red-light district.

I guess if I still believed in some degree of order and direction in the universe, I couldn't call myself a complete atheist.

The image of that young woman's bloodied face flared across the screen in my mind.

But as long as one human being could do that to another, I'd have trouble believing in a benevolent god who claimed we were made in his image.

~

Jacobs knocked on my half open door. It was mid morning and I was working on my third cup of coffee.

"Might have something, Chief?"

I motioned for him to come in, and noted with interest that he closed the door.

"I ran the crime past the Jacksonville PD."

Ah, thus the closed door. He didn't want his fellow detectives hearing him admit that my new policy was working.

The previous Chief of Police had maintained an adversarial relationship with Jacksonville PD. I was determined to change that.

"They got two possible matches," Jacobs said. "One two months ago, rape and homicide. And one farther back that was just rape, but the girl survived."

I winced a little inside at the "just rape." There is no such thing as "just rape." It's a crime equally heinous as murder in my book. But now was not the time to lecture this man.

"So we know our vic was raped?"

"Oh, uh, yes, ma'am. The M.E. called earlier to let me know that. Autopsy's scheduled for tomorrow."

I stifled a sigh. Downside of a small city force, no M.E. of our own. We depended on Jacksonville to do our autopsies, which thankfully were few and far between.

"You tell the M.E.'s office that it might be related to some of their open cases?"

"Yeah, that's why they moved it up from Friday."

A curse word escaped my lips before I could catch it.

Jacobs grinned.

I frowned at him.

His face smoothed out into cop mode. "I was gonna go talk to the gal who got away."

"I'll go with." I started to push up out of my desk chair.

"Wha'?"

"I said, I'll go with you." There was a terse edge to my voice, but I decided that was okay. I stepped around my desk toward the door. "Keep in mind, Jacobs, that we're outside our jurisdiction."

He looked at me funny, as if he was trying to figure out if that was my only reason for going, to make sure he didn't step on any Jax PD toes.

I resisted shaking my head. It was going to take awhile for this crew to get used to the idea that I was not a retired-in-place burnout like their old boss.

ABOUT THE AUTHOR

Kassandra Lamb has never been able to decide which she loves more, psychology or writing. In college, she realized that writers need a day job in order to eat, so she studied psychology. After a career as a psychotherapist and college professor, she is now retired and can pursue her passion for writing.

She spends most of her time in an alternate universe with her characters. The portal to that universe, aka her computer, is located in Florida, where her husband and dog catch occasional glimpses of her.

Kass has completed ten full-length novels in the Kate Huntington Mystery series (set in her native Maryland, about a psychotherapist/amateur sleuth), plus four Kate on Vacation novellas (with the same characters). She is also the author of the Marcia Banks and Buddy cozy mystery series, about a service dog trainer and her sidekick and mentor dog, Buddy. There are six novels and three holiday novellas out in that series, which is set in north central Florida. A seventh novel and a Valentine's Day novella are planned for late 2020/early 2021.

To read and see more about Kassandra and her books, please go to https://kassandralamb.com. Be sure to sign up for the newsletter there to get a heads up about new releases, plus special offers and bonuses for subscribers.

Kass's e-mail is lambkassandra3@gmail.com and she loves hearing from readers! She's also on Facebook (https://www.facebook.com/kassandralambauthor) and Goodreads (https://www.goodreads.com/author/show/5624939.Kassandra_Lamb) and hangs out some on Twitter @KassandraLamb. She blogs about psychological topics and other random things at https://misteriopress.com.

Kassandra also writes romantic suspense under the pen name of Jessica Dale.

Please check out these other great *misterio press* series:

Karma's A Bitch: Pet Psychic Mysteries
by Shannon Esposito
Multiple Motives: Kate Huntington Mysteries
by Kassandra Lamb
Maui Widow Waltz: Islands of Aloha Mysteries
by JoAnn Bassett
The Metaphysical Detective: Riga Hayworth Paranormal Mysteries
by Kirsten Weiss
Dangerous and Unseemly: Concordia Wells Historical Mysteries
by K.B. Owen
Murder, Honey: Carol Sabala Mysteries
by Vinnie Hansen
Blogging is Murder: Digital Detective Cozy Mysteries
by Gilian Baker
To Kill A Labrador: Marcia Banks and Buddy Cozy Mysteries
by Kassandra Lamb
Steam and Sensibility: Sensibility Grey Steampunk Mysteries
by Kirsten Weiss
Never Sleep: Chronicles of a Lady Detective Historical Mysteries
by K.B. Owen
Bound: Witches of Doyle Cozy Mysteries
by Kirsten Weiss
At Wits' End Cozy Mysteries
by Kirsten Weiss
Payback: Unintended Consequences Romantic Suspense
by Jessica Dale

Plus even more great mysteries/thrillers in the *misterio press* bookstore.

Made in the USA
Monee, IL
29 July 2025

22162632R00125